Bad
Hair
Day

To Martha,
in honor of her father and his legacy of faith.
And because she told me,
"I think you can do more."

Bad Heiress Day

ALLIE PLEITER

Steeple
Hill
Café™

Published by Steeple Hill Books™

STEEPLE HILL BOOKS

ISBN 0-373-78533-X

BAD HEIRESS DAY

www.SteepleHill.com

Printed in U.S.A.

Acknowledgments

It is an author's job to take the kernels of truth everyday life offers up and spin them into a compelling story that somehow takes us beyond daily life. The details and plotlines bubble up from an author's imagination, but the stories that touch us most do so because they spring from people and situations we all know. As such, this story belongs to all of us who have lost our parents, wrestled with an estate and come out stronger for the struggle.

First and foremost, my thanks must always go to my husband and children, for they are on the front lines of my daily life. They endure the crankiness and the rapidly multiplying stacks of paper that invade our house, and hear me continually talking about book characters as if they were real people. Although you told me I was "calmer for this one," Jeff dear, I doubt that made it an effortless task. For the many times you've walked beside me as I trudged through first drafts and rewrites, thank you. For my children, Mandy and CJ, whose choruses of "Allie Pleiter, Famous Writer" are the best cheering section any mom could hope for—may I someday live up to the moniker with which you've blessed me. My special thanks to you, Mandy, for saying "Yes, Mom, you've GOT to buy a tiara now!"

To my friends and extended family, who continue to offer up gobs of support whenever needed. Had I a crate of tiaras, you'd all get one of your very own...and may still.

To Karen Solem, my agent and wise counsel, who has been advising me to write this book for years before my muse finally kicked it out of me.

To my editor and instant friend, Krista Stroever, for believing in me from the first ten pages, and for loving Friendly Fribbles as much as I do.

To the city of Cincinnati, and its lovely people. You lured me once years ago, and rekindled the affection again as I returned to write this book. I hope I have done you proud—and not botched too many of the local details. My thanks to Bill and Lorraine Downing at the Grace and Glory Bed and Breakfast, who were my gracious and encouraging hosts during a frenzied writing-and-research visit.

To Len Harrison at LVM Capital Management, who patiently answered far too many "what if" questions, and to several attorneys at Huck, Bouma et al. who did the same.

And finally to God, for the gift, the grace and the guidance. Without those, I am nothing but a clanging cymbal. May the words You have given me draw others closer to You.

Chapter 1

Chocolate, Grease & Diet Coke

Cincinnati, Ohio
September 15, 2001

"Lovely man."

"Such a waste. Sixty-five is still so young these days."

"I'm sure his faith was a comfort to him."

Platitudes—sincere and otherwise—were flying fast and furious in the narthex of the Ohio Valley Community Church. One woman spent a whole ten minutes telling Darcy Nightengale what a pillar of the community her father had been. The next woman smiled as she told Darcy how the universe now welcomed her father in his new state of pure energy. After that last "unique" remark, Darcy's husband, Jack, softly hummed the General Electric theme, "We bring good things to life" in her ear. It made her laugh. A small laugh, but it was a gift none the less.

Somehow, the fact that a joke could still be made—in the current state of both the world and the family—was a foothold of hope. The Tuesday of this week, September 11, had been a day of national tragedy. Thousands lost their lives. Darcy had lots of company mourning a loved one.

For Darcy, though, September 11 was more still. September 11 was the last day she saw her father's eyes. The last day he spoke. For a man who'd been dying for months, Paul Hartwell chose a really lousy last day on Earth. It was like a cruel afterthought to lose her father in the early hours of September 12. The day *after* the world shook on its foundations. Darcy remembered looking up from the hospice center bed in the roaring, breathless silence, and wondering if anyone would even notice.

But they had. The church was crowded with friends offering their sympathy. It had been a rough day. Between the ceremonial pressure, the endless handshaking and the spurts of intense conversation, Darcy was running on adrenaline. After the months of dying, Dad's death felt more like the finish line of a long and weary marathon than any kind of mourning. She had stood beside Dad and seen him through to the end. Literally. When she dared to be honest, Darcy admitted that woven in through all the grief was a clear gleam of relief. Jack put his hand on the small of her back, as if holding her up, as an older woman told tales of Paul's kindness to her little dogs.

"That's the last guest," came a deep voice behind her. Ed Parrot was the epitome of a funeral director, subdued and dignified. Except that he had a voice like Darth Vader and a body just as large. The fact that he always wore a black suit just intensified the effect. It made for a creepy image every time he spoke to her—as if the telltale Vader breathing sound effect would kick in at any moment. He took her hand in his with an experienced clasp. With an exhale he looked into her eyes and said softly, "It's over."

Over. What a potent choice of words.

His expression told Darcy that he meant both the best and worst of it. Here was a man who knew how grueling the rituals of grief could be. The time would come soon enough when the small box of ashes would go to their final spot, but this day's duties were done.

Done. The word hung in Darcy's thoughts like the last chord of the Beatles' "A Day in the Life"—the one that echoed on at the end of the record for what seemed like forever.

"Kate's in the driveway," Jack said suddenly, loosening his tie. Darcy noticed that Jack and Mr. Parrot were exchanging looks. She raised an eyebrow.

"She's going to go take you to dinner. The kids and I will head back home—I rented a movie for them and bought a vat of popcorn."

She blinked. It hardly felt like time to hit a restaurant, but she couldn't even form a coherent protest.

Jack kissed her lightly on the cheek and pressed his hand into the small of her back again. "Go, hon. You need it."

In that moment, seeing her own weariness reflected in Jack's eyes, Darcy realized she did.

Boy, did she.

Only a best friend like Kate Owens would know to do this, and only Kate would dare.

When Darcy walked out the church's back door, Kate was in her little red Miata convertible. On the passenger seat was a pair of Darcy's jeans, a T-shirt, sneakers, the instantly recognizable red-and-white stripes of a bucket of Kentucky Fried Chicken—extra crispy, Darcy was sure, with extra biscuits—and a box of chocolate-covered graham crackers. Darcy wanted to cry for the understanding of it all. Jack and Kate knew, even before she knew it herself, that what she needed most at this moment was to unwind and do something that felt normal.

Kate's smile made words unnecessary. She winked back a tear and said, "We'll hit Graeter's Ice Cream Parlor if you're still hungry later, but for now, let's get out of Dodge."

"You betcha."

Kate reached over and opened the door. "Get in, girl." She pulled the car out through the parking lot's far exit so that they didn't have to pass any of the lingering guests Darcy saw talking to Jack. Jack was earning Husband of the Year points for this one, to be sure.

Speeding onto Victory Parkway, the evening's cooler air washed over Darcy like a balm, whipping her hair and streaming around her upstretched fingers. The weight of the last two hours slowly eased up off her shoulders. Of course, wiggling out of the control-top panty hose within thirty seconds of being in the car helped matters, too.

They stopped at a United Dairy Farmers convenience store to switch clothes in the ladies' room, ditching their somber suits for the familiarity of jeans and T-shirts. Darcy felt as if she began to breathe softer air.

They ate on benches in Overlook Park, the quaint pond behind them, the river valley stretching out before them. In a silence broken only with sighs, the pair watched the Ohio River wind its way under the bridges. The serene scene spread out in postcard-style perfection. Bit by bit the evening sky appeared, washing the landscape in pastels and pinpricks of light. You'd never even know New York was still smoking.

Kate licked her fingers loudly and she threw yet another bare drumstick bone into a paper bag. "We just raised our cholesterol a dozen points, you know."

Darcy chuckled. "I don't care. I've never enjoyed a bucketful of drumsticks so much in my life. But shame on you for getting all dark meat. We'd probably have added only five or six points if you'd have sprung for all white."

"No way. This was pure indulgence. White meat would have been too responsible. And just for that ungrateful remark, I'm going to eat all the cookies!" She made for the package, but Darcy lunged first.

"Over my dead body!" she yelled, then stopped short at the choice of words. They both held still for a moment. Oh man, just when she'd actually almost forgotten about it for a while. Even her own language couldn't get out from the death all around her.

Kate tore open the cookie package and handed a stack to Darcy. "It rots," she declared sharply. "It just rots. All of it. Your dad, those terrorists, the planes. My kids think they're going to be blown up if they go to the mall. It all just *rots*."

Darcy had to admit "rots" was putting it rather bluntly, but there was a useful truth in Kate's choice of words. Fourth-grade-style vocabulary aside, it felt good for someone not to try to put a sympathetic, comforting spin on whatever they said to her. It *did* rot. No amount of greeting card-worthy verse would change that. "It does," Darcy agreed. "It rots. It *rots!*"

They looked at each other. "It rots!" they yelled together, listening to the satisfying way it echoed over the steep hillside. So they did it again. Granted, it was childish and undignified, but it felt wonderful. When they began to laugh from the ridiculousness of it all, Darcy didn't care who else in the park stared. No matter what the shape of the world this week, she needed to laugh far more than she needed to care who saw it.

"Oh, if Thad could see me now, he'd turn purple from embarrassment," Kate said behind a mouthful of chocolate and graham cracker.

"That son of yours has heard worse. Actually, by the eighth grade, Thad's probably *said* worse." Darcy plucked another cracker from the plastic sleeve. "Actually, I think 'rots' is rather restrained given the circumstances. I can think of far worse words that apply. A dozen or so, to be exact."

They fell quiet again for a while, pondering the sorry state of the universe.

Kate finally broke the silence. "I went to the safe-deposit box."

"And…" Darcy's heart did a small, tense somersault.

"Well, it was just like you said. They weren't going to let me near the thing until I showed them the letter you wrote and about twelve forms of ID."

"I suspected as much."

Kate turned to her. "Dar, why did you want me to do this? This is your *dad's* box we're talking about. Private stuff and all. Why me?"

Darcy leaned back against the bench. "I dunno. It just seemed like one too many things to do. There's been so many picky details in the last couple of days I just couldn't handle one more."

Kate leaned back to meet her eyes, not letting her off the hook. Darcy knew Kate would get into this with her. "So have me fetch flowers or drive Aunt So-and-So someplace, but why the box?" Kate pointed at her with the half-eaten end of a graham cracker. "I know you, Darcy. You're avoiding something. What did you think would be in there?"

"I don't *know* what's in there," Darcy said, more sharply than she would have liked. Why did Kate always have to know her so well? Of course she was avoiding it. With the bombshell that'd been dropped on her at the lawyer's office, she was terrified to find other secrets lurking in her dad's private affairs. She thought she knew everything about her dad, that nothing had gone unspoken between them. It had been a comfort of sorts as she was forced to watch her father's long, agonizing exit from life.

Just goes to show how wrong a person can be.

Dad had left a great big secret for her to find. Intentionally hid it from her—at least that's what it felt like. Now she discovered Dad had left strict instructions with Jacob the Kindly Lawyer for her to remove the contents of the box upon his death. What now? What else was going to come crashing down upon her head?

Darcy didn't want to ignore her dad's instructions, but she surely didn't think she could handle another startling revelation at the moment. Things were feeling as if she were on *The Jerry Springer Show* as it was.

Kate wasn't backing off for a second. "Darcy. You knew something was in there. Something big and worth going to all this trouble to avoid."

"Okay, okay, you're right."

Kate was getting up. *No, Kate, don't get up. Don't go get whatever it is now. I can't handle this now.* Kate was getting up anyway, trotting back to the car to flip open the trunk and pull out a small, official-looking box.

Don't make me open it. Not in front of you. Not today.

Kate sat back down, plunking the box squarely between them. "Look Dar, I put the stuff from the bank into this box. I know what's in here. There's no body, no bloody knife or anything that looks like Colonel Mustard did it with the pipe in the library. There's no long-lost cousin, no crown jewels. There's two bibles, a stack of what looks like wartime love letters between your parents, some collectible-looking coins, and a letter addressed to you. And as near as I can figure it, there must be some reason you wanted to open this with me instead of Jack, and today can't get much worse, so you might as well get it over with."

Darcy stared at her. She didn't get it, did she? After all she'd been through this week, and what she'd learned at the lawyer's office, a mere letter was worth a *dozen* bloody knives in this family.

"Look," insisted Kate, not letting up even though Darcy glared at her, "I got four more boxes of cookies up in the car. We have enough grease, Diet Coke and chocolate here to get over a crisis of monumental proportions." She pushed the box over to Darcy. "You've been looking like you're ready to explode for three days now. Jack told me something was up but he wouldn't say what. I only know that he's worried enough about you to willingly handle two kids who are jumpy and crazed because they've just had to sit through a funeral. Maybe it's time to light the fuse and let it go off now before somebody gets hurt."

Kate wasn't being mean. She was being loving in the rarest sense of the word. Willing to stand by and watch it get ugly if it meant helping her friend through a tough time. And Kate was right—she *was* ready to explode. Jack had said much the same thing. It's probably why he agreed to this little picnic in the first place. If she didn't get it out somehow, it might—no, it probably would—come out in a way that everyone would regret.

Darcy put her hand on the top of the box. A sensation close to an electric shock pulsed through her fingers. Somehow touching it, that ordinary sensation of cardboard, made it both easier and frighteningly real. She took a deep breath and then let it out again. Kate wrapped her hand around the paper cup of Coke, settling in for a good spell of listening.

"There's something you need to know. First, I mean. Well, you don't actually *need* to know it, but I need someone besides just Jack to know and you're elected, Miss Nosy Pushy Best Friend."

Kate nodded.

Darcy exhaled, staring at the river. "I found out something about Dad when I went to the lawyer's office."

"I gathered as much."

Darcy tried to find an eloquent way to put it, but couldn't. She opted for blunt. This was Kate, after all. "Dad was…well, rich."

Kate thought for a moment. "Yeah, well I knew he was well-off. I mean, he had good medical care and you weren't getting all worried about money like any of my other friends with sick parents, but so?"

"*Really* rich."

"Like Regis Philbin 'Is that your final answer' really rich? What are we talking about here?"

"One and a half Regis Philbins to be exact. And that's after taxes."

Kate gurgled unintelligibly and dropped her Coke. "*Your* Dad? Mr. Coupon-clipper Dad?"

This time it was Darcy's turn to merely nod. Kate's shock felt comforting. It made her feel more at home with the shock waves she'd been feeling since she'd known.

"No, really, Darcy. You've got to be kidding. There's no way your—excuse me but you know it's the truth—*tight-wad* of a dad could be a millionaire. The guy drove an eight-year-old car."

"I know. I couldn't believe it. I don't get it, either. He had so much. There was so much he could have done that he didn't."

Kate stuffed another cracker in her mouth and offered Darcy the box. "Whoa, Dar. This is big stuff. What are you going to do?"

"I don't know. I don't know yet. I had no idea Dad had that kind of money. It's actually scary when you think about it."

It flashed back at her before she had a chance to even name it. An avalanche of angry scenes. Dad arguing with a clerk over not getting the senior discount. Eating dinner at 4:00 p.m. to get the early bird special. A million little—okay, she was going to use this phrase—*cheap* impulses that used to drive her crazy back when Dad was well enough to be up and about. Buying store-brand knockoffs when what she really wanted was honest-to-goodness Oreos. Why would a man with enough money to live three lifetimes spend—no, not spend—*waste* so much energy penny-pinching? Her throat began to tighten. There was so much lost. She turned to Kate. "I'm mad at him for doing this. For hiding it and springing it on me like this. It's not fair to make me deal with this now. I thought we'd cleared the air completely between us, Kate, but he kept this huge thing from me." The words came spilling out, pouring from the open wound in her heart. "Why would he put me through this? I feel like I'm on some sort of sick, twisted game show and it's his doing. Sure, it's a cartload of money and I suppose that's good. It solves a lot of problems. But it's bad, too. I've spent the last week wondering what else don't I know. Are there more secrets lurking out there waiting to do me in?" The tears sneaked up on her before she had a chance to stop them. Darcy slumped against the bench, lay her head down on Kate's shoulder, and cried. For both the hundredth time and the first time.

Kate stroked her shoulder and let her cry, fishing tissues for her out of her purse because Darcy had gone through every one of the dozens of tissues she'd stocked her pockets with this morning.

"I don't know," Kate said finally, and Darcy could hear the strain in her friend's voice. "I think you may have been better off with something like *The Princess Diaries*. He should have left you queen of something. I was only joking about the crown jewels bit, but now I'm thinking…"

"I know, I know." Darcy laughed, glad to have her friend's thoughts follow her own. "I was thinking I need a tiara or something."

"It's gonna change your life forever, Dar. I mean, think about it. Okay, I realize his methods—" she narrowed her eyes for emphasis "—rot, but the game show metaphor isn't all that far off. You're loaded. Think about all you and Jack can do. Mike can go to that snazzy math academy you've been eyeing for all these years."

Kate had hit the nail on the head. "That's just it, Kate. Mike can go to Simmons Academy now. But Mike could have gone to Simmons Academy all along! Dad knew how much we wanted him to be able to do something with his math skills. He *knew* we couldn't afford to do it. How could he just sit there and not help if he had all that money lying around?" It was unkind, but it was spilling out of Darcy and she didn't care. "One point six million is enough for three lifetimes Kate, and he knew he didn't have much more time. He's known for two years. Why, why, *why* did he feel he had to keep it from us? And you know what? I don't even care about the dollar signs, I care that he kept such a big, huge, important thing from me. From *me!* I could change his bedpans but I couldn't be trusted with his finances? Why keep secrets now, of all times?" Darcy crossed her arms. "It hurts. It hurts a lot."

"It rots."

"Yeah, it rots all right."

Kate kicked her legs out in front of her and giggled just a bit. "But at least it rots all the way to the bank."

God bless Kate. Darcy knew she'd done the right thing in telling her. She bumped Kate playfully with her shoulder and sighed.

"You have no idea why he'd do this? Hide this from you?"

"Not one. Not a one." Darcy stuffed an entire graham cracker in her mouth.

"Well, at least now I understand why you weren't in any hurry to open that box. You've got a license to be gun-shy on this one."

"Tell me about it."

"You know, Dar," said Kate, pulling up one knee to sit facing Darcy on the bench, "you're forgetting something."

Darcy turned to look at her friend.

"What if the why is in the letter?" she offered. "What if it's not a time bomb, but an explanation? Mr. Lawyer Guy said you were to open the box shortly after your dad's death, right?"

Darcy nodded, her brain straining to put the pieces together. What if there was some kind of reasoning, some explanation in the letter? Darcy wasn't sure she was ready to see it. But another part of her began to give in to the curiosity. Knowing why would help the coping process a lot more than chocolate graham crackers.

"You know what?" Kate offered suddenly with a smirk. "I was wrong. We *don't* have enough chocolate to deal with this. It's gonna take a whole gallon of Graeter's mint chocolate chip to cope with this baby." She began gathering up the food and wrappers. "And on the way, you can tell me what Jack said about all this."

Chapter 2

The Twelfth of Never

"Four more spoonfuls and then I'll open it. I'll save the rest of my ice cream sundae for the aftermath." Darcy was feeling better bit by bit.

Kate counted down Darcy's spoonfuls and added a drumroll to the last one for effect. There, in the front seat of Kate's car in Graeter's Ice Cream Parlor parking lot, she took a deep breath and pulled the lid from the box.

Kate was right. It did look ordinary. She didn't know if she expected some hand to come out and grab her like something from *The Addams Family,* but it looked tame enough. She started with something safe, like the coins.

"Gold," Darcy said as she pulled one from the wax paper envelope that held it. "From Africa. At least I think it's gold—it's heavy enough. I'll have to take them someplace to have them appraised. Dad told me he got these when I was born." There were four of them, two pairs of different kinds. *Okay, safe enough. Nothing shocking there. Good.* She laid them gently back into the box.

The first Bible was soft and worn, the aged leather flaking off a bit in her hands. It was a woman's bible, with swirly lettering stamped on the elegant beige of the cover. Her mother's. Darcy realized she'd never seen her mother with it. She imagined it tucked in a nightstand drawer next to a velvet jewelry box and hankies.

Mom. Her death in 1982 seemed like ages ago now. As a shy seventeen-year-old, it had been so hard for Darcy to come to grips with the automobile accident that had taken her mom's life. Actually, it hadn't taken her life, just made her give up on the life she had until it ebbed right out of her.

Maimed.

Darcy had always thought that was an odd choice of words for people to use. Her mother's left hand looked just as it always had, but it was rendered lifeless. Limp and useless. Her mother had survived all the other bumps and bruises, and had lived for years after the accident, but never gave a hint of ever recovering. Or even wanting to. Clara Hartwell had been a violinist, and life without a left hand didn't seem worth living. "But it's just a *hand,*" Darcy remembered thinking, even arguing with her mother.

All arguments, all pleading, all encouragement had proved as useless as Clara's fingers. It had been a hideous, awful time.

"Mom's," Darcy offered to Kate, surprised by the lump in her throat when she spoke. "I've never seen it before." She ran her hands through the impossibly thin pages, fingered the faded red ribbons that were meant to mark pages. Each ribbon left a pale-pink line on the page it had sat in over the years. Darcy ran her fingers across the monogram gracing the bottom corner before she laid it back in the box.

She recognized the second Bible. Hard-bound, it was tattered and dirty. This was the small Bible her dad talked about carrying through the war. The one he carried for years until he wore it clean out and Darcy gave him a new one for his birthday. Thumbing through it, Darcy saw hundreds of tiny scrawled notes in the margins. Names of people. Question marks and exclamation points with arrows to particular verses. "Harry—forgive him" was one, with an arrow to a passage in Luke which read "But he who hath forgiven little loves little."

Darcy looked up. "Dad's."

Kate said nothing. There wasn't anything for her to say, really. Except maybe "So, open the letter." Darcy was glad she didn't say it.

There it was. Sitting in the corner of the box. Small and thick, with "Darcy" in her father's handwriting on the front. His handwriting the way it used to be, before his letters got sloppy and shaky from weak hands. This penmanship was strong and careful.

Darcy felt Kate's hand on her shoulder. "You know, if you want to be alone, I could go get more ice cream or something. Maybe you need to do this in private."

Darcy swallowed hard. "No. I think I need you here. I'm not going to read it aloud or anything—at least not yet, but I don't think I want to do this by myself. You just sit over there and polish off that fudge, okay?"

"Got it."

"Okay. I'm gonna do this."

"I'm right here, kiddo."

Darcy counted to five and then slid her finger under the back flap. The paper was still strong, the seal still solid. Darcy guessed it was written about two years ago. Just about when her dad's diagnosis was finalized.

She pulled up the flap and slid the papers out. Five sheets—filled on both sides—appeared. Small, stationery-size—the kind nobody used much anymore because it didn't fit into computers, and who even *wrote* letters anymore?

Unfolding the pages carefully, she let her eyes travel up the lines of dark-blue ink until they hit those fateful words: "Dear Darcy,"

All right then, here we go.

Darcy read the letter.

Dear Darcy,

I've been wondering, as I sit down to write this letter, just how upset you will be when you read this. If you're holding this paper, it means I'm gone now, and you've been to see Jacob. And you've learned the one piece of my life I've kept from you. And, I assume you're not happy to learn I kept such a thing from you. I had reasons, and you will learn them before this letter is done.

I'm not feeling sick yet, but I know I will be. I know, too, that you will have been there, for you're that kind of person. They tell me the end won't be pretty, but I will step out in the faith that I have in you and thank you now for sticking by me when it got messy. I wonder if I will have even known, when it is time, everything you have done on my behalf. If I didn't, and somehow didn't recognize or acknowledge your care in the end, forgive me. I know it now, and I'll take these lucid moments to thank you. The words hardly seem sufficient for what I can only imagine is coming, but I have no others.

Darcy's chest heaved in a sob. How she had longed for that last, clear, look of acknowledgment from her dad in those final hours. It had never come. He was far away and already lost to her and looking frightened. She ached from his death all over again. For the body now reduced to ashes, the spirit long since left. She forced herself to continue reading:

I worry about you now. I'd have never said it before, but I worry about you and Jack through all this. The strain is sure to be huge. Jack's so independent, and our tiny family is about to become as dependent as it gets. Know that I have prayed for you and Jack and your marriage. And I will continue to send down blessings and prayers after I am gone, because I have a feeling that's when things will be the worst. I'm not kidding myself to think I'm not making things harder by what I've done.

All right, little girl, I've sidestepped the issue long enough. This letter, as I said before, is to tell you why I've done what I've done. No doubt by now you know the extent of my financial assets. I'm sure you've eaten a gallon of Graeters—if you've not eaten three by now...

Darcy laughed at her father's foresight. It helped to stem the tears lurking like an undertow just beneath the surface. "He's betting I've eaten Graeter's already." She offered the explanation to Kate just to break the aching silence.

"He knew you" is all Kate replied, her eyes tearing and her sundae untouched.

...and I'm sure you're in shock. Probably mad, too, for we never kept secrets from each other. Wondering, if I know you, what else you don't know about me. Let me put your mind at rest, Darcy, and tell you this letter is all there is. There are no other secrets. I didn't like keeping this one much, but I had reasons.

Where did it all come from? That's a painful episode in your mother's and my history that I hope we've successfully shielded you from. There were discussions—arguments really, and bad ones—after your mother's accident. I knew, just by how she was talking and acting, that Clara had no intention of continuing to live. Some people are strong enough to recover from a tragedy like that. Clara wasn't one of them. No amount of convincing from the doctors could change her mind. They even had some lady with two prosthetic legs come and talk to your mother, but she wouldn't hear it. To her mind, her body had been so badly damaged that she didn't want to be *in* it anymore. I was angry with her for wanting to leave me, to leave you, over her one hand. But you know Mom and her music, and what it did to her to have that taken away from her. Clara needed someone to pay for the awful thing that happened to her.

In truth, I began to as well. Clara just plain stopped being my wife and your mom when her hand stopped working. We argued all the time—I hope you don't remember how much.

Drivers didn't have to have car insurance back then. So, when we won the lawsuit against the driver who hit Mom's car, it cleaned the poor guy out. Our $250,000 award meant he had to sell his house, his car, everything.

Clara was glad we ruined his life for hers. I was, too. But even all that money couldn't bring your Mom back to us. I woke up one day, after she was gone, and realized I hated how much her vengeance had become such a part of me.

I should have realized earlier and tried to talk her out of it. In truth, Darcy, I suppose I didn't want to stop her from doing the one thing she seemed to feel was left on Earth for her to do. I suppose I thought it might keep her with us for a bit longer if she felt she still had some purpose. I loved my wife and was blinded by grief into letting her do anything to keep her alive.

I told her once, in a moment of anger, that I would give it away. The money, that is. I wanted to, after I realized it didn't help. Having lots of money never meant much to me, anyhow. My experience has been that money never solves problems, only makes new ones.

Well, Clara went so hysterical she ended up back in the hospital and almost died. So there, with her life on the line, it seemed, she made me promise not to give it away. On my honor. Before God.

Even Clara never got what she wanted. Despite taking everything Harry Zokowski had, we ended up with only $150,000. But that was still a lot of money back then. To me, though, it was just a reminder of how vengeful I'd become, and I wanted it far from my hands. The life insurance and casualty insurance more than paid for her bills anyway, what use did I have for one lonely old man's life savings in exchange for my lost wife?

By now you've been to see Jacob, and you can trust him—even if he is a lawyer. Jacob has kept the money for me, and seen to its wise investment over the years. Over time, he convinced me to let him take some of the interest off the money for when things get expensive with all those medicines and nurses I'm sure I'll need. I didn't much like it, but it made sense to me, because it means I won't be a financial burden to you and Jack. Jacob has the authority to draw off funds whenever he needs to ensure that my accounts have enough to pay the bills. That's why you've only seen the accounts you've seen. At least up until now.

So now, if I guess correctly, you're looking at something over $1.5 million. Can you believe it? It feels like a fortune, but it's not. It's not, Darcy, and don't fool yourself into thinking that it is.

I could never give it away, Darcy, I promised your mother. But *you can*.

I don't know what your life will be like in my last years, so I won't require you to do this. I won't command you to do anything. I don't have that right after all I've just put you through.

But I *can* ask you to. Give it away, Darcy. Do this for me. I know that sounds crazy to you right now, there's so much you and Jack could do with that kind of money, but don't keep it, honey. Take your Dad's advice this time. It's ill-gotten money, no matter what the legal system says. Keeping it will keep you from moving on. I'm not sure I can explain it, but the cost is dear. You've already lost so much in this life. Don't let this money take away anything more. Whatever you think it will buy you is an illusion, anyhow.

I don't expect you to understand this right away. Please don't do anything yet. Just talk to Jack, talk to people you trust and who are right with God, seek

His wisdom, and know I am praying for you every moment. Now I can mean it when I tell you I'll love you forever. Remember when I used to sing to you "Until the 12th of Never, I'll still be loving you"? Now it's true, and never forget it. God loves you, Darcy. Loves you still. Your faith will always lead you to the right decisions in life. That's the best treasure I can leave you.

I love you. I've always loved you. Your mother has always loved you, even when she couldn't show it anymore. God loves you always. I will love you forever, sweetheart, beyond the 12th of Never.
Love,
Dad

Darcy closed the pages, her face streaming with tears. "Oh, Daddy," she said quietly, and dissolved into sobs on Kate's shoulder.

Chapter 3

Little Orphan Heiress

The little red Miata pulled into the driveway just after eleven. The living room lights were off, but Darcy could still see the TV's flickering colors. She wondered which James Bond movie—Jack's favorite indulgence from the video store—he had chosen. *Live and Let Die,* most likely, or maybe even *You Only Live Twice,* because that one started with James Bond's own funeral.

"You have Jack to help you with this. That man's a dream. And me. I'm dreamy too, aren't I?" Kate put her arm around Darcy. "Dar, you're going to be okay. You know that, don't you?"

"No." Darcy let her head fall back against the car seat.

"Look," said Kate, "why don't you let me take the kids tomorrow morning so you and Jack have some time to sort this out. They've canceled soccer practice and Thad is going nuts because I won't let him turn on the TV." Kate rubbed her eyes, and Darcy thought for the first time how long this day had been for her, too. "I don't want him seeing all the stuff that's on right now—some paper showed a photo of someone *jumping* from the Twin Towers yesterday." She shook her head. "Everybody needs a distraction—something normal feeling. The kids can get together and play and then I'll take them out for pizza."

The images from the paper had left Darcy feeling cold herself. "The gates of hell" one fireman in New York City had called it. Her father was to have spent his last day at the gates of heaven, not watching the gates of hell open up in New York City and Washington, D.C. It killed her inside to know that such a gruesome day had been Dad's last hours on earth. Cruel.

"Dar…?"

"Yeah. That's probably a good idea."

"I'll pick them up at nine-thirty. Go get some sleep. It'll all still be here in the morning. All of it."

Darcy picked up the chicken bucket and the bank box from off her lap. She sat still for a moment. "Thanks."

Kate just nodded.

Jack looked up to see Darcy coming through the front door, her hands full of clothes and boxes. She looked better. Exhausted, spent, but some of the tension had eased from her shoulders. He'd have to thank Ed Parrot for his suggestion next time he saw him.

Darcy tilted the boxes so that the bucket of chicken slid to the coffee table in front of Jack. "Let me guess," he said, pulling off the lid, "extra crispy, all drumsticks."

She smiled, sort of. "There's even a few left. Dig in." There was an explosion on the television and she turned to it. "Let me guess, *Live and Let Die* or *You Only Live Twice?*"

Jack grinned. "Both. It's been that kind of day. Plus, it was two-for-one at the video store." They knew each other so well. He paused in thought before asking softly, "How are you?"

Darcy kept staring at the television. "I don't know. Okay, I suppose. But not really. Tired."

An idea struck him. "Go get your pajamas on and come watch. The bad guy is just about to reveal his plan for world domination." They used to do it all the time. Zap up a bucket of popcorn and watch Bond flicks in their pajamas.

Darcy returned, clad in soft pink cotton, and sat down beside him. Without a word, he wrapped one arm around her. With his other arm he pulled the throw from off the back of the couch and tugged it over her. She lay her head on his lap and exhaled. He felt her soften against him as he stroked the blond waves of her hair. How long had it been since they'd had time to do this?

Just as the last drumstick was gone and 007 was getting his girl, Jack looked down at Darcy to notice she'd fallen asleep. Her breathing was soft and peaceful. The knots gone from her shoulders as she lay against him.

When the movie was over, he hit the VCR remote and watched the blank blue glow of the TV screen fill the room. He wrapped his arms around her shoulders and legs and picked her up. Jack held her there for a moment, the sensation taking him back. Back to when they were younger, before kids and middle school and dying parents and flaming office buildings. They would watch Bond movies on the couch and Darcy would always fall asleep. Always just half an hour before the end. The feeling of her asleep against him was warm and familiar. He'd scoop her up on those nights, like he did just now, and carry her to the bedroom.

There, in the blue glow, that younger woman returned. So much had changed. It'd been months since he'd seen her look like that. She'd been exhausted and beaten down by the endless care of her dad. It was like the life was draining out of both of them at the same time. She'd aged a dozen years in the last two months. Their life had dwindled down to Paul and everything else fell second to him.

And so much of everything else fell second to him.

She smelled of chocolate. They'd been to Graeter's. Mint chocolate chip, if he knew her.

And he did. There was a small smudge of it at the corner of her mouth.

He kissed her forehead softly. She made a soft sound that hummed through him. No matter how unfair to Paul, Jack yearned to be the most important man in her life again.

"Movie's over," he said quietly.

They lay together later in the moonlight, listening to the night sounds waft through the open window. The moon had seemed harsh and cold when she'd been up nights with Paul. Now, the light poured rich and creamy through the window to play across Jack's shoulders. She laid her hand on his chest and turned to rest her chin on it. Jack put an arm behind his head so he could look into her face. He smiled as he fingered a lock of her hair.

"Jack?"

"Hmm?"

"There's something I need to tell you."

"You've been spending your nights with another man." It was a tasteless joke, but somehow Darcy was glad for the irreverence. Everything had been so very serious for so very long.

She swatted him softly with her free hand. He caught it in his and held it. "No, seriously. There was something in Dad's safety deposit box. About the money."

That got his attention. "More stuff we didn't know?"

"Well, not exactly. It was a letter. From Dad to me. For me to open after he died."

"The guy had a flair for drama."

Darcy couldn't suppress a small smile. "This does sound like a bad novel, doesn't it?" She paused, formulating the right words in her head. She hadn't even wrapped her own mind around her father's request, much less figure out how to explain it to Jack. "I'm not sure I even get it myself."

Jack cocked an eyebrow, encouraging her to go on.

"Well, for starters, he told me where the money came from. It was from a settlement on Mom's accident. She sued the old man who hit her—or at least started to—before she died." Darcy's throat tightened a bit at the thought of her mother, so bitter, angry and hopeless.

"I had a feeling that's where it came from. Your dad was tight with a buck, but all that couldn't have come from just clipping coupons. I figured it was from insurance settlements, though, not from lawsuits. Paul doesn't seem the suing type."

"There was a time when he was. Or Mom convinced him to be. He says—*said*—he tried to stop her." Darcy still couldn't get used to talking about her father in the past tense.

"And…" Jack was trying to help her, but somehow that only seemed to make it harder.

"They cleaned out the guy who hit her—he had no insurance. Once they got the money, though, Mom was already too far gone. Dad stopped wanting it, I guess. Hated what the lawsuit did to him, how it only ruined another life. Oh, I still don't really get it. But he ended up promising her he'd never give it away."

"So, what? He just hid it?"

"That's a good way to put it, I suppose. He hid it. All these years. Never touched it."

"Well, at least he had the good sense to find an interest-bearing hiding place."

"I suppose. It seems sad, in a way."

"It's amazing when you think of it. All that money, just waiting, sitting. If I ever wanted to teach Mike about the magic of compound interest, I've got the ultimate real-life example. I've been thinking a lot about this Dar, and we're going to have to do some serious research on how to manage it. The stock market is already taking a nose-dive from the attack, and if we go to war, who knows what will happen? There's a guy at work who's really into all that stuff—"

"Jack," Darcy stopped him. "There's more."

"Okay."

"He asked me to give it away."

Jack's eyes flew wide open. "He what?"

"The letter asks me not to keep the money, but to give it away. He couldn't—he'd promised Mom—but I can. At least that's how he put it."

Darcy could feel Jack's chest tighten under her. Hadn't she had the same reaction when she read the letter? "Well, that takes a lot of nerve. After all you've been through, after keeping it from you—from us—in the first place."

"I know, I'm sick to death of bombshells going off around here."

"Let me get this straight." Jack's hand left hers to rub across his eyes. "Your dad leaves you a small fortune, but you have to *give it away?* First you play nurse, now you have to play Santa Claus? I tell you, Dar…"

"I think he had good intentions."

"I've got a thing or two to say about his methods."

"I'm still not sure just why.…"

"I just don't get it. Was he not in the room when we were talking about struggling to find college money for the kids? It hasn't exactly been easy street around here since you quit your part-time job at the library so you could spend more time with him. You practically shut down your life—*our* life—to take care of him. And he pays us back with a stunt like this? Who does this to their own daughter?"

Darcy slid off Jack and sat up, her own anger growing. It wasn't fair. This was a lousy thing to do, no matter how many dollar signs or good intentions were involved. "I don't know, Jack. I don't get it. I've read the letter a dozen times and I still don't get it. Why on earth did he need to pile *this* on top of everything else I've had to handle?"

Jack pulled himself up to a sitting position, his elbow jabbed onto one bent knee. "I've put up with a lot from your dad over the years, Dar. I've put up with his weird mission trips and Bible speeches and all the cancer stuff and who knows what else, but this takes the cake." He stared right at Darcy. "Since when is it okay to be religious and deceptive at the same time?"

Darcy could only repeat the phrase that had been echoing in her head all day, "I don't know. I don't know anything anymore."

"Darcy, it's Aunt Jenny."

Oh, no. Not Aunt Jenny. This woman had single-handedly started dozens of family arguments.

"Good morning, Aunt Jenny," was all Darcy could manage, still holding a box of Pop-Tarts in her other hand. She could already hear the usual hurt edge in the woman's voice.

"I just had to call and ask, what were you thinking, child? How could you be so hurtful to the rest of your family? You *know* we couldn't get there for the memorial service. They've only just now opened up the airports again. Honestly."

"Look, Aunt Jenny, I know…" Darcy picked up a Handi Wipes and began mopping up crumbs in an effort to keep from jumping down Aunt Jenny's throat.

"You know I would have wanted to be there. We're all that Paul had left. Would it have killed you to put off the service until *the family* could come pay their respects?"

All that Paul had left, huh? "Aunt Jenny…" For a second, she considered that hanging up might be the wisest course of action—she was sure to say something she'd regret if Aunt Jenny kept it up.

"I just wanted to ask how you could be so inconsiderate. Why, Charles is just livid." Darcy could imagine just how livid Uncle Chuck could be. The man rarely got off his La-Z-Boy for anything. One of Aunt Jenny's favorite tactics was to project her self-righteous anger onto Chuck—whom everyone knew to be permanently disinterested—as if he were some sort of emotional ventriloquist's dummy. Darcy doubted that Chuck had done much more than hoist a beer in her dad's honor and tell Jenny to go buy a nice card and send flowers.

And she hadn't even done that much.

Darcy wrung out the cloth, trying not to visualize it as Jenny's neck. "There didn't seem to be much point in waiting. We didn't know how long travel would be disrupted. We can always have a nice little family service in the summer."

"How very *convenient* for *you*. I don't see the hurry in all this."

Darcy whirled around at the harshness of the woman's words, the phone cord knocking over a glass of juice Paula had left too near the edge of the counter. Her patience shattered with the glass. "I'm sorry you're upset, Aunt Jenny, but Dad had said his goodbyes. Perhaps you should have paid your respects to him *while he was still alive*." She hadn't intended to be so cruel, but her anger at all the people who stayed away because it was hard to be with Dad came tumbling out. Jenny had never come. Not once in two years. "You never *once* came to visit him while he was sick, why start now?"

Jack looked up from the breakfast nook and began to ease himself off the chair. Aunt Jenny's wounded silence filled the phone. Darcy shut her eyes, fighting for control. Acting like this wouldn't solve anything. She didn't fight Jack when he took the phone from her hands.

"Jenny, perhaps we should leave this conversation for another day. You can understand it has been a hard time."

"Jack, I'd have thought you would have been—" came the woman's shrill voice through the receiver.

"I'm sorry, Jenny, but Darcy and I have an appointment and we really need to go."

Darcy shut her eyes. She heard Jack mutter something less than kind as he thrust the handset back into the cradle.

"You knew she'd react that way," he said as he bent over the broken glass, picking shards out of the puddle of orange juice with his fingers.

Darcy sniffed. "I can hope."

"It's gonna get worse when she finds out about the money."

"She's not going to find out about the money," Darcy replied. It was hard enough to deal with her own reaction, she wasn't going to add vicious Aunt Jenny into the mix.

"Dar—"

"I'm not dealing with her. Not now. She's been invisible for two years, she doesn't get to show up and play loving sister now."

"Yes, I know she's horrible, but she was horrible before. She's always been—"

Darcy cut him off. "Who's side are you on, anyway?"

He tossed the shards into the garbage. "Yours. Ours. But we're all just going to have to try to be reasonable...."

"Don't do that!" Darcy snapped. She wasn't ready to be reasonable. She'd been reasonable and responsible and reliable for months, and she'd been repaid with deception and death. There was nothing reasonable about that. She'd earned the right to act out. To be unreasonable.

But not to Jack. For God's sake, he didn't deserve this. She wasn't handling this well. Tears tightened her throat.

"Jack, I'm..."

"Not handling this well," he said softly, as he stepped over the juice puddle to take her in his arms. "But it's only your first week on tour as Little Orphan Heiress." He'd coined the term late last night after they lay in bed talking. It was so crass, so full of disrespect for the situation at hand, that it made her laugh. Awful but truthful. She should have slapped him on the cheek for the hideous remark, but somehow she loved him for daring to say it. For the absurd honesty of it. "We've got a lot to work out here, and that last remnant of your bonkers family isn't helping." He kissed her forehead. "But I'm on your side, here, remember?"

"No, I'm on the side. *You're* standing in the middle of the orange juice."

Chapter 4

Comfortably Drastic

Despite death and national security, Monday came.

After seeing everyone off to work and school, Darcy sat alone in the quiet of her deserted kitchen, watching the steam make graceful curls out of her teacup. The frenzied desperation of the last week had filtered down to a kind of dead calm. A low tide, still and dry. Darcy remembered the feeling from her childhood home on the Gulf Coast. A flat void of mud and tidal leftovers, baking to a slightly foul smell in the hot summer afternoon.

Low tide.

If life had a low tide, she had hit it.

Her dad was right about one thing: the money meant almost nothing in the face of her life's tangled messes. It offered no real comfort, just complication. Darcy wondered if the odd sensation of useless abundance had struck her father when the lawsuit had been won. Money, she guessed, was a poor substitute for a living wife. She sure knew it was a poor substitute for a living father.

The house gaped open and empty around her. She wondered, aimlessly, when the last time was she washed this bathrobe? Or when was the last time she'd bought anything new for the house? Had a haircut? Put on lipstick?

The idea rose in her chest and surfaced with a small, quiet, pop. Today was Monday. Mike had science club, Paula had dance lessons. And, for once, it was everybody else's turn to carpool. She cast a hopeful eye at the kitchen calendar, grateful to see a blank square. She had the whole day.

Granted, there were about two dozen responsible things Darcy ought to be doing today, not counting the massive stack of paperwork for her father's estate.

But responsibility wasn't coming along today. Darcy Nightengale was going to be her own best friend today, and the rest of the world could just wait until tomorrow.

She grabbed her address book and the yellow pages and made three phone calls, not taking no for an answer on any of them.

She was out the door in seventeen minutes flat.

"Mercy! What have you done with Darcy Nightengale? I know she went in there half an hour ago. Where'd you put her?" Kate let the magazine she was holding fall into her lap. Darcy reveled in the way Kate's eyes lit up. Kate's look was exactly the way she felt.

Ernestine came up behind her. Ernestine, whom she'd never met before today. Yet, the minute she sat in her salon chair, Darcy felt one of those instantaneous, giftlike connections with the woman. Ernestine picked up immediately why Darcy had come to the salon and seemed to know just what to do. A large woman with complicated black hair and a South Seas type of accent, Ernestine winked at Kate and made a clucking sound with her tongue.

"It does do wonders for the woman, don't you think?"

Kate nodded from above her pedicure. "Dar, you look *wonderful.*"

"Comfortably drastic," Darcy quoted, using Ernestine's perfect phrase for what she needed. Turning to the mirror, she admired again the oh-so-up-to-date flippy thing her hair was doing. "I'm just hoping I can achieve the home version. What do you think about the color? I've never done highlighting before."

"It suits you. Really. Hey, when do I get to do 'comfortably drastic'? And Ernestine, would you consider moving closer to Cincinnati? Tomorrow? One look at Darcy and I could garner you a full client base in about forty minutes."

Ernestine smiled. "You drove out here once. You'll drive it again. I don't plan to be going anywhere. And as for you, redhead, I get my hands on you in twenty minutes—after your toes dry."

"Mmm," sighed Kate, wiggling her toes, "I can hardly wait."

The idea to come here had sprung itself on Darcy in a heartbeat. She'd scrambled through the yellow pages to find a full-scale salon sufficiently out of town and ordered the works for two. She wanted no chance of encountering a judgmental eye wondering why a grieving daughter was popping for beauty treatments two days after the funeral.

Darcy eased into the pedicure chair next to Kate and accepted a fantastic-smelling cup of tea. "I feel like a snake shedding its skin."

The hip young man filling her tub, who looked suspiciously like a relative of Ernestine's, gave her a wide grin. "I am looking at these heels and thinking you are not too far off. These feet have been through a lot, mmm?" Somehow he managed to make such a potentially judgmental comment come off as warm and understanding. That made Darcy sure he was a relative of Ernestine's.

"Uh-huh." Both women agreed simultaneously, and then broke into a giggle fit worthy of middle school girls.

"Oh, I can't believe how good this feels," murmured Darcy as her feet slid into the warm bubbles. "I swear, I feel like I've just joined the human race again."

Kate looked at her. "I think you have. Welcome back." She hesitated just a moment before adding softly, "We've missed you."

She had been gone, hadn't she? Lost to a world of crisis and catheters. Far away from many of the people she loved. Who loved her. Caught up in her dad's ever-tightening world until she couldn't see beyond its edges. And Darcy was just now coming to see the cost. That didn't mean the attention she gave her father wasn't worth it, but somehow—maybe even for her own sanity—she'd managed to ignore the consequence of that drastically narrow focus.

She fingered her wispy hair again. "Do you think Jack will like it?"

Darcy was sure Kate was going to say something like, "He's missed you most of all." But she didn't. As a matter of fact, she didn't say anything. She just sneaked her hand over to give Darcy's hand a quick squeeze. The gesture said a million things at once.

Something was happening. Something was seeping into Darcy's skin along with the creams, lotions and treatments. The outward pampering was becoming a foothold of sorts back into a life she'd almost forgotten. The non-urgent facets of life. Something inside her was remaking itself. Coming up for air out of the deep sea of crisis. It was hard to describe and felt a bit shallow coming from hand cream and hair dye. But it was there. And remarkably potent. Almost magical in how the outward care changed her on the inside.

"I'd have to say you've pretty much covered Christmas and my birthday on this one. I'm definitely liking the best-friend-of-heiress gig. Although, I'm rather certain this isn't what your dad had in mind when he told you to 'give it all away.'"

Darcy's heart felt like it stopped beating momentarily. *There.*

Yes, that. That was it.

Kate kept gushing on about marvelous everythings but Darcy didn't hear her. She was staring into thin air, watching the pieces of an extraordinary idea weave themselves together in front of her.

As if it wasn't even her own thinking. As if the concept came pouring down out of somewhere to coat her consciousness. Faces came into view. Faces from the hospice center. Hands cracked and drying from the disinfectant and endless washing. Bodies aching from nights in vinyl armchairs. Drawn cheeks and red eyes. The haphazard griminess of clothes and bodies roused in the middle of the night for what might be a loved one's final hours. Unkempt. Ignored. Unnurtured while nurturing someone else. They were like dried leaves, all of these people—herself included, colorless and brittle and swirling at the mercy of the death's unpredictable wind.

Within the space of four seconds she could name six women who needed this as much as she. Needed that inexplicable renewal that comes from caring for a body long overlooked. And the faces and names kept coming. Piling into her thoughts. The gallery of faces became like walking through a brown and sere garden....

...And...

...And...

She'd just been handed water.

Gallons and gallons of it.

Darcy's body hummed with the realization. She stretched her limbs, practically testing their pliancy. She wasn't dry and brittle anymore. Certainly not on the outside, and less than she had been on the inside. There was something about this reckless luxury—the pampering, the time with Kate, the permission to do something nice for herself—that *healed* her.

"Kate. Oh, Kate, I've got it."

"Got what?"

"The Dad thing. What I'm going to do. I've got it."

"Who knew a good manicure could solve life's major problems?" quipped Kate, staring a bit quizzically at Darcy.

"I got it," Darcy said again softly, still reeling from the power of this idea. And it was powerful. She recognized its power the moment it sprung into her thoughts.

"Okay," Kate said slowly, cueing, "So you got it. And it is…"

"Time to do something with this amazing red hair of yours, madam," came Ernestine's voice from the next room. Her wild braids popped around the doorframe. "It's Kate, isn't it? Come, lady Kate, let's see what we can do for you."

Kate eased up out of her chair. "Dar, you look like you're going to explode. You okay?"

"Fabulous," said Darcy. "I'll tell you all about it over lunch."

* * *

Darcy didn't even remember the rest of the pedicure. Her brain launched somewhere far away. This was the right thing to do. She knew it, down to her newly cranberry toenails. It felt right. The plans kept zinging into her thoughts until she was working it out to the small details by the time Kate appeared from under Ernestine's magic hands.

And appear Kate did. Ernestine was an artist. Kate's hair had always been beautiful before, but it was just plain stunning under Ernestine's hand. Silky red layers framed Kate's face and made her look younger. In the space of twenty minutes Kate had gone from suburban mom to babe. Major, head-turning, knock-your-socks-off babe. Kate knew it, too, for a swingy little bounce had found its way into her walk. In fact, it was edging closer to a strut. Who could argue with the woman? Darcy had to admit she felt the same way.

"Man alive, Kate, Don is going to go nuts when he sees you tonight. You look fantastic."

Kate admired herself in the same mirror that Darcy had. "I do, don't I? Ernestine, *you* sure you won't move to Cincinnati? *Today?*"

"You sure you're going to come back to me again?"

"Uh-huh," confirmed Kate, still eyeing herself in the mirror from different angles.

"Then I don't have to go anywhere, now do I?"

"No, ma'am, I think I'd probably crawl over broken glass to get back to you."

Ernestine clasped her hands together like a teacher making an announcement. "Now, you go two doors down to Stephano's for lunch, there are some splendid salads waiting for you and some dessert that's going to make you feel like the treasures you are. I've had his chocolate mousse, dears, and it's absolutely heavenly. Off with you now. You come back at one-thirty for facials and massage."

"*Oh.* Oh, this *is* fantastic. I'd ask for seconds if I didn't feel like such a pig already. And even that might not stop me." Kate was leaning back, eyes closed, savoring the chocolate dessert before her.

"Worth every despicable calorie," murmured Darcy, her own mouth full of the spectacularly smooth, silky mousse. The meal had been wonderful. What she'd eaten of it, that was. She'd spent the majority of the time outlining her brainstorm to Kate. Darcy was glad Kate seemed to like the idea as much as she did.

"Really." Kate finished off another spoonful and licked her fingers. "I love your idea of giving women under the strain of care a day of respite just like the one we're having. Who knows better than you what happens to people when they spend such a long time in dying-loved-one mode? It's taken so much out of you, Dar. And not just you. Jack and the kids, too."

"I know," agreed Darcy, thinking of the way Jack looked the other week. "Even with everybody trying to make the best of it, things have been wearing pretty thin at our house. Jack and I have argued more in the last six months than in our whole marriage. I'm fried, he's tired of my being fried, the kids act up, and no one wants to say anything because how can you blame a man for dying? Nobody wants it, but it…*rots*—" she pointed her spoon for emphasis on their new catchphrase "—just the same."

Kate leaned in. "But you see, that's the great thing about this. It *does* rot and you can't blame anyone. Near as I can tell, there's this sort of unwritten rule that you can't get angry at it. You have to be noble and enduring, because it's your parent and all, but it shreds people from the inside out." Kate sucked in a breath and looked down, as if she hadn't meant to be so direct about the state of affairs at the Nightengale house. "It's been hard to watch all of you. There's nothing I can do to make it better. Your dad was going to die, you had to practically put your life on hold to deal with it, and there wasn't a thing I could do to change it. If someone had given you a nudge to take care of yourself, the kind of reminder you're talking about, then things might not have gotten so bad."

Darcy swirled her spoon in the rich, brown ripples. "Things have gotten 'so bad,' haven't they?" she asked softly.

"Jack's been a saint, but he's human. You can see the frustration in his eyes. Look, Dar, no one can blame anyone. There doesn't seem to be a painless way to do this. Damage happens. I don't know that I wouldn't turn into an absolute shrew under the circumstances. I'd doubt anyone can guess what it's like to go through what you've been through."

"Things are still messy. But I *feel* better. Loads better. Maybe if I feel better, than things can get better. Or at least I can start making them better." She paused for a moment before adding, "Dad had his daughter's attention for a long time. Maybe it's time Jack gets his wife back."

Kate winked. "Oh, but he's not getting his wife. He's getting a new, improved version. I'd give anything to see the look on his face when he sees you."

They laughed. And Darcy realized things were *already* on their way to getting better. She pulled a pen from her purse and snatched a paper place mat from the next table, flipping over to the blank side. She wrote a number one in a big, bold hand.

"First, I think we need to run a test. See if every woman gets the same boost from the pampering. Today ran us about four hundred dollars, including lunch. It's got to be the women and a friend—this would be no fun alone, and I'm betting these ladies haven't had lunch with a friend in weeks, if not months. If we pull two thousand dollars, we can run a five-pair test group. I thought of more than six names off the top of my head from women at the hospice center. They run a gamut of ages, too, so we can try a good mix." She wrote "Test Group" in capital letters after the number one.

"Ernestine?" Kate suggested.

"She'd be fabulous, but I think we'd better stick closer to home. Any ideas?"

"We can ask Ernestine to suggest someone, but I have a friend who does the spa thing all the time. The lady's nails are perfect every waking moment. She'd know where to go." Kate admired her own newly perfect nails.

"Okay, but not too posh. We want really nice, but not too over the top. I wouldn't want to sit in the pedicure chair listening to a bunch of country club types talk about their latest trip to the Virgin Islands, would you?"

Kate pointed her spoon at Darcy. "Good point."

Darcy penned a number two. She spread her hands on the table, her mind whirring. She didn't even have words to describe the sparkling sensation in her chest. "We need a go-between. Someone to let the women know they're receiving this gift. I think we have to do this anonymously."

"What?" balked Kate. "You don't want to be known as the patron saint of martyr beauty?"

"That's a good one," Darcy replied, laughing. "I'll put it on my business cards. But I'm sure we need to do this without anyone knowing who we are. And we need someone who can convince these women that this is on the level, and that it is important and worth taking the time. Someone from the hospice, like…Meredith. She's the hospice center's executive director. Oh, she'd be perfect. She's got that sage-wise-woman quality about her that makes you listen to what she has to say." Darcy wrote "Contact—Meredith?" beside the two. She looked up to find Kate staring at her. "What?"

"Business cards. Dar, that's the first joke I've heard you crack in nearly three months."

Darcy thought. "It is, isn't it?"

"And what's with the 'we'? Nobody left me a fortune to give away, you know," Kate added, hesitantly.

Darcy stopped short. She'd never even considered that she ought to ask Kate if she wanted to be involved. Perhaps that was a bad assumption. But she needed her. Badly. She looked at Kate intently. "You're in on this, aren't you? Kate, I can't do this without you. You've *got* to be in on this."

Kate's smile was as rich as the mousse. "You betcha. Wouldn't miss it for the world." She held out her hand. "Partners."

Darcy shook it, manicure to manicure. "Maybe *co-conspirators* is more accurate. But that sounds too…I don't know…too criminal." Darcy pondered. "What'd Robin Hood call his buddies?"

Kate narrowed her eyes, thinking. "The Merry Men, wasn't it?"

"Ick. We need something better than that."

"Bandits of Beauty?"

"Ugh. Even worse."

"Drive-by Pamperers."

Darcy laughed. "That sounds like we're chucking diapers out of a minivan window. Definitely not."

"I'm stumped."

"Me, too."

Kate folded her hands under her chin. "Well, how do you feel? What word would you give to what's happened to you today?"

Darcy considered the question for a long moment. She finally said, "Healed. Put back together. Restored."

"Restored. I like the sound of that. That fits."

Without another word, Darcy put her pen to the top of the page and wrote, "The Restoration Project."

Kate nodded in agreement. "So it is written, so may it be done."

Darcy raised an eyebrow. "Where in the world did *that* come from?"

"*Prince of Egypt.* Jessica watches it constantly. She loves the funny camel faces."

Darcy held out the paper. "'So it is written.' Massage, partner dear?"

Perhaps it would have been wiser to wait until she had it worked out better before telling Jack. Dinner had been great fun. Jack's ogling of the "new and improved Darcy" was a terrific high. Jack took in her hair and nails and generally saucier new demeanor with manly fascination. She couldn't even remember the last time she'd surprised Jack, much less with the kind of surprise that made him look like he'd give anything to have the kids somewhere else for a few hours.

All of which went out the window when she mentioned she'd had the beginnings of an idea of what to do about the money. Darcy hadn't realized, until just that moment, that Jack had never even considered going along with her dad's instructions. Granted, she still felt a long way from sure about her father's request, but she hadn't moved it completely from the realm of possibility—the way Jack obviously had.

What started out as a whopping pile of money was quickly turning itself into a whopping load of conflict. *Oh, great. Just what we need.* When she told him about The Restoration Project, Jack stared at her as though she'd mentioned it might be a nice idea to sell the children into slavery. He was still holding the glass of Cherry Coke halfway to his mouth, frozen in astonishment.

"You're serious," he said, almost under his breath.

"Well, I don't know yet. It's just an idea."

Jack ran his hand through his hair the way he always did when baffled. "I never thought…"

"Yes, well, *that's* pretty clear." Darcy amazed herself at how her dander got up so quickly defending an idea she'd not even settled on yet.

Or perhaps she had. Her mind raced back to the sensation, the energy bolt that shot through her when the idea first came. As though someone had opened up the top of her head and poured something warm and sparkly into it. No, Darcy Nightengale wasn't ready to say no to this, even though she wasn't completely ready to say yes. She sure wasn't ready to have it totally knocked out of consideration. Darcy turned, pacing the living room, groping for the words. "Jack, I don't know what I'm going to do…what *we're* going to do," she corrected herself, "about this. But I have to tell you, this idea just does something to me. I'm not sure I can explain it yet. But there's something there. Something I really want to think about."

Ugh. She wasn't making sense. Ah, but one look at Jack told her he was already putting things into neat order. Usually, she loved him for his ability to take control of things. To make sense of chaos. To put life in order. He'd been the anchor that kept her from going completely over the edge during the craziness of Dad's illness. He was Jack.

But this whole thing had defied perfect sense from the moment she opened that envelope. One of the tiny sparkles left in her chest from this afternoon kept insisting that it would never be about logic. It was a leap of faith of an altogether different kind.

Leap of faith? Darcy had never used those words before. Those were Dad's words. *What was going on here?*

"Are you telling me you want to give the money away, Dar?" His tone was an unnerving mix of question and statement.

"No, I'm not saying that at all. I'm saying I don't know what to do yet. I don't even know what to *want* to do yet. I'm not ready to say yes to Dad's request, but I'm not ready to say no, either. I mean, we don't have to decide now, do we? We don't have to decide a year from now." She turned and looked at him. "But I really like this idea. Couldn't I at least try it? See what happens?"

Jack was trying. Darcy could practically see his brain stretching to get around the idea of giving away some of the money. It was like watching Paula try to hug the big oak tree in the backyard—she would try mightily to get her arms around the thick trunk, but her fingers would always be just out of reach of each other. Dad's view of the world was always just out of Jack's reach.

Mostly out of hers, too. Until this morning.

They stood there, thinking hard, staring at each other, until Paula barreled up the stairs from the den. "Daaad! Mike keeps telling me to go away!"

Mike's rebuttal came howling up the stairway. "I'm trying to do my homework and she's bugging me. She wants to play with my calculator and she won't quit it."

Darcy glanced at her watch—eight-fifteen. Consideration of the Nightengale brand of philanthropy would have to wait. Baths and bed were a more pressing concern. Not to mention the small mountain of dishes still gracing the kitchen counters.

Little Orphan Heiress may have a new killer hairstyle, but she was still sadly lacking in maids and butlers.

Jack cracked her a smile. Something in his eyes told her he'd had the same thought. "Which do you want? Kids or dishes?"

Both might ruin the new manicure, but at least she could put on rubber gloves to do the dishes. "I'm opting for the sink and gloves, honey." She wiggled her fingers for effect.

"Gloves, huh? Well, all right, Paula-bear, let's get your shower started. We gotta give mom's manicure a fighting chance at survival."

Chapter 5

The Paul Hartwell Memorial Parking Lot

Darcy drew her finger around the curved edge of her coffee table. "How do I feel? I don't know. I don't imagine I feel anything different than any other person in this boat."

Doug Whitman said, "I see," in that I'm-not-going-to-comment-one-way-or-another-so-you-say-more kind of tone she knew psychiatrists were prone to use. Darcy didn't suppose she could blame Pastor Doug; they were only passing acquaintances. Whitman liked her Dad; it was clear from both his eulogy and the string of stories he told her today. Darcy wished, though, that the guy had been less comfortable with the gaps of silence in their conversation. He hadn't even bothered with the customary "How *are* you?" usually accompanied by a firm clasp of her arm and a polite show of concern. The kind of question that implied anything too deep in response would be unwelcome.

The kind she'd heard a dozen times a day in the week since Paul Hartwell slipped his mortal shell and upgraded to Heaven. No, Pastor Doug went straight to the *real* questions, the ones that required *real* answers.

"How do your days feel?"

Like hours. Like nanoseconds. Like endless blank journal pages. Darcy wasn't sure which answer would get Pastor Doug off her back, and off her couch, and out the door fastest.

"Feel?"

"Yes. What is it like for you to get through the day this week? Hard? Easy? All of the above?" Doug kept trying to poke his straw through the lemon floating in his ice tea. The effort he put into the pursuit was almost amusing.

"I don't know. They feel…plain." She took a drink while she searched for the right answer to satisfy him but not open up a deeper conversation. Doug clearly wasn't going anywhere until he'd either speared his lemon or "connected" with her somehow. She made a mental estimation that it would be eleven sentences before the word Jesus came up in conversation. "Empty, I suppose. I've spent so much time in crisis mode that it feels…well…odd to be doing normal stuff. Good, but odd. I keep waiting for the other shoe to drop, then I stop myself and realize it already has."

Doug shuffled a bit in his seat. "Was there anything about Paul's death that surprised you?"

Now, there was a loaded question. How much to reveal? If Darcy spoke of the inheritance, would Pastor Doug kick right into Building Campaign oh-but-we-need-that-new-nursery-wing mode?

"No." The minute the word left her mouth, Darcy knew it had too much bite. Now there was no way the good pastor was going to back off his ministries. She took out her regrets on a Mint Milano, biting the crispy cookie rather than indulge the urge to bite off her own tongue.

He reached for a cookie himself, far too comfortable with the silence. His eyes took on just a shade of a faroff look—was he *praying* for her? Getting God's permission to pry further? Did he *need* permission? Wasn't prying an occupational skill for reverends?

"Darcy…" he began.

Darcy anticipated the patronizing tone of voice, that politely compassionate edge that colored nearly everyone's attempts to "comfort," ready to jump down his throat the minute she heard it. "*I understand how you must feel… Time will ease your pain, let me tell you about the time my… I'm sure your children are such a comfort to you.…*" Darcy'd heard it all—and believed about two percent of it. She could smell it coming a mile away by now.

"…are you surprised at how angry you are at Paul for leaving the way he did?"

What?

"I think I would be. Hospice is never as peaceful as we imagine it will be. The dying leave us long before they're dead. I'd be weary and bitter, and probably more than a little ticked off if I were in your shoes."

Darcy nearly choked on the cookie. Before she could stop herself, she blurted out, "Are you *supposed* to say stuff like that?"

Doug inspected the chocolate inside his cookie. "I'm not *supposed* to say anything. I mostly try to figure out what's true, and go from there. Near as I can tell, the truth very rarely turns out how we think it's supposed to be."

A sharp, white-hot crack split through Darcy's chest. Yes, she was angry. Livid. And everyone was so busy giving her permission to grieve, to cope, that she hadn't realized until this very moment that no one had given her permission to be royally ticked off. Except for Jack, who seemed to be ticked off enough for the both of them, forcing her into defending Dad's indefensible actions. No, nobody had given her a chance to spout off. Like it had at the park, the anger erupted out of her, unbidden and unstoppable. Darcy didn't really want to be so exposed in front of this man, but the force of what he'd started was more than she could stem. Half in self-defense, she sprang up off the couch to pace the room.

"Yes." That one word opened the gates full force. "I am. I'm *really* mad. I did everything a good daughter's supposed to do. I turned my life inside out to take care of Dad. And I *wanted* to—I didn't do it out of some weird only-child obligation, I wanted to take care of him, to keep him comfortable."

She ran her hand along the fireplace mantel, half gripping it, half wanting to knock things off it. "But he wasn't comfortable. He was delirious and drooling, and pulling his bedsheets off in fear of something and choking and making sounds like he was drowning and…it was awful. It wasn't supposed to *be* like that. He was supposed to have a peaceful end. Meeting his maker and all. Going home to Jesus. But no, it was just *nuts*. People were running everywhere and everyone was freaking out because of the terrorist attacks so it was like no one even *noticed* he was dying. Noticed he was *gone*."

She stopped, her back to Doug, catching a sob. Her mind replayed the sound of his last breath. The halting, broken rasp. Then, the trailing, endless exhale.

It had been so far from what she expected, what she wanted.

It *all* had been so far from what she expected.

"How could he let me go through all that and then do what he did? How could he let me do all that disgusting stuff, handle all of those medical—" she searched for the word, trying not to be graphic "—*indignities,* and then hide his checkbook? How could he not trust me with this? How could he spring this on me and live with himself!"

The illogic of her last phrase, the way death kept winding itself into her speech like some sort of mean joke, stung Darcy.

She turned to look at Doug, half surprised that he wasn't reaching for his coat and eyeing the door.

"Am I mad? Yes. I'm furious!"

Again, he said nothing, just looked her straight in the eye. No judgment, not even surprise, just looking.

Embarrassed, Darcy plopped back down on the chair, snagging a tissue on the way around the end table. She tried to blow her nose as politely as possible, dabbing her eyes. "Well," she offered, "you asked."

Doug folded his hands. "Yes, I did. And I'm glad you answered. You need to talk about this kind of stuff. It will eat you alive if you pretend it isn't there. It isn't disrespectful, it's just human." He looked up, and for an awful moment Darcy thought he was going to clasp her hand or some other pastory thing, but he simply continued. "Look, Darcy, if Paul left you with debts, we have some people who can offer you some good counsel in that area. It happens. You wouldn't be the first to find out how expensive it is to die."

The fiscal cat was practically out of the bag now. Might as well tell it all. Even if it did end up as the Paul Hartwell Memorial Parking Lot.

"No, it's not that. Actually," Darcy added, almost laughing, "I think that would be easier. There are no debts. Just the opposite. I went to a lawyer just after Dad died—Dad told me I had to, you know, back when he was still…*with* us mentally. The lawyer told me Dad had a whole bunch of money he'd never touched. Tons of it. And, well, now they're *my* tons of it."

Darcy looked up to check Doug's expression. He looked genuinely surprised. That somehow made her feel better. "Well," he offered, "that *is* big."

"Yeah, you'd think. But evidently it wasn't big enough for Dad. He had to take it a step further." She took a deep breath before she continued. "Now, not only do I have one point six million shiny new dollars, I have to decide if I'm going to do what he says to do with it."

Doug paused a long while before he asked, "What *did* he tell you to do with it?"

Darcy hedged. The Paul Hartwell Memorial Parking Lot and Hospitality Wing played across her vision. But Pastor Doug didn't seem to be waxing predatory in front of her. She was gaining a sense, unfounded or not, that she could trust him. After all, Dad had.

Well, to a point. Which was as much as he'd been with her. Why not tell him?

"He told me to…he *asked* me to give it away. It was money won from a lawsuit over my mom's accident. He didn't want the money, but he'd promised her he'd keep it. It's complicated. Anyway, he promised he'd keep it, but since I never made a promise like that, he says I can give it away like he always wanted to." Darcy felt an odd, nervous laugh slip from her lips. "Death's a good way to pass the buck, it seems."

She felt stupid for laughing, uncomfortable at revealing something he could so easily pounce on. Darcy waited, watching for dollar signs to appear in his eyes like some Looney Tunes cartoon. But he kept looking at her. *At* her. Not mentally calculating the tax benefits of a major donation, just looking at her. It was the weirdly warm smile on Pastor Doug's face that stumped her most. "Literally," he quipped.

He *quipped*.

Darcy was so surprised, it took her a full thirty seconds to get the joke. A joke. Not at her, but *with* her. *Yes!* she thought, another person who found the situation absurd enough to joke about. Maybe Doug wasn't so bad after all. Perhaps the Paul Hartwell Memorial Parking Lot and Hospitality Wing and Community Baptismal Pool wasn't such a bad place to dump a fortune. Maybe it wasn't so bad he knew.

He pulled his hands down over his chin, shook his head a bit, and chuckled. "Your dad was a surprising man. Every time I was sure I'd figured him out, he'd throw me a new curve. I have to admit, though, this is a good one—even for him." Doug looked up at her. "Darcy, I haven't the foggiest idea what I'd do in your place. What are you thinking you'll do?"

I'm sure I know what I'd be doing if I were in your place, Darcy thought. *I give it ten minutes tops.* "Well, Jack and I have been discussing the issue practically nonstop. Everybody seems to have an opinion. And there are a lot of options."

Doug pinched the bridge of his nose. Then he got a "Say, I've got an idea" look on his face. This guy was good. Not even three minutes, and it looked genuinely spontaneous. Darcy decided she didn't really blame him. He probably had a furnace on the brink of death, stained nursery carpeting, two dozen committees to fund and all those poor hungry souls to feed.

"Darcy, I have an idea for you."

Darcy smiled. Not even a month into Little Orphan Heiress and she could smell 'em coming already.

"We have a couple in our church…"

…*Who feed tribes in Africa and teach them fractions,* Darcy finished in her head.

"…who deal with this sort of thing every day. They are quite wealthy, but they seem to know how to handle it well. Ed's a self-made man—grew a fortune going from selling newspapers to buying printing companies. I can't help thinking you'd like them. And I'm sure they'd like to meet you. Maybe they can help."

Darcy fought the urge to shake her head. "Huh?" was all she gulped out.

"Okay, it was a bad suggestion. I'm sorry to pry, I was just thinking—"

"No, wait, back it up a minute. You just…um…surprised me. Who are these people again?"

"Ed and Glynnis Bidwell. A couple—an older couple, actually—from our church. They have sizeable financial resources, but in my estimation they seem to know how to keep it in perspective. It was just a hunch…I'm sorry if I—"

"He's not Chairman of the Contributions Committee or anything?"

"Ed? No, he'd never— Wait…Darcy, did you think I was going to ask you to give your dad's money to the church?" He was putting the pieces together right in front of her. Astounding. Truly, the idea hadn't entered the guy's head yet. What kind of pastor *was* this guy?

Darcy shut her mouth, realizing that it was hanging open. Do you tell a white lie to a pastor?

"Ugh. Of course you did. Why wouldn't you? Oh, Darcy, I'm so sorry I gave you the wrong impression. I don't know what your dad told you about me, but in truth I am the most abysmal fund-raiser in history. Please, please believe that I knew nothing about what he left you. Oh, I've botched this."

"No, really," Darcy said, just because he looked so mad at himself.

"No, I should have said something right off the bat when you told me. I was just so…so…dumbfounded." Doug stood up, pacing the room. Honestly, he looked like he was going to walk over to the wall so he could pound his head against it. "No, look, Darcy, I want you to know—*right now*—how I see things. If Paul had wanted our church to have that money, I know he'd have told you so. Paul himself used to lecture me about how I need to be more aggressive in seeking funds for the church. No, Paul's got something else in mind for you. He's—he *was*—a man who never left things to chance when he had an idea. If he didn't tell you where to donate the money, then I truly believe he wants *you* to go through that decision process. And, even though my Stewardship Committee would probably boil me alive if they heard me say it, I've a good guess that it's not Ohio Valley."

"I don't really know what I'm—we're—going to do yet. Really."

Doug sat back down. "I don't think you *can* know what to do yet. That's a huge, broad issue. Darcy, I really think the Bidwells could be helpful to you. Will you let me give them your phone number? If you don't like them or they're not helpful, you can never see them again, but I don't think it will go that way. You'll really like Glynnis. Please, Darcy, will you let me do this for you? After I've been such a jerk?"

Who could say no?

The pastor left after a dozen more apologies, not one sentence of Christianese, and not a single plea for money. Who'd have thunk it?

Chapter 6

Heiress Lessons

Jack practically craned his head out the window to take in the snazzy sports car in Ed Bidwell's driveway. It was small and shiny—a take-no-prisoners red color—and slick enough for its own Bond movie. "Wow. Getta load of that thing, will you?" Jack had been none too keen on keeping this brunch date, but Darcy smiled to herself at Jack's sudden change of heart. Evidently Pastor Doug knew just how to get Jack Nightengale's attention. Or Someone Else did.

Not quite ready to chalk it up to divine intervention, Darcy surmised that all well-to-do men indulged in fancy cars. A testosteronized version of the three-stone, multi-carat ring every well-to-do woman seemed to own. The rings in the magazine and television ads, with adoring husbands shouting their affections in Italian streets and other wildly romantic venues.

Her brain flashed a quick, unlikely scene: Jack, in black turtleneck—unheard of—and leather sport coat—fat chance—and hair with just a touch of gel to make it look truly dashing—possible but not likely—by the Tuscan seashore. Crusty bread and Brie replacing Doritos and onion dip, a deliciously small black velvet box in his hand. Surging waves of violin music filled the air. With an elegant flair and a twinkle in his dark eye, he flips the lid to reveal one of those anniversary rings that are supposed to let you know he'd marry you all over again. Three whopping stones, cuddled next to each other in a bed of gold. Dazzling. Adding elegance to any hand, even one picking Play-Doh off the couch cushions….

"Dar?"

Jack was already out of the car, standing outside her door, hand ready to knock on the window if that's what it took to get her attention. How long had that little day-dream gone on?

"Oh, I get it," Jack said, "I'm supposed to open the door for you and such now. This is a high-class affair."

Darcy fumbled with her purse. "No, I just… My mind went somewhere."

"No kidding." Jack actually looked a little nervous. Darcy had to admit she felt the same. The whole setup felt odd and unnatural. Jack nudged Darcy with his hip, a gesture he'd done when they first dated. "Can I get one of those?" he said, pointing to the four-wheeled wonder.

"A two-car garage? Sure, hon." She nudged him back. Wow. She couldn't even remember the last time they'd done that to each other.

"Very funny." Jack ran a fidgety hand through his hair as they started up the walkway to the Bidwells' front door. "This feels weird. I don't know about this. I mean, we don't know these people from Adam."

"I know. But it's one brunch. Maybe they're really nice. It couldn't hurt. Besides, if you behave, maybe Ed will let you near that car...."

Jack rubbed his hands together in a let-me-at-'em gesture just before he pushed the doorbell button. "Think there's a butler?"

Darcy giggled just a bit. "Jack..."

The door swung open to reveal Ed Bidwell. Or a man who Darcy guessed was Ed Bidwell. He didn't look anything like she was expecting. He looked more like everybody's favorite grandfather than a printing magnate. He had a round, jovial face framed by a balding wreath of white hair. Gold wire glasses, hosting a pair of rather thick lenses, gave his water-colored eyes an oversize, magnified appearance. He had on an ordinary-looking plaid shirt and khakis, but Darcy noticed his belt and shoes were of a thick, soft, expensive-looking leather. He held his hands out.

"Jack. And Darcy. Saw you come up the walk. Ed. Ed Bidwell. Come on in. Come on in." He called down the hall as he took Darcy's coat. "Glyn, honey! They're here!"

"I can see out the windows just the same as you, Bid. I'm coming." Both their voices held the tint of a Southern upbringing, but softened from what sounded like years in the Midwest. Glynnis Bidwell came down the hall, tossing a dish towel on a side table as she did.

She was the pepper to her husband's salt—all dark but graying hair and wide brown eyes, her skin olive-colored to his fair skin. They were like a pair of ceramic salt shakers, the two of them: same size, same jovially heavy build, same sparkle in the eyes. They looked like the kind of couple you'd ask to play Mr. and Mrs. Claus at the church Christmas bazaar. That is, if *Better Homes and Gardens* ran your church Christmas bazaar.

"Darcy, so nice to meet you. I'm Glynnis Bidwell." She reached out a friendly hand. Well manicured, still damp, and boasting a one-stone ring. It was, however, a rather large stone. Darcy chided herself for even looking.

"See you've met Ed. And you must be Jack. Glad to meet you, too. Don't think I didn't see you eyeing Ed's baby out there in the driveway. Go on, Bid, show your toys off. I'd much rather have the two of you out of my hair than in the kitchen anyway." She shooed the men off as if telling her grandsons to go play in the yard.

Ed smiled, not bothering to hide his enthusiasm. "Glyn never misses anything." He winked at Jack. "Makes it hard to misbehave, but God must've known I needed watching, hmm?" Jack shot Darcy a quick you-didn't-tell-me-they-were-one-of-those looks, hopefully too quick for Glynnis to catch. "Like Coke, do you Jack? I got a thing for Cherry Coke. Keep a whole fridge of it in my garage. Can I stand you a drink, sir?"

Jack put up no resistance whatsoever as he let Ed Bidwell guide him into what must surely be a Man's Wildest Dream of a garage. Cool cars and Cherry Coke. Maybe Someone *had* known just how to put those two together.

Darcy looked back from watching them leave to find Glynnis eyeing her with one hand on her hip. *Ouch*. She *had* seen Jack's quick glance. Funny though, she didn't seem annoyed. More like she'd just received confirmation of a suspicion. "Jack wasn't itching to come here, was he?"

"Well," Darcy hedged, thinking she should be polite, but also quite sure no one pulled anything over on Glynnis Bidwell, "all of this has got us rather…baffled."

Glynnis shrugged a bit in her orange cardigan, fastening the two bottom buttons. "The world's a baffling place these days. Don't blame you one bit for feeling like someone's just shook the inside of your snow globe." She looked up from her buttons. "If even half of what Doug's told me is true—and I know he's only told me the half of it—then you were up to your eyeballs in sticky issues even before the world went on red alert." Glynnis turned, tucked Darcy's arm in the crook of her elbow and headed toward the kitchen. "Let those boys drown themselves in sugar water." She snatched the dish towel as she went past. "I've made us some ice tea."

Darcy wondered if the sugar water remark was a joke as she watched Glynnis dump not two but *four* spoonfuls of sugar into her own ice tea. "I like life sweet. And I think saccharin is for the birds, even if my thighs might be thinner for it," she said, catching Darcy's glance. Man, this woman did not miss a trick.

Glynnis plopped herself down onto the counter stool beside Darcy. The Bidwell kitchen had a comfortably cluttered feeling—as if there was too much fun in life to be tidy. It was well decorated, but with an eclectic, impulsive eye. Glynnis surely had a thing for chickens—they were everywhere—on potholders, drawer pulls, wallpaper border paper, and an abundant collection of chicken figurines lined up like a henhouse above her cabinets. If a kitchen could be bustling in a house with only two people, this was it.

"The hens…" Glynnis began, catching Darcy's sweep of the room. "Yes, well, I must admit there are a lot of them. Bid gave me one as a joke once, saying I should never become a biddy old hen because my name already had a *bid* in it and now I already had a hen." She pointed to a rather riotous ceramic one given a place of obvious prominence overseeing the sink. "Things just sort of snowballed from there. Soon this place became a henhouse." She offered

Darcy a wink. "If the sky should happen to be falling, I've got enough Chicken Littles in here to be the first to know."

Glynnis settled in closer to Darcy and wrapped her hands around her ice tea glass. "Sounds like lots of your sky has already fallen, my dear. I am truly sorry to hear about your dad. Paul and I didn't travel in the same circles, but he seemed like a good man. Cancer's an awful way to go. Are you doing okay?"

Even though a hundred people had asked her that question in the last month, Darcy knew Glynnis really *meant* it. Darcy found herself liking Glynnis Bidwell almost immediately. There was something wonderfully transparent about her—one look and you knew just what you were getting. "I'm not even sure I know what 'okay' is supposed to look like now," Darcy replied with a small smile.

"I don't expect you'll know anytime soon. It's important to have good people around you at a time like this. Have you got good friends helping you out?"

Darcy stirred her tea. "One really good one. Some people try to be nice, others don't seem to know what to say. Only a few people know about…the money part. Mostly I haven't had time for friends lately." She put the spoon down, noticing it was a heavy, solid silver. Someone once told her the mark of a true Southern lady was that her silver set included ice tea spoons. Darcy wondered when her mind had begun cataloguing such obscure details about people. "It's odd to have so much time now." She continued, "I feel like I can't remember what to do with it."

Glynnis pushed a plate of crackers toward her. Darcy dunked one into a bowl—chicken patterned—with dip in it. "It'll come back," the older woman offered in warm tones. "It'll all come back. But I imagine a few things are changed forever in your life now. You're not the same person you were before Paul died. You've got new responsibilities and challenges ahead of you now." Glynnis took a cracker and absolutely loaded it with dip before popping it into her mouth. "Listen, hon, lots of money is fun, but it has its own problems—and not everyone understands that. Things can get kind of messy before you find your balance.

"Bid and I, well, we got used to it bit by bit. Not that we didn't make a colossal mess of things in places along the way, but we had a chance to learn as we went. You, you and Jack have a whole different ball of wax. Everything all at once is no picnic. You need lots of good counsel if you're going to see it through." She drowned another cracker in dip. "It's a funny little niche Bid and I have carved for ourselves, helping people deal with big finances, but we like it. It's no accident Doug hooked us up, you know. God's been sending us people for years now, letting us help them over the—how does Bid say it?—'the big bumps that come with the big bucks.'" She chuckled as she selected another cracker for saturation. "That's my Bid. Always has a way with a phrase. Now, Darcy, tell me more about your dad...."

"Play golf, Jack?' Ed Bidwell snapped the tab on his Cherry Coke with a satisfied grin.

"No, never could quite find the time." Jack pulled the tab on his own can.

"Good." Bidwell hoisted the can in a salute. "Hate the game, myself. All those men chasing that silly little ball around a hunk of nice landscaping. Ah, give me a horsepower over a good tee time any day." The man looked lovingly at his sports car.

Jack had to admit, it was one lovable car. A beauty, and brand spanking new from the looks of it. Hadn't he seen one of those on the cover of *Car and Driver?* "What is it?"

Ed walked out into the driveway with the swagger of a man who felt king of all he surveyed. "That, my young friend, is a Ford Thunderbird. Hot off the line. Packed to the gills and gleaming in the sunshine." He continued to spout off a collection of technical specifications that made Jack's head swim. Jack could just picture the car zipping through the windy streets of Mount Adams, Cincinnati's upscale, steep-hilled section…

…and skidding all over the place. This was a car that belonged on the autobahn, not slipping down the hills in a Cincinnati winter. Totally impractical.

But one fabulous little car anyway.

"'Course," Ed continued, as if reading Jack's thoughts, "she'll be about as useless as a woman in high heels when the weather turns cold. But that first day of spring, when the weather gets warm enough to pull her out again and put the top down, well, that's a day I'm looking forward to with a huge hunk of pleasure."

Jack had to nod.

"I'll get another month out of her at least, but I don't think she'll hit the streets after October. Too much salt on these hills. Wouldn't want to rust these lovely curves now, would we?"

"No, sir." Jack thought about the blotches of rust gracing the "curves" of his car. It would practically be its own salt lick by February. The transmission was getting ready to give out soon, too. Not to mention the sad shape of the tires on Darcy's van—they might not last the winter, either.

Ed plucked a handkerchief from his pocket and rubbed at a nearly invisible smudge on the front headlamp. "How's Darcy holding up now that her dad's gone?"

Jack wasn't sure how much he wanted to get in-depth on this topic just yet. He gave his standard response. "As well as can be expected. We've known this was coming for so long, it mostly feels over. She gets blue some days, then on others she's her old self again."

Ed didn't look up from the headlamp, moving to inspect the other instead. "Dying's hard on a family. On a marriage, even. Glyn and I had more fights the year her mother died than we'd had in our entire marriage until then." He turned to look at Jack. "'Course Glyn's mom was a stubborn old battle-ax, and Paul was a saint, hmm?"

Jack wasn't quite sure what to make of that last remark. Was Ed speaking well of the dead, or inviting Jack to share his honest opinion? He sure didn't know this guy well enough to read between his lines. He sipped his Cherry Coke to bide a bit more thinking time.

"You're a smart man, Jack."

"Pardon?"

"I know half a dozen fellows your age who wouldn't have seen that comment for the minefield that it was." He laughed, folding the handkerchief back into his pocket. "You knew there was no real safe way to respond to a remark like that. I could spot it in your eyes. I like a man who knows that sometimes the best answer is not to answer at all."

Jack eyed him, half annoyed, half impressed. "Do you always test people for their conversational—" he searched for the right word "—agility so quickly after meeting them?"

"Only if I think they're worth it, Jack my boy, only if I think they're worth it." Ed tossed his Coke can into a large recycling bin clear across the garage in one perfect long shot. "I think I'm ready for lunch."

Chapter 7

The Torture Man Cometh

Kate pulled up a stool to Darcy's kitchen counter as they shared a cup of tea. "So the Bidwells have a nice house?"

"Really nice. Jack was drooling over the guy's sports car. Nice furniture, the works. *Real* art, not just prints from a superstore. She had silver ice tea spoons, even."

Kate made a dour, uppercrusty socialite face and stuck her pinky out.

"No, it wasn't like that. I mean, that's what I was expecting, but she was really nice. The house was gorgeous, but it was a…comfortable sort of gorgeous." Darcy sighed. "It's hard to describe. It was really a lovely afternoon."

Darcy could tell that Kate had caught the edge to her voice. "But…" Kate cued.

Darcy sighed and stirred her tea again. "It just seemed to make everything worse."

"Worse how?"

"They were so perfect, so happy, so…compatible." She looked at the colored plastic handle of her teaspoon and thought of Glynnis's graceful flatware. "I could look at them and see what could be…and see what isn't." Darcy put down her spoon. "Isn't, isn't, isn't."

Kate sighed. "You guys fought again last night, didn't you?"

"It's so funny, Kate. Jack talked to Ed Bidwell, I talked to Glynnis. Ed and Glynnis are so in sync with each other, so agreeable, and yet Jack and I came out of that visit with two completely different viewpoints. No, let me rephrase that. We came out of there with the same viewpoints we've had all along, only just farther apart than before. How can that happen? It doesn't make sense. It should have made things better, but it made things worse."

"Jack still on the investment bandwagon?"

"More so than ever. If I didn't know better, all he and Ed Bidwell talked about were the miracles of compounded interest. I think he told Jack the interest off his latest investment strategy bought that shiny new car Jack was eyeing."

"Ed Bidwell's a pretty big honcho. Maybe it did."

Darcy eyed her. "You're not helping."

"Okay, tell me about this Glynnis lady. All I know about her is what I see on the charity ball page of the newspaper. She's a bigwig at the art museum, isn't she?"

"From the looks of her walls, she sure is." Darcy leaned in. "She was so…cool. She launches all these incredible projects and mentors people and looks so happy and…you just want to hate her but she's too nice to hate."

"Must be nice."

"She's done such amazing things with what she's got. She can look back on her life and tell me story after story of people she's helped, things she's done, differences she's made in people's lives."

"And you want that."

Darcy stopped and stared at Kate. *Want.* Yes, she wanted that. She wanted what Glynnis had, what Glynnis did, how Glynnis changed her world. Even though she'd felt the emotion, and had even expressed something like that to Jack last night, Kate had somehow nailed it. Kate always nailed it. "Yeah," she said softly, surprised at the hurt in her own voice, "I want that."

The women sat in silence for a moment. "Did you tell Glynnis about your idea? The Restoration Project?"

"No, I wasn't ready to for some reason. You're the only one who knows." Darcy pressed her fingers to her brow. "I don't know, Kate, it sounds so stupid. It's not like you can change the world with a good haircut."

Kate got a sassy look on her face. "Oh, I don't know about that. Don might argue with you there."

"Don enjoyed the new do huh?"

"I got two whole compliments yesterday. He can't seem to stop touching my hair."

Darcy gaped at her. Don wasn't exactly a man given to compliments and hair touching. This was high praise, indeed.

Kate tossed her hair like a shampoo ad. "And I owe it all to Darcy Nightengale and the wonders of The Restoration Project," she added with infomercial-quality enthusiasm. "Maybe I need to give a testimonial to Jack."

Darcy sent her a mock glare. "You stay away from Jack." She took a sip of tea. "He did hip-check me yesterday in the Bidwells' driveway."

"Hip-check?" Kate's eyebrows furrowed a moment. "You mean that little side-bumping thing he used to do to you all the time? The thing that bugged you so much when you were dating?"

"Yep."

"I thought you hated that."

"I thought I did, too. Until he did it yesterday. It was…I don't know…something from another time. A piece of memory from when we were young and gushy. Instead of old and responsible."

Kate squinted her eyes, calculating. "So Jack hip-checked you. Okay, not exactly changing the world, but I think it qualifies as a solid spark." She straightened in her stool and planted her hands on the table. "I think this is just going to take some time. Talk to him again. If your eyes look to him like they do to me when you talk about this idea of yours, I don't see how he can say no. Maybe he just needs time to come around."

"I don't know. Oh, Kate, maybe this whole thing is just plain stupid."

"No, no, Dar, it's not. It's not, and you've got the hip-checks and—" she winked "—I've got the hair touching to prove it. You're onto something, girl. I know you are. *You* know you are. And it's not stupid." Kate gave Darcy her own version of a hip-check. "Promise me you'll try to talk to him again tonight, will you?"

Darcy nodded as the phone rang.

Kate grabbed her purse and took a couple of gulps of tea for the road. She mouthed "See you" and waved over her shoulder as she let herself out the back door. Darcy picked up the receiver.

"Mrs. Nightengale, this is George Tortman at Nichols School." Tortman, Tortman. Darcy strove to place the name. Torture Man. The kids called him Mr. Torture Man.

Because he was the Dean of Discipline at Nichols Middle School. Now what?

Darcy forced her voice to sound casual and upbeat. "Good afternoon, Mr. Tortman. What can I do for you?" More like, What are you going to do to me, Torture Man? Surely no good could come from a call like this.

"I need to speak to you about Michael."

Nope, no good at all.

"He did what?"

"He wrote on his desk."

Jack snapped his tie off with something close to disgust. "Mike got a detention for writing on his desk? How bad can that be?"

"Well," Darcy tried to soften her voice as she folded a fourth bath towel, "he wrote a lot. An entire song. Well, the words to a song, actually."

Mike kicked his dress shoes onto the closet floor. "Why am I sure it wasn't 'Mary Had a Little Lamb'?"

"Mike covered his algebra class desk with the lyrics to a rock song. A rather depressing, anxious one. Social angst, heartbreak, despondent slacker kind of stuff."

"Great."

"Evidently at first they thought Mike had written it. The song I mean. That the words were his own. Which, of course, sent the school counselor into action. You know, recent death in the family and all." Darcy snatched another towel from the laundry basket and began folding it aggressively. "Only when things began to heat up did he admit it was just song lyrics."

"Oh," moaned Jack sarcastically, "that makes it *so* much better."

"I made Mike show me the lyrics off the CD liner sheet. They weren't violent or anything like that, just rather depressing. Dark and dreary."

"Lovely. Did he say why he did it?"

"He…said he was bored." Darcy hesitated, knowing this would just broil up the whole Mike-needs-to-go-to-private-school argument on top of everything else.

Jack blew a breath out sharply. "Can't he just twiddle his thumbs like the rest of the world? He's never done this before."

"Even Mr. Tortman admitted they haven't been completely happy with this new math teacher," Darcy offered, not at all sure that was the right thing to say.

"That's no excuse. This is dumb, Dar. Even for Mike."

"I don't think he ever thought anything like this would come of it."

Jack looked at her. "So you're defending him?" This was getting nowhere fast.

"No, Jack, I'm not defending him. I'm just trying to figure out how this happened, same as you."

"I *know* how this happened. Mike needs more challenge. We've been saying that for months. When is the last time he's even brought math homework home? He finishes everything in school. Early. He hasn't brought home anything lower than an A- in math for two years and I never even see him putting in much of an effort. We can't let this slide. He could be doing so much more than coasting. Mike's got to have someone teaching him at his level."

"I *know*," Darcy shot back, stuffing the towels into the linen closet as if she were loading a cannon. "I said the same thing to Mr. Torture Man."

Jack looked at her. "Mr. *Who?*"

Darcy hadn't even realized she called him that. Oh, no, had she called him Torture Man to his face…uh phone, too, without realizing it? There's something that should really help the situation. "Mr. Tortman. The kids call him Mr. Torture Man."

Jack started to laugh, despite himself. "You didn't call him Mr. Torture Man, did you? You know how you are with names."

"No, I'm sure I didn't." When Jack made a face at her, though, even she started to laugh. "A least I'm pretty sure I didn't."

"Let's hope so." The tension in Jack's shoulders softened a bit. "Look, I've had a lousy day at work." He came over to her, helping her with the last towel. "This isn't a new argument, Dar. We've been talking about this for over a year. You know Mike needs a more advanced education—at least in math—and who knows what other subjects. For crying out loud, we were so frustrated last spring when those test scores came back. We both said he should be at Simmons Academy, not at Nichols. Back then it was impossible. Now, it may be an option for us. Lots of things may be options for us now." He stared at her, a tall dark pillar of sensibility. "Are you going to let a goofy idea of your dad's stand in the way of this family's options?"

Well, that was the question of the hour, wasn't it? Trouble is, it wasn't just Dad's goofy idea. Darcy had a relentlessly goofy idea of her own. One she wasn't sure her husband, Mr. Sensibility, would ever understand. She barely understood it herself.

The confusion must have been obvious, for Jack just sighed. He turned to lean his back against the closet door, letting his head fall back as well. "You're still grieving. You've been through a huge trauma. You're exhausted.

Can you just *consider* the possibility that I may be able to see this more clearly than you can right now?"

He was right. There were barrelfuls of emotions tangled up in this. She knew he saw it all in the pure science of facts and figures. He had it all covered, caged up inside sharp edges of prudent finance. No one in their right mind would argue with his thinking.

So why was she so angry?

Chapter 8

Loose Ends on the Loose

Darcy turned the page on her kitchen calendar slowly, almost with ceremony. October. It was a new month. It felt somehow important, and then again not at all. Time was marching on, and that was a good thing, wasn't it?

The first of the month had seemed like a good day to make the appointment when she'd scheduled it. A day to close out some things and start up others. Now, staring at the notation of "8:30 a.m.—Meredith" on that first square, it felt entirely too soon. Her dad had been gone a few weeks. Since his last day, Darcy had not set foot inside the hospice center. She didn't want to return now. The sights, the smells, the sounds, the faces all felt like they'd wash up over her, drag her out to sea in a tidal surge of emotion.

Who could blame her? Who wanted the memories of such a place? She hadn't really thought of it as bad when she was there—just the opposite, as a matter of fact. It was an entire institution fighting against the tide—forcing comfort into discomfort, making peace from terror, insisting on dignity in the face of so many indignities. Now, though, it loomed in the shadow of memory. Dark and awful in all its peach-colored softness.

Darcy had tried to avoid returning to the hospice, but the papers had to be signed, and a few overlooked personal items needed to be collected. She'd asked Meredith if they couldn't meet at Darcy's house. Meredith had declined. Darcy had then offered to buy Meredith lunch at one of her favorite restaurants. Meredith wasn't placated. "I'll take you up on lunch at The Palace over the holidays," she had said, "but you and I both know you need to come here for this."

She didn't want to go.

She had to go.

If only for the slim chance that it wasn't as bad as she remembered it. At first, Darcy took Jack up on his offer to come with her. He'd even offered to go *for* her. Darcy knew, though, somewhere in the back of her mind, that sending someone else—even bringing someone else— wouldn't make this go away.

She pulled on her jacket with hollow-feeling hands. Hands that slipped instinctively into her coat pockets for the car keys—and found the worn smoothness of her father's key chain. She'd linked it to hers. A memento, a sliver of life's ordinary trappings, a piece of her father's day-to-day existence. *I miss you* heaved out of her chest with her breath. *Are you happy now? Is heaven wonderful? Is heaven there?*

"Are you okay so far?" Meredith Sorensen had a voice like a soft blanket. It wrapped around Darcy and made her feel better, even when Meredith was delivering the worst of news. The woman was an extraordinary soul, perfectly suited for her job as director of the hospice center. She was tiny, a little plush-toy dynamo of a woman; passionate about her work and the people it touched. Darcy had often wondered how Meredith could be surrounded by death and still be so full of life.

"Sort of," she replied. "This paperwork is incredible. I don't know how I'd have sorted through it without you."

Meredith smiled behind her wildly colored reading glasses. "You'd have found a way. But I'm glad you don't have to." She slid yet another stack of papers toward Darcy. "Here, sign these three where the Post-it notes are, and that will be the last of them."

Darcy signed. "No more after this?"

"No more from me." She pulled off her glasses and let them dangle from the beaded chain around her neck. "I'm sure your father's lawyers will have more to sign once the estate goes through probate, but I have a feeling Paul left no loose ends there."

You have no idea, Darcy thought, wondering when she would stop feeling like a walking time bomb of secrets. "Sure" was all she said.

Meredith pushed back her chair. "Let's walk back and get Paul's things."

Darcy's chest tightened. "Walk back? You don't have them here?" The office was bad enough. She wasn't ready to walk the residence hallway.

Meredith was not at all taken aback by the response. "They're back in the east lounge. Besides," she said, coming around the desk corner, "Angie's here and she wanted to see you."

Angela Denton. Angie Denton had been a friend of sorts. Her husband Bob moved in a couple of months before Paul got really bad. Angie and Bob were Jack and Darcy's age. An accomplished couple who'd chosen world travel rather than start a family. "Bob's taking this particular one-way trip without me," Angie used to quip. If you could call it quipping, for she never could quite get the joke out without choking on it.

With horror, Darcy realized she hadn't once checked in on Angie during the weeks since Dad's death. "Oh, Meredith, I've never…"

"It's all right." Meredith stopped her with a hand on Darcy's arm. "She understands. Really. But I think she'd really like to see you."

"Bob?" Darcy almost didn't want to ask.

"A few days. Probably not much more. He's only conscious an hour or so a day now."

Darcy's throat tightened. "Oh…I, Meredith, I'm not sure I can do this."

Meredith's hand tightened supportively around Darcy's arm. "Yes, you can. You of all people can, because you know what it's like. She needs to see you, Dar, to know that you can come out of the other side of this."

Darcy began to tear up. "I'm not out, I'm not on the other side of this."

"All the better not to be in the middle alone. You can just stand in the doorway and cry if that's as far as you can go. Angie won't care what you do. Come on. I'll be right beside you. It will be good for both of you."

Darcy felt almost ill as Meredith began to lead her down the hallway. The scent of this building, the particular combination of medical aromas combined with the many homey touches Meredith added, was like no other. Just breathing the air seemed to suck Darcy into a time warp, back to the days when all the days were in here. When life divided itself into time at the hospice center, and time waiting for the center to call her.

With surprise, Darcy discovered that it wasn't that bad. At just that moment, sucking in a deep breath to steady herself, she realized that she didn't regret the time spent here. This was a good place. An important place. No, the time in here, with her dad, was not wasted time. Hard time, but not horrible time.

The wasted time, Darcy realized with a shock of clarity, was the time spent outside of here still thinking of here. It was a good thing to be here with Paul, but it *had* taken over her life. So much so that the time away from here was still spent constantly thinking about Paul. While she physically left the hospice, she never *mentally* left the place.

The door to Bob's room, just across the hall from where Paul had lived, was left ajar. The room seemed tiny as Darcy peered in. It was like when people go back to their elementary school to visit as an adult. They remember it as enormous and mythic, yet everything seems small and ordinary upon their return. Just as they remember it, but then again not at all the way they remember it. Darcy half expected to find drinking fountains that came up to her knees.

Inside the room, Angela held the time-honored posture of watchful loved one. Sitting in a vinyl chair, head leaning on one hand, slumped shoulders, facing Bob. Darcy's body remembered the posture almost involuntarily, the way one mother will involuntarily rock when standing near another mother rocking an infant.

"What kind of day today?" Darcy gulped out. It was how they greeted each other, because "How are you?" seemed so stupid in such a setting.

Angela uncurled herself and turned with a thin but warm smile. "Not too bad. Better, now." She came up and gave Darcy an enormous hug.

She looked awful.

It was inconsiderate, inappropriate, it was downright mean, but Darcy's first thought at seeing Angela was, Did I look like that?

Oh, lovely, Dar. The woman is about to lose her husband and you're playing fashion police? Darcy wanted to stomp on her brain cells for reacting this way, but it was about so much more than whether Angie had combed her hair yet today. It was the uncared-for, neglected, starving look of the woman that made Darcy's heart ache. Not because sweats and old T-shirts were involved, but because Darcy knew all they represented. It was all there, all instantly recognizable: the neglect and tension and sleepless nights and uneaten meals and mind-numbed wanderings that one set of overworn clothes represented. She knew: she had a closet full of such clothes.

The overwhelming urge to fold Angela in a huge hug, dip her in warm, soothing water, and wrap her in scents and softness and beauty washed over Darcy in a wave she could neither explain nor ignore. She'd planned on her memories of Paul being hard, but her memories of herself were harder still.

Her throat tightened under the depth of emotion that had passed over her in the split second of Angie's greeting. "Angie…I'm…I haven't…"

Angie stopped her. "Don't." She heaved in a get-it-together breath and held Darcy at arm's length. "You look really good."

"I'm okay. Some days are easier than others."

"How are Jack and the kids?"

"Good, too. Coping, same as me, although they choose some…challenging ways to show it."

Angie managed a chuckle. "I'll bet." She looked Darcy in the eye. "Is it hard?" There was no need to finish the sentence with *after it's all over?* Darcy knew what Angie was asking.

You could tell the truth in this place. "Yeah." Darcy thought of a million examples, but none of them seemed to be important just this moment. "Up and down. I think it goes up and down for a while." Darcy's eyes strayed toward Bob. He seemed even thinner than before, more pale. Meredith used to say you could tell when a soul was packing up and leaving home, that it showed on a body. Darcy could see that Bob's soul was just about out the door. "It's easier in some ways," she said to Angie while still looking at the hollow of Bob's cheekbones. "Harder in others, but easier in some." She returned her gaze to Angie. "Is he comfortable?"

"He does that wheezing thing more, and there are times I know he's talking but I can't hear what he's saying. I think he dreams a lot. No Thrasher Basher, though, so I'm glad for that."

Thrasher Basher was the sickly joking name they gave to Paul when he began to have convulsions toward the end. His delirium would send him into fits of grasping, moaning and other decidedly heartbreaking activities that made Darcy crazy. After one particularly gruesome episode, Darcy had lost it and yelled at Paul in her frustration, telling him to "quit playing thrasher basher and just *die* already." When Darcy was mortified at her own response, beating herself up for her lack of compassion for a dying man, Angie had come into the room and ceremoniously knighted Paul "Sir Thrasher Basher." The name stuck. It was odd what passed for humor in this place.

"Are you ready?"

Angie sighed. "Yes. No."

"Have you called?" *Calling* was slang here for making the gather-the-family call. The call made when it looked like only days or hours were left. It was a rite of passage of sorts here. Everyone else in the center would come around for support when someone "called." Some people had been through it three or four times if a patient was particularly unpredictable—which seemed cruel to Darcy. Oddly enough, there had been no call for Paul. Those who might travel couldn't, phones were crazy in the height of the terrorist attacks, and those who were close by and cared enough had already said their goodbyes. Darcy felt a twinge of jealousy—Bob was getting the peaceful, attended death she had hoped her own father would have. Again, it was odd what passed for blessings in this place.

"Not yet. Tomorrow maybe. A couple of people need to fly in."

"When's the last time you ate anything more than a Snickers bar?" Darcy found herself rubbing Angie's hand. The compulsion to take care of this woman's poor, overtaxed body was so strong it was nearly a physical ache. Maybe, just maybe, this was the force that drove Meredith. Darcy didn't quite understand what was happening to her lately. But it was happening, and it refused to be ignored.

"They brought me breakfast." Angie inclined her head to a tray of predictably untouched food that sat in the corner.

"I mean real food. When's the last time your hand saw the inside of a Skyline Chili bag?"

A wisp of a smile crossed Angie's taut face. "Oh, wow, ages."

"I can fix that," Darcy offered, fighting the urge to reach out and smooth Angie's hair. "Let me fix that."

"Okay."

They talked for a few minutes more, not really about anything important because in here the really important stuff transpired without words. The real communication took place over a plumped pillow, a rubbed shoulder, an offered tissue or a sigh of recognition.

Every single moment, the ache in Darcy's chest doubled. By the time she and Meredith left the room, Darcy thought she would burst from her own skin. Her heart would incinerate in two seconds if she didn't talk to someone about The Restoration Project. Without any hesitation, she grabbed Meredith by the arm and pulled her back into her office.

"Meredith," she began, almost breathless, "you have to help me do something."

"Do what?"

"Well, it starts with one of Dad's loose ends...."

Chapter 9

Joan of Arc, but with Hot Dogs

The river spread before her, glazed in the afternoon sunlight. The last of October's strong sun warmed her like a comforting blanket. Darcy could see why this had been one of her dad's favorite places to think. In the days of his demise and in the days since his death, she'd come to think of this landmark perch atop the steps of Immaculata Church as her spot as well. A haven passed down from one generation to the next. Standing here, atop the dozens of famous steps that led up to this tiny church on Mount Adams, she could reach easily back into her memories. Soon, November's winds would turn the pathway cold and slippery, but for now, she could let the warmth take her back to the dad that was. Not the sick one, but the healthy one. The wise, wonder-filled father who could unravel life's thorniest knots. She'd come up here a lot lately.

Usually, the altitude gave her a sense of perspective. Not today. Today, Darcy felt as though she were standing on the edge of a very high precipice, contemplating a leap so large it made her head spin. If she had hoped time would calm her spirit and make the crazy craving of The Restoration Project go away, it hadn't happened. Talking with Meredith today had only made it worse.

Not a single part of her life fell into agreement with this idea. Not one.

But it didn't make one ounce of difference in how she felt.

"I'm insane," Darcy pronounced to the last bite of her chili dog. Now, it seemed, even fast food had joined the conspirators to set her on this path, for handing the bag of chili dogs to Angie had added to the obsession. As Angie took the bag of food from her, Darcy had the inexplicable urge to grab her hands and smother them in soft, warm cream. They were so dry and cracked. So used and used up. "I'm nutters," she reiterated, reaching for the plastic cup of iced tea. "Dad, what are you doing to me?"

Darcy looked at her watch. She had a little over an hour and a half to figure life out. After that, the bus would deposit Paula on her doorstep and the hurricane that was after-school activities would begin. Darcy needed a plan. She needed a path, like the set of steps winding up the hillside before her. Something to get her up this impossible mountain of an idea.

She imagined the church members standing at the bottom of this hill, hoping to build a church at its top. Everyone in town knew the church's famous story: the parishioners had climbed the mountainside to the site of this church as a show of faith. The chapel had faced all kinds of obstacles to its construction. It had started out as a path, then someone built wooden steps up the hillside. Then the wooden steps became concrete. Construction of the steps led to construction of the church.

The path was a symbol, standing for a journey of faith. Had anyone known what that first footpath would eventually become? Foreseen the thousands of people who would tread those steps over time? Or were they just trying to do what needed to be done? What did it feel like to lay that first plank, knowing where they wanted to go but not at all sure they could get past the obstacles to get there? How many doubts arose?

Pastor Doug's comment about Dad wanting her to go through this decision process popped into Darcy's mind. What if Dad's request was his staircase, his vision and path when he gave her that money?

Really, Darcy thought, trying to dismiss the thought as she flattened the container that held the chili dog. That's making a bit much of it, isn't it? Your father didn't send you on some kind of self-discovery pilgrimage. This isn't *Lord of the Rings;* no one's handed you a save-the-world quest. This is Cincinnati and you're eating chili dogs until the school bus comes. Don't go all epic when you've got to get your third grader to Girl Scouts in two hours.

Darcy knew, though, even as those nice sensible thoughts came to her, that they were useless against the thump of her heart.

I need to do this.

I need to do this. I need to do this.

All the common sense in the world wouldn't fight this idea, and Darcy knew it. So what now?

A small statue of Mary atop the landmark church caught Darcy's eye. Before she could stop herself, Darcy found herself thinking, *Is this what it felt like for you? Sure, you had an actual angel show up and hand you your orders, but your task was a whole other ball game. I'll bet*

God's plan made no more sense to you than Dad's plan does to me. And I'm not even sure this is Dad's plan.

Then, as if her insides were having an argument with each other, another thought stopped that one dead in its tracks: This isn't Dad's plan.

It's yours.

Given to you. She recalled the sensation that overtook her when the idea had first come. A complete, electrifying, power surge that hatched the idea, fully formed, inside. Like a revelation.

Darcy's hands shot off the railing, alarmed at her own thinking. *Oh no.* She wasn't going to go in that direction. No way, no how was God telling her to do this crazy thing. She began pacing around the sidewalk, fighting the tidal wave that she didn't want and couldn't seem to stop. *No, no, no.*

That was the kind of thinking that made people sell their houses and go live naked in communes waiting for aliens to come take them home. Darcy Nightengale was a housewife, not a hobbit. Oh, no, we weren't going there on this one. That was just…plain…

Inescapable.

Darcy sank to the top step, clutching the sack of hot dogs like a life preserver. Suddenly every action, every thought since she found out about the money, seemed to slide into its place along the path. She could see them in her mind—the trip to the spa, Kate's reaction, Angie, Meredith, even Glynnis—falling into a pattern. Connecting through some sort of amazing thread to this place, these stairs, this moment. Like stair steps, laid one by one up the path to where she now sat.

No. Not me. She wanted to run down the stairs and run

away. Every bone in her body wanted to deny what she now knew she couldn't.

This sort of stuff was supposed to happen on moonlight nights with stars and angels and shepherds biding in the fields. In Italian grottos and biblically picturesque mountaintops. To other deeper, stronger, far more appropriate people.

Not on Cincinnati hills with chili dogs.

I don't believe enough. Darcy cried into her paper napkin. *I'm not even sure I believe at all.*

The world stopped. A horrible, wonderful halt that brought the whole universe to an incredible breath-holding standstill.

At that moment, Darcy knew.

Yes, she wasn't sure she could believe enough.

But she *wanted* to.

If a mustard seed was all God claimed he needed, well, that was about all He had to work with here.

A mustard seed of wannabe faith, a hunk of money, a sack of chili dogs, and Darcy Nightengale.

No way, no how was this going to work.

Darcy glanced at her watch, suddenly aware that she had no idea how much time had passed. It was 2:20.

Exactly—almost to the minute—enough time to get home and catch the bus. Not exactly the Archangel Gabriel in glowing robes, but a good omen none the less. Still having not a single idea how to deal with all this, Darcy gathered up the cup and wrappers and made her way back to the car.

All the traffic lights did not suddenly turn green at her arrival. Life did not suddenly fall into place. Just the opposite; the car began making a strange new noise when making left turns—evidently the fridge was taking in recruits. God did not come down from the heavens and appear in front of her.

As a matter of fact, the closer she got to home, Darcy wasn't even sure she knew what had happened. Only that *something* had happened. Something that she had not chosen, but rather something that seemed to have chosen her.

Oh, she thought as she pulled the back door open, I'm so not ready.

Life, however, didn't seem to really care. Paula came bursting through the door, backpack, jacket and lunchbox flying in all directions.

"Mooom! I'm starving! Betsy Cooper says I have too many freckles to be a nice person and Peter Nemski called me a walnut-brained dinosaur. I need five empty coffee cans for Girl Scouts and I lost my library book again."

Darcy slid the plate of peanut butter cookies across the counter just as Paula hurled herself into the stool. "Coffee cans for Girl Scouts this afternoon?"

"Yep."

Darcy mentally inventoried the recycling bin. No coffee cans. "How long have you known this, Paula Nightengale?"

"Since last time."

"Since last time *two weeks ago?*"

"Yep." Paula didn't seem to see how that was a relevant point.

"I don't think we have five coffee cans." Darcy sighed, firing up the Mom Who Fixes Everything persona. Last time, it was old jeans and a washed white T-shirt on twenty minutes' notice. How hard could a few cans be? When Paula's face began to register catastrophe, Mom sprang into action. "Calm down, Paula bear. What are the cans for?"

"I dunno. We're making somfin." Evidently the coffee can shortage had not curbed her appetite for peanut butter cookies. Rather the opposite, Paula now had one in each hand and was alternating bites.

"If you can tell me what you're making, then maybe I can find other cans that will work just as well."

"Mooommm, Mrs. Hapson said we need *coffee* cans." Peanut butter cookies evidently did little to muffle whining.

"Mrs. Hapson is a grown-up, she can adapt. Tell me what you're making."

Within ten minutes, Darcy had identified that luminaria were the project in question, and managed to persuade one little girl that soup-size luminaria were just as beautiful—perhaps even more so—than coffee-can-size luminaria. Two more peanut butter cookies sealed the deal, and they went on to tackle larger subjects such as why people with freckles could be as nice if not nicer than those without freckles, and that Mom was absolutely certain her daughter did not posses a walnut-size dinosaur brain.

All with twelve minutes to spare before Mike exploded through the door with his own backpack, lunchbox, hunger and demands.

Darcy sent Paula off to her room to change into the scout uniform, set vanilla cookies and a glass of orange juice out to await Mike, and turned her attention to scavenging the recycling bin for a quintet of soup cans.

As she gathered the last of the cans, Darcy froze. Mike wouldn't be needing any snack, because Mike would not be barreling through the door at any second, because today was the day Mike was serving detention.

Again.

This time for drawing an alarmingly detailed scene of terrorists bombing Cincinnati with water balloons from a B-52 airplane they'd apparently stolen from the air museum two states over. Algebra class was turning into a carnival of imaginative bad behavior from Mike. All while still pulling straight A's on every test.

Darcy sighed, making a mental note to look up something like *Difficult Lives of Bible Heroes* on Amazon.com. She was four hours into her reluctant partnership with You Know Who, and life didn't seem to be improving much.

You were expecting Peace on Earth, Good Will Toward Darcy?

Well, now that you mention it, yes.

Darcy checked the front door to make sure the hidden key was under the second step, just in case Mike forgot his house key, and then herded Paula, five cans in hand, into the car for Girl Scouts.

When she got back into the car, having successfully refrained from screaming when Mrs. Hapson mentioned Paula needed only *two* cans of *any* size, Darcy noticed the voice mail icon on her cell phone was flashing. She punched the code to hear Jack's voice. "I want to talk to you tonight. Can we find some time?"

Jack wanted to talk. Wow. Maybe Peace on Earth Good Will Toward Darcy *was* in the works. What if Jack had experienced a change of heart, and could now understand what this crazy idea meant to her? Darcy's heart did a Maxwell House-size leap in her chest, just as it had done on the church steps. She tried to call Jack back, but got his voice mail instead. She left a brief message saying she'd stop at the video store on the way home and get a movie to occupy the kids and make sure all homework was done before dinner.

Fasten your seat belt, Darcy, it's going to be a red-letter day.

Time ran like molasses until Darcy found herself pushing Play on the DVD player at seven. Paula was duly bathed and pajama'd, Mike had, through what Darcy could only interpret as divine intervention, been cooperative all afternoon. He'd even knocked off the majority of his homework during detention, and showed her a copy of the reluctant "Sorry I drew on school property" letter he'd been asked—ahem—forced to write. One zapped bag of popcorn and a quart of Kool-Aid later, Darcy settled herself into the living room love seat beside Jack.

It was going to be a wonderful moment. She'd grabbed a minute between Girl Scouts, social studies vocabulary, and chicken casserole to change into a nicer shirt and brush her hair. She'd picked up the living room a bit so that it actually looked like a living room, not the place where everybody's stuff seemed to be dumped on the way to the kitchen. Impulsively, she'd set out a plate of cookies and even made decaf after dinner—French vanilla, Jack's favorite flavor. If this was the moment God was going to walk into her life and begin guiding her on her quest, Darcy wanted it right. It seemed the proper, grateful thing to do.

Jack made a little noise of pleasure as he sipped his coffee. He had something big to tell her; the tension in his shoulders kept him from sitting back against the cushions the way he normally did. She waited, watching him rehearse the words in his head.

Darcy had rehearsed her own gracious response. She would tell him how hard it must be for him to understand such a strange idea. How much these past months must have worn on him, with so much trauma in the house. How supportive he had been as a husband, how much she owed him for continuing to show yet more support. She loved him so much for what he was allowing her to do. She was so sure he would come to see, someday, how really amazing this whole project would be, how lives would be changed.

"Darcy, hon…" he began. What a strong man it took to change such a firmly held opinion, to go so completely against his sensible nature. She admired him, at that moment, working to find the words.

"Yes, Jack." She played with the cuff of his shirtsleeve. Turned up. He worked so hard to support this family.

"The company implemented a hiring and wage freeze today. Effective immediately."

Whatever was inside her chest evaporated in a poof she would have sworn she could hear. Darcy could only gulp.

"Everyone's afraid to build inventory because the economy is so bad." He pulled his hands down over his face and let out a weary sigh. "That raise we were hoping for at my annual review next month isn't going to happen. Not now, and not anytime soon."

It was going to be a red-letter day all right. Stop sign, stop light, caution, warning, flashing-ambulance-light red.

Chapter 10

Ain't Nobody Here But Us Chickens

"And then he said, 'It's a good thing we have your father's money to fall back on at a time like this.' As if that were a given, as if totally disregarding a dying man's last wish were something that didn't even need discussion." Darcy blew her nose on the tissue Glynnis handed her and added it to the six others in her lap.

"I know that must have been a jolt to hear." Glynnis put the clever rooster-themed tissue holder—goodness, the woman even decorated her Kleenex boxes to match—back on the counter. She poured more ice tea.

"I…I wasn't crazy up there on those church steps, was I? I mean, it felt so real, so…important…I was so sure. Sure of something I'd never think of…I just don't think of that sort of thing in my life, despite Dad's faith. It was…I don't know…so *unignorable*." Darcy looked at Glynnis. "Is that even a word?"

Glynnis smiled. "Does it matter?"

"I suppose not. But Glynnis, if I was so sure, how come

everything went to pieces? Within *hours?* God doesn't get to pull stunts like that." She winced a bit at her own presumptions. "Does He?"

Glynnis chuckled. "God is God, hon. Which means He pretty much gets to do what He wants whether we like it or not. And no, I don't think you're bonkers. I believe you felt everything you said you did yesterday afternoon. God's not in the habit of dialing wrong numbers, Darcy. He got your attention because He *wanted* your attention."

"Then why'd it all go so wrong?"

Glynnis took a long swig of tea. She thought for a moment. "Well, now, who's to say it's all gone wrong?"

"What do you mean? If Jack was against The Restoration Project before, he's twice as opposed now."

"Oh, I wouldn't argue with you there. But getting a nudge from God isn't the same thing as having the way swept clean before you." She looked at Darcy, her brown eyes shimmering. It was amazing; the woman could hug you with her eyes. "Plenty of folks have had huge, enormous obstacles thrown in the path God called them to take. Lots of hurdles bigger than Jack Nightengale."

"Why?" Darcy felt she was practically whining like Paula. She did feel like stamping her foot and throwing a good old preschool-style tantrum.

"Try to look at it this way. If it were easy, everybody'd do it."

Darcy shot Glynnis a nice-try look.

"Okay, try this, then. Maybe the part about it seeming impossible is one of the important parts. That's why they call it 'faith,' Darcy, instead of 'agreement.' If it made sense, if you could plot your way from point A to point B with ease, there wouldn't be much faith in it, would there?"

"I suppose."

"No supposing about it. God seems to have big plans for you, Darcy Nightengale, and that means you're gonna have to get some big-plan faith." Glynnis poked Darcy in the arm. "Would it help you to know that I was in the middle of gardening yesterday afternoon—pulling the last of the mulch out over the beds—and God stopped me right in the middle of the vegetable patch to pray for you? Told me clear and simple to stop right then and there and get down on my knees for you? I'm no spring chicken. I don't haul this body down on my knees for just nothing. Fact of the matter is, I wasn't the slightest bit surprised you called me this morning. I was going to call you anyway, to ask you what in heavens name you were doing at 2:10 yesterday afternoon." Glynnis planted her hands on her hips. "How do you like them apples?"

Darcy hadn't heard someone say "How do you like them apples?" since her great-grandmother. She simply sniffed, unable to respond.

"Well?"

"Well…"

"Well, what *were* you doing at 2:10 yesterday afternoon?"

"Eating a Cheese Coney with mustard and onions."

"And…"

"And sitting on the Immaculata Church steps."

"And…"

"And deciding that the Restoration Project was something I was supposed to do."

"And…"

"And…thinking I was feeling that…that God wanted me to do it."

Glynnis sat back in her chair, having successfully excavated the answer she was seeking. "If you're looking for a burning bush, that's already been done. Near as I can tell, you've got all the evidence you need. What you need now is a little bit of faith."

Like a mustard seed. Hadn't she thought that herself, coming down off the hillside?

"I guess."

"No guessing. It's the most sure thing in life there is. Now, you finish the last of that ice tea, I'll whip us up some sandwiches, and you can give me all the details about this little project of yours. You want ham and cheese with that revelation, or just ham?"

Over sandwiches on—of course—rooster plates, Darcy told Glynnis every last detail about The Restoration Project. Everything from the magical moment in the middle of a pedicure to Kate's willing partnership to Angie and even Mr. Torture Man. Most of it for the second time, Darcy realized by the time she'd finished. It didn't really surprise Darcy that Glynnis was a good listener. She asked a few poignant questions, smiled in all the right places, but mostly just let Darcy spill it out. Best of all, Glynnis's face showed only wonder and support—not skeptical analysis or that certain look Darcy had come to recognize as someone questioning her current emotional stability. Darcy didn't need anyone thinking she was losing her grip on reality—she was pondering that just fine on her own.

"So that's when Jack told me they'd had the hiring freeze. Then he said that there'd be no raise next month. And we really needed that raise." Darcy looked down to see that while Glynnis had finished her entire sandwich, Darcy had managed only one bite of hers. How long had she been talking? Darcy guessed she'd broken a dozen social rules in monopolizing the conversation like this, yet it was clear Glynnis didn't mind. No, in fact, Darcy could swear the look on the woman's face was one of pure enjoyment. As if she got a kick out of doing this sort of thing.

What sort of thing *was* this exactly?

"It's amazing," pronounced Glynnis when Darcy had finally finished her monologue. "I'm just so excited for you, child."

"Excited? How can you be excited? I'm terrified. I feel stupid. Irresponsible. It's like I'm trying to defy gravity or something—I just don't see how this can work."

"The Restoration Project is a good idea, Darcy. Don't ever doubt that. You've had an experience—an intense, life-changing experience—in taking care of your dad. Not many people have the kind of perspective you now have. You, best of all, know what it is that people going through that sort of thing need—and you know that it is something most people wouldn't even think of. Or wouldn't think is important. They're all busy bringing casseroles or sending greeting cards. I can't agree more with what you have in mind."

"You'd be better at it than me. Maybe you should do it. I mean, you've already got the money—I can't believe I said that. How rude."

Glynnis just laughed. "Not rude at all. Yes, I have money. It's nothing I don't already know, hon. And I'm rather glad you said it—everyone thinks it's some kind of intimate subject you can never talk about." She examined the last crust of her sandwich before popping it in her mouth. "And you're right—I could do The Restoration Project, and I doubt Bid would have a single word to say against it. But there's one big problem."

"What's that?"

"God didn't ask me. He asked you. Your dad asked *you* to find a place to give the money away. Like I said, God doesn't get wrong numbers. This, Darcy Nightengale, is your baby."

"I suppose."

"Now you need to stop saying that. Stop saying 'I suppose.' Say yes. Clearly and with conviction."

"Yes," Darcy managed to agree.

Glynnis eyed her with mock analysis. "Weak, but it will do for starters."

Darcy took a big bite of her sandwich, mostly because she thought it might keep Glynnis from making her say yes again.

"And another thing—you'd better start praying about this a lot right away."

Darcy stopped chewing. Even when Dad was at his worst, she wasn't exactly the praying type. Exactly how big a spiritual overhaul was God planning here?

"What am I saying?" Glynnis continued, "I mean *we'd* better start praying about this. Finish your sandwich, hon, there's no time like the present."

"Now?" Darcy said, before she realized her mouth was still full.

"Of course now. Did you think you needed an appointment?"

Darcy quickly swallowed. "I…um…don't do this sort of thing well. Actually, I've not done this sort of thing at all."

"Paul Hartwell was your father and you don't know how to *pray*?"

Darcy backpedaled. "No, that's not what I mean. It's not that I don't know how. I mean everyone knows *how*. I just don't do it in…groups. Out loud."

Glynnis swept her hand around her henhouse of a kitchen. "Do you see anyone here but us chickens?"

Darcy knew, without a shadow of a doubt, that she was cornered.

"If it'll make you feel better, I'll do most of the talking. You can do most of the agreeing. But you're not getting off the hook completely. I'll hold you to at least two complete sentences, and 'Yes, Lords' do not count."

There, at the counter in Glynnis Bidwell's kitchen, feeling like she'd rather be anywhere else but there right now, Darcy bowed her head and let Glynnis take both of her hands in hers.

I don't think I can do this.

"Lord," Glynnis started, "I know Darcy doesn't think she can do this, but you and I both know she can."

Darcy hoped her gulp was too soft to hear.

"Thank you, Lord, for calling Darcy. For showing yourself to her and for helping her through such a difficult time. You are a powerful God, a mighty fortress, and we are so thankful to be in Your care. We know we can trust Your plan for us, even when it seems impossible. For nothing is beyond Your power, Lord.

"But Father, there seem to be a mountain of obstacles in Darcy's path. Now we know that all things work together for good for those who are called according to Your will, but that's hard to see from here. Help Darcy to trust in Your work, to see Your hand in how the details are playing out." Glynnis squeezed Darcy's hand, a silent cue for her to add something.

Squinting her eyes shut hard, Darcy took a breath. "Help me…help me not to be so scared, so confused."

Glynnis's hands wrapped themselves more tightly around Darcy's—a silent encouragement. "There's a lot to be scared and confused about, Lord. Work in her marriage. Move between her and Jack, and let there be peace and understanding between them. Protect Jack's job, if that's Your will, and ease his stress. Guide Darcy in how to be loving and supportive. And I ask, Lord, that you send huge portions of encouragement and peace to Darcy. Put people in her life who will help her along this path. Bless the partnership she has with Kate, and give them a clear vision of where to go from here. I'm going to ask, Lord, that you send them an *unignorable*—" Glynnis had a laugh in her voice as she quoted Darcy's uncertain adjective "—sign of encouragement. Something Darcy will know, without a doubt, is You.

"Keep Mike in Your care, Lord. Show him better ways to use the fine mind You've given him. Send a guide or a teacher into his life who can focus his attentions, and protect him from further trouble." The cue of squeezing came again.

Darcy didn't have to take such a deep breath this time. "Watch over Mike."

"I thank you, Lord," continued Glynnis, "for bringing Darcy into my life. Thank you for allowing me to be part of this marvelous thing You are doing in her life. Thank You for all You do for Bid and me, for all the blessings we enjoy. Keep Darcy and me safe in Your care until we can meet again, and clear the path for us to be together again soon. In Jesus' precious name we pray, Amen."

"Amen," Darcy added, with surprising ease. When Glynnis pulled her into a warm, long hug, the world seemed a tad brighter place.

And so it was that Tuesday Morning Prayer in The Henhouse began.

Chapter 11

Taking Everything Personally

If Darcy was expecting God to come down from Mount Adams and give her life a makeover, it didn't happen. In fact, hardly any of the external circumstances in Darcy's life moved at all from that first hesitant prayer at Glynnis's kitchen counter.

For the most part, life had settled itself into a sort of abnormal normality—different, and yet still the same. The widespread panic of September had faded to a quiet state of alert, a background stress rather than front-page hysteria. Still, everyone had the collective sense that this holiday season would be different from any other they had known.

It was true for Darcy as well. Things had not shown much improvement at Jack's work, and the state of his office was taking its toll. He came home later each night, sometimes even bringing work home with him. More than once she had found him shooting baskets in the driveway very late at night. Jack found his solace underneath a basketball hoop. It had always been that way. When Jack needed to think, to work through a problem or to burn off a case of nerves, he did it with a ball in his hands. Jack's best man had told Darcy he shot hoops for two hours the night before their wedding. That, Darcy supposed, was a far better coping strategy than to down a quart of ice cream, which is what she had done.

"Lunch tomorrow?" Kate called out the car window as she dropped Paula off from soccer practice one Thursday afternoon.

"Can't." Darcy winced. Kate had a talent lately for asking to go to lunch when Darcy had a lunch planned with Glynnis. They still met in The Henhouse every Tuesday, but more often than not, Darcy found herself needing Glynnis's wise counsel again before the week was out. Like clockwork, Kate would ask to go to lunch that same day. It was pure coincidence, but Kate was starting to get miffed.

"J.L.'s?" Darcy offered, feeling bad. J. L. Tanenbaums's Tea and Spice Merchants was a favorite hangout of theirs, but it wasn't lunch and they both knew it.

"Sure." Kate didn't sound so happy.

"Two okay?" She had an edge to her voice, as if she was asking Darcy to check her packed social calendar.

"Fine. My treat."

The look in Kate's eyes told Darcy that had been the exact wrong thing to say. Ugh, why were things so strained between them lately? Even the excitement of continued dreaming about The Restoration Project had a strange tension to it. It showed up in little things, like how Kate referred to the inheritance now as "your fortune." She used to refer to it as "the fortune," and always as a bit of a joke. It didn't have that bit-of-a-joke sound to it anymore.

Why did everything suddenly seem to have a monetary agenda? Was Darcy just oversensitive, or did it really sound like she was trying to buy off skipping lunch with Kate? Darcy shut the front door with a stronger slam than usual. Why was Kate suddenly taking everything so personally? She wasn't blowing Kate off. It's just that Glynnis had a perspective Darcy desperately needed right now.

Kate had never gotten this way about all the time demands of taking care of Paul. Didn't Kate understand how much was shifting in her life? How much she'd rather *not* be meeting with lawyers and insurance people and school counselors? She could barely balance her checkbook; now there were all kinds of forms, and people, and statements to organize.

And then there was the family. Even the kids were picking up on the tension in the house. It had been simpler to explain the tension of Paul's last days—they understood the concept of being very, very sick. How do you explain terror-based economics, probate court and the peculiar financial-legal predicament of Paul Hartwell's Last Will and Letter to the Heiress, to *kids?*

You'd have to understand it yourself first, of course.

Great. No help there.

Darcy used to think life "before"—while Paul was still alive—as so much harder. She would catch herself longing for the days—and feeling intensely guilty for it—when Paul's fight would be over, he would rest in peace and life would return to normal.

No normal to be had here, lady.

Darcy sighed, picking Paula's gear bag up off the foyer floor where she'd left it. She longed for another impulsive, girlfriendy spa day with Kate.

Somehow, she was sure suggesting such a thing would only make things worse between them.

Lord, fix this. Little prayers like that would shoot into her day lately. SOSes to God, Glynnis called them. Glynnis said that an honest three words were better than a mouthful of stuffy show-off prayers. Darcy hoped she was right.

Glynnis hadn't been nearly as much help over lunch as Darcy had hoped. Darcy parked her car in front of J.L.'s with a knot in her stomach. She wanted to get things back to where they were, but how? The only sliver of solace she had was that she had prayed over the tea date with Glynnis, and Glynnis had said she would pray starting at 2:00 p.m. With a prayer champion like Glynnis on her knees at this very moment, Darcy felt like maybe she had a chance.

Ditto whatever Glynnis is saying, Darcy shot up to heaven as she hit the automatic door lock on her key chain and headed into the store.

Kate had already bought her tea, even though Darcy had offered to buy. She was sitting at their favorite spot, the far window table. Darcy grunted. It never used to matter who bought before. Why did it matter now? The knot in her stomach tightened as she ordered ginger plum tea and two—no, four—shortbread cookies.

She slid the cookies onto the table and sat down. "I'm sorry I couldn't do lunch today," Darcy offered. And she was. She hoped it showed.

"It's okay," Kate replied, but it was clear it wasn't okay.

Darcy set her purse down on the windowsill beside her. "Did Thad make the traveling soccer team?" Kate's kids excelled at sports. Darcy's kids participated, but every coach wanted one of the Owens kids on their team.

"Yep." Kate sat up a little straighter. "Center forward. Don's practically strutting."

"I can imagine." She imitated Don's New Hampshire accent. "That boy's got skills." It got a chuckle from Kate. Good. They both sipped their tea to fill the gap in conversation. Darcy pushed the waxed paper with the four cookies on it to the center of the table. "You're looking sugar deprived. As your best friend, I prescribe at least two of these, maybe even a third." She picked up one of the cookies. "But this one's mine, so don't try anything sneaky."

No response.

"It's the best dunker, and you don't even dunk your cookies."

Kate shrugged her shoulders.

Stop trying so hard, will you? Darcy chided herself.

"Is Glynnis Bidwell a dunker?" Wow, you could have chopped the cookies with the edge in Kate's voice. Darcy was guessing even Kate was surprised at how sharp it sounded.

"I…um…I don't know actually."

Kate looked up. Darcy felt like it was the first time she'd really made eye contact since she walked in the door. Kate had that look, the one that showed she was testing the truth of Darcy's words—evaluating if it was just a polite lie to spare her feelings.

"I've never actually seen her drink anything…dunkable. I mean nothing hot. She just drinks vats and vats of ice tea. So, there are cookies involved, but no actual submerging takes place." It was the truth. Darcy hoped Kate could see that. "I'm not dunking with another woman, if that's what you're asking." It was supposed to be a joke, but it came out all wrong.

"I'm not asking." Kate's voice was tight and curt. More uncomfortable silence.

I don't deserve this, Darcy thought, snapping her cookie in half. I didn't do anything wrong. I get to have other friends, don't I? She needed every friend she could find lately, not someone who was going to ask her to punch a time clock. Why did this have to be so hard all of a sudden? Darcy let her cookie fall onto the table and sat back in her chair. "What's going on here anyway?" she blurted out, hurt and angry.

Kate eyed her. "I could ask you the same thing, Darcy."

"Ask me? How can you not know what's going on with me? My life is turning itself inside out and you know it. You've been beside me for half of it. I'm trying to put all these nutty pieces together, to keep my family from imploding in on itself, to figure out what my dad thought he was doing, to figure out what I'm going to do about it, and you ask me *what's going on?*" An old lady buying English breakfast tea turned to glare at them. Darcy lowered her voice. "I'm hanging on by my fingernails, that's what's going on." She let out an exasperated sigh. "How did... Why has it gotten so weird between us lately?"

Kate sat back and crossed her arms. "How would I know? I haven't seen enough of you to know what's gotten weird. I hardly see you at all. You're off with Glynnis Big Bucks or lawyers or tax gurus or whoever it is you see to solve all those family fortune problems you've got now."

"That's not fair."

"Isn't it?"

"You think I'm having *fun* with this? You think I'm running around shopping for tiaras? There's miles of paperwork and Jack is a walking ball of tension and I don't know what I'm supposed to be doing. It rots, and the last thing I need is you turning on me because I have lunch with Glynnis."

"Do you stand Glynnis up for lunch, too? Or is it just me?"

"I do *not* stand you up for lunch."

"You *have,* Dar. Twice in the last month alone. Okay, once was for here, but you've brushed me off twice this month." Kate whipped out her pocket calendar, ready to prove her point. "Once on September 28 and again on October 9."

Kate was right. Darcy knew it the moment the dates were spoken. She had brushed her off. Not intentionally, but forgotten just the same. But, come on, Kate could have called. Could have said something. Could have done something than just sit there and stew on it. "You're keeping *score?*" she snapped out.

"I never thought I'd *have* to."

"Do you have any idea how complicated things are for me right now?"

"No, I'm sure I couldn't imagine." Kate's smug edge was really starting to get on her nerves. She hadn't asked for any of this.

"I'm not any different. I'm still here, Kate, it's still me."

"You are different, Dar. You're *really* different. You're so far away I don't even know what's going on anymore. Wake up. It's all changed and it's not going back to whatever it was before."

"No. Things have gotten complicated, but they haven't changed. Look, I'm sorry about those days, but it's not like I'm intentionally *ignoring* you."

Kate stared into her teacup. "Did you know that Thad broke his finger? That Don got passed over for a promotion two weeks ago? That my aunt's been diagnosed with breast cancer? Did you know any of those things, Dar?"

Darcy couldn't respond.

"No you didn't know any of that because you weren't around. You're…well, you're around less now than when you were dealing with Paul. You're off on your big quest, making your new friends, and the rest of us are just standing around watching." Kate grabbed a cookie, pointing at Darcy with it. "Do you know how many people in the neighborhood lost their jobs last month? Five. *Five,* Dar. But you don't see it. I know you're going through a lot, but the rest of us aren't exactly having a picnic of it, either."

What do you say to a speech like that? Darcy's throat started to tighten. She didn't have the emotional skin to take that kind of a lashing right now. "It's not like that," she finally said, almost in a whimper.

"It is. It is and I hate it."

A long, raw silence hung between them. Darcy stared at the table. Kate stared out the window. Darcy wanted to both hug Kate and punch her in the stomach. Kate couldn't turn on her now. She needed Kate too much. Or not enough. *Oh Lord, how did this get so messy?*

"I…" she started softly, completely at a loss for what to say.

Kate sniffed and grabbed her purse. "I gotta go. I didn't want to get into this but…look, I just got to go."

Darcy grabbed her arm. "Kate, don't…"

Kate pulled away. "Not now, Dar. Maybe later, but not now." She hurried out the door without a single look back.

Darcy sat, staring at the two remaining cookies. She wanted to throw them across the room. To kick the table over, to stand in the doorway and yell "It's not my fault!" to the universe.

Eating two cookies was a poor substitute, but it was easier to stop yourself from crying when your mouth was full.

* * *

Jack hit the Send button on his e-mail, trying not to wince. Oh, well, better to do it electronically than in person. Still, he didn't see how there was any good way to relay to his boss the news that their largest client had just cut this quarter's order in half.

Everybody was cutting their orders in half. Some were cutting them out altogether. Parco Industries' remaining half an order had been a testament to the strength of the relationship Jack had built with them.

At least Jack hoped his boss would see it that way. The stress was really getting to some of his staff.

He couldn't blame them. It was getting to him, too.

He caught the reflection of an unfamiliar shadow in his monitor and spun his chair around to see someone standing in his doorway.

His wife.

And something was very wrong. She'd been crying—or trying not to cry, he guessed. She'd held herself together through the front lobby and down the hallway and was going to make it about four inches into his office before it all came loose. What in the world...?

"Dar? Hon, what's wrong?" He jumped up and pulled her into the office, his hands holding her wobbling shoulders steady. He kicked the office door shut with his foot and steered her into the guest chair. Thankfully, he hadn't been planted in some cubicle yet—he still rated four walls and a door—for now.

She started to shake her head. "Jack, I'm sorry, I shouldn't have come here...."

"Is everyone okay? Did something happen to the kids?"

"No, they're fine.... Oh, it's stupid, I'm dumb to come here." She was crying now. Hard.

Even though he'd been half expecting her to come unglued one of these days since Paul's death, he hadn't expected it to be here. "Dar, you're a mess. What happened?"

"I had a…I had a huge fight with Kate."

Jack's response traveled from relief, to annoyance, to amused concern in the space of about ten seconds. Part of him was ticked at her bringing something like this into the office; the other part of him was glad to be the place she had run to. Even if it meant she ran here. He let out the breath he hadn't realized he was holding and handed her another tissue. "Come on, you never fight with Kate."

"I know." It came out as a moan.

He pushed a stack of files aside and leaned against the desk corner beside her. "What about?"

"About me."

Well, he doubted that. These days most of the spats in his life were about everything but the argument at hand. Everybody was short-tempered with everybody, and it didn't really matter why. Dar and Kate were as thick as thieves—too close to have an actual fight between them; it had to be something else just now coming to the surface. "You fought about you?" He tried to keep the skepticism out of his voice. She was really upset.

"She says I've been blowing her off. Things have been…I don't know…tense between us. It's never been weird between us and suddenly now everything is strained."

Truth be told, he'd seen this one coming. It had "too much Glynnis Bidwell, not enough Kate Owens" written all over it, and it had been brewing for the better part of a month as near as he could tell. Better to go slow, just ask her questions until he got all the details. Even though he knew the answer, he started with, "Well, *did* you blow her off?"

"I didn't mean to. It's not like I'm ignoring her or anything."

"But you did blow her off? Even if you didn't mean to do it?"

Darcy sniffed. "I suppose. Yeah. I forgot about a date, twice." She looked at Jack. "But that's not the same thing as standing her up. Jack, she even whipped out her calendar to show me the dates. That's going a bit far, don't you think?"

"That is far, even for Kate. She must really be mad."

"She told me that everything is different now, that I've changed, that I spend all my time with Glynnis. Jack, it sounded like Paula and her friends, 'You like so-and-so better than me!' What's gotten into her?"

Jack knew exactly what had gotten into her. Good for Kate, he thought to himself, for coming out with it. How many times had he bit the same sentiment off his tongue when Dar had spent every waking moment with Paul? He had wondered how the strain of all this was going to show once life settled down. Everybody had their own way of coping with Paul's death. Dar's fixation on this project of hers had been her coping mechanism. Sure, there were worse ways to handle grief, but he had to admit he was hoping she'd get over this particular idea.

"I thought you and Kate were in on this idea of yours together."

"She is. She was. But it's not about that…at least I think it's not about that." Darcy blew her nose. "She's jealous of Glynnis. Of my friendship with Glynnis." Her eyes grew narrow and sharp. "Like I'm going to haul off and have new rich friends now. Mutate into some sort of socialite."

"She's hurt you forgot the dates. It's a natural reaction, Dar."

"No, it's more than that. She thinks I don't care about her anymore."

"I doubt that."

"It's what she said." Darcy accepted another tissue. Jack tried to check his watch unobtrusively, glad it was Thursday. Thursday was his boss's day at the other building. He hooked the leg of his desk chair with his ankle and pulled it up next to Darcy's chair. He sat down in it, and began rubbing her wrists with his hands. She had the most exquisite, tiny wrists. He could feel her pulse when he held them, tapping lightly against his fingers. He began to work his way through the problem.

"Did she tell you why she thinks that? If I know Kate, she had a dozen good reasons all lined up ready to go."

Darcy nodded. "Oh, she had her argument all laid out, that's for sure. She had a shopping list of family news I'd managed to miss." Dar looked up at him with shimmering eyes. "Did you know Don was passed over for a promotion?"

"He told me, yeah."

"And that Thad broke his finger?"

"Uh-huh." Darcy's response told him this was not the answer she was hoping for.

"And that Kate's aunt has breast cancer?"

Jack was almost grateful he could say, "Hadn't heard that" to that last one.

"Well, I sure heard about it today." Darcy blew her nose again.

"Look, you and Kate have been friends forever. I think you'll find a way out of this. The whole world's a ball of tension these days." Jack swept his hands around the office. "There have been fights here between people I've never seen fight before. Tension does nutty things to people. Kate and Don are no different."

"I suppose. I have been in my own little world for a while."

Now there was an understatement. Jack chose to let it slide. "You've been through a lot. Nobody blames you for taking care of Paul. It was a good thing you did." He lowered his voice a bit, wondering just how far to go with this. "But lots of us have been out here, slugging it out in the rest of the world, waiting for you to come back. Kate's been holding you up for a long time. Maybe she just wants a little holding in return."

"You're right. It's not been fair to her, has it?"

"It's not been fair to anyone. Life is pretty much unfair all over town these days."

Darcy looked at him. "I can't bear the thought of not having Kate."

Jack smiled. "I'm sure Don's having the same conversation right this very minute—that Kate's on the phone with him, just as upset." He brushed a lock of honey-blond curl out of her eyes. "Honestly, you women."

He saw her smile. It felt good to be the one to make it better for her. He loved how she leaned on him, how she let him play knight in shining armor. It had been hard with Paul—there were no fixes to be had, no way to solve things for her, and he had hated that about it. "How 'bout I call Don and set up B-ball for Saturday afternoon? The guys can tear up the court and you and Kate can get back to whatever it is you do together."

"I'd like that."

"I'm in this for me. I can't have you crying in my office every day until you patch things up." He took her hand. "You're lucky it's Thursday as it is, and Mr. Big Shot's at the other plant." He was teasing her. He'd have rescued her any day of the week. He ignored the e-mail notification signal that came in over the computer.

"My hero."

Man, how long had it been since he'd heard that? "Take a little advice from your hero?"

"Okay."

"Make good and sure the next lunch you eat out is with Kate Owens, and not Glynnis Bidwell."

She looked at him.

"I'm right, Dar, and you know it." He was right. She was spending hoards of time over at the Bidwells', and it was starting to put ideas into her head. Some of which worried him. She was a tangle of emotions yet, not half-healed over Paul's death. Now was no time to get all fired up to do something drastic.

And drastic, it seemed, was a standard Bidwell operating mode. "Hey, wait," he said as she gathered up her purse. "I've got another idea...."

Jack always had the best ideas for fixing stuff like this. At his suggestion, Darcy stopped at the United Dairy Farmers convenience store and bought Mint Milano cookies. She wrote "I'm sorry" in black marker across a package and slipped it into Kate's mailbox.

She inhaled a second package on the way home in the car.

Every great idea can always be improved—a bit.

Chapter 12

It's Never Just a Ball

That Saturday was one of October's spectacular last hurrahs to warm weather. A last blast of sunshine and autumn-colored glory before winter took over the Ohio Valley. It had even been warm enough to grill lunch out on the deck. Darcy and Kate, having had a good long string of "I'm sorry's" and honest conversation over lunch—yes *lunch*—on Friday, sat staring out the kitchen window. Jack, Don, Mike and Thad were going father-and-son two-on-two at the basketball hoop in the driveway. Paula and Jessica were up in Paula's room creating a Barbie dynasty, and all felt right with the world. It was one of those glorious fall days, the kind that made you want to don a sweatshirt and sneakers, kick back in your deck chair, and wish Monday would never come.

"I swear Mike's grown half a foot since school started," said Kate, laughing at a wild jump shot from one of the boys as they watched through the kitchen windows.

"He eats like he's growing a foot a second. Last night he ate three double cheeseburgers. That's got to be a week's worth of fat grams in one meal." Darcy pulled a second pair of diet colas from the fridge, fondly remembering the days she didn't have to count fat grams.

"Oh, to be young again." Kate accepted the can from Darcy's outstretched hand. She popped the tab and made a toast. "To the boys."

"The boys. May they hoard their fat grams wisely."

"As if. How many brats did Jack eat, anyway?"

"Three. They're his favorite. I owed it to him after— well, after this week." They'd talked long and hard on Friday about the argument they had in J.L.'s. It felt good to get it all out on the table, to have them both on the same side of the challenge again. And they both had work to do. Kate needed to remember that life was not all hunky-heiress-dory for Darcy and that grief wasn't a four-week stint. Darcy needed to remind herself to check in on the rest of the world and to take the time to keep relationships strong in all the transition. Jack's prediction, by the way, had been correct: Kate *was* sniffling on the phone to Don at the same time Darcy was using up Jack's office tissues. No doubt about it, life would hold its share of challenges for both of them in the next few months.

"Jack's a good guy," Kate replied leaning back against the counter. "Speaking of which, what are you planning to get him for his birthday?"

The refrigerator gave out a high whine and a series of menacing clunks. "Think he'd go for a new fridge?" Darcy quipped.

"Sure. Then he can buy you another vacuum cleaner for your birthday. It'll be an appliance extravaganza. I think

Little Orphan Heiress and her Mr. Moneybags can do better than that, though."

Darcy was sorry she'd ever leaked the nickname to Kate. She chose the most annoying times to use it. Not to mention she'd taken to calling Jack Mr. Moneybags—behind his back, of course. But the names meant the returning of joking about it, which Darcy welcomed. It meant they were finding their way back to normal. Or the new normal, whatever that was. Personally, Darcy thought Ed Bidwell made a better Mr. Moneybags—right now Jack was so concerned about finances she was thinking she might be lucky to get to buy him a present at all. There were times, like last Thursday, when Darcy loved Jack for his calm sensibility. Then there were times—times when a bit of imagination or dashing was called for—that she wanted to strangle him for it.

Global crisis or not, Darcy Nightengale wasn't in the habit of skipping birthday presents. Darcy loved presents. Buying them, giving them, pondering them, helping other people pick them out, you name it. Even if they had to be teeny tiny, birthday and Christmas presents were nonnegotiable in her world.

It was another one of those things Jack never quite understood.

"Believe it or not, I don't know what I'm going to get him. I've got another week, though."

"You don't know yet?" Kate had good reason to be surprised. Darcy usually planned presents weeks and weeks in advance.

"I'm stumped. Really. There's just been so much going on between us, nothing seems to be appropriate, and I don't want to give him just anything—especially after all we've been through." Darcy took a long swig of her soda. "This one has to be good."

"Don't suppose we can kidnap him to Ernestine's to give him a makeover?"

Darcy laughed. Jack and a manicure—the most unlikely combination on earth. "Very funny. But you know, I'd like to do that sort of thing—not the makeover part, but the…I don't know…*spark* of it. I want him to feel the same spark I did when we were there. To catch the idea of it. I want him to understand The Restoration Project, to get why it's so important to me, to understand what it can do for people."

"Pretty big agenda for a birthday present."

Darcy looked out the window again. "Tell me about it."

"Too bad everyone expects better of you than a gift card. You've a reputation to maintain. You can't give wimpy presents like normal people—you've been too perfect at it before."

Cries of victory erupted from the driveway, pulling the women back out the door onto the deck. From the looks of things, Thad had just made a spectacular shot, securing the game for Team Owens. The guys stood around the hoop, gesturing and pounding each others' backs, deep in playback analysis.

"Man, that was such a cool shot!" Thad was evidently as thrilled with his game-saving swish as the rest of them. "Mr. Nightengale, this ball really rocks. Do you have it pumped up to a different pressure or something? It feels different than mine."

Kate and Darcy grinned at each other. Jack's obsession with quality sports equipment was about to get a major shot in the arm. Not that it needed it. Don's kids may be heavy on the talent, but Jack's kids always had the best of equipment. The man scanned sporting goods catalogues the way most men looked at power tools. Even Paula's tiny soccer shin guards were the best the Nightengales could afford.

"It's an indoor ball, Thad. They're more expensive, and they wear out faster playing out here, but I love the way it feels in your hands. Makes all the difference, doesn't it?" He held it up for inspection. "The skin gives you a really good grip."

Thad, true to the nature of any fourteen-year-old basketball star wannabe, eyed his dad. "Can we get one of these?"

Don smirked. "Thad, if we got every piece of the Nightengales' sports equipment you've asked me for, we might not have enough left over to get you a car anytime this decade." That brought "Ooos" from the men. Don even dangled the car keys out of his pocket for emphasis.

"Very funny, Dad. It's only a ball."

Moans of "Don't say that" rose up around the boisterous group. To Jack, it was never "just a ball" and everyone knew it. Jack shot the ball into Thad's chest and within seconds a new game was underway. The pure exuberance of it made Darcy smile.

"Oh." Kate made a strange sound.

"Huh?" Darcy looked at Kate. She was staring at Jack. Hard. With a really odd look on her face.

"Oh, man, that's it…that's *it!*"

"What? What?"

Kate grabbed Darcy's arms and began to pull her inside the door. "Oh, I got it, Darcy, I got it. I've got the absolutely perfect birthday present idea for Jack. You're going to love this. You *are* so going to love this. Get in here!"

"It was awful, Glynnis. I didn't think it would be so hard, going to Bob Denton's funeral. But I walked in there,

and I saw that casket, and it all came rushing back at me."
Tuesday Morning Prayer in the Henhouse had hosted a
packed agenda for the last two weeks.

"Are you really surprised?" Glynnis handed her another tissue. Glynnis simply kept a box on the table now.
Darcy wondered if "tissues for Darcy" had its own line
item in the Bidwell family budget these days.

"I thought I'd handle it better. I wanted to be there for
Angie. She looked awful. Even worse than when I saw her
last at the hospice."

"She's hurting."

"I keep thinking about how alone she must feel. I lost
Dad, and it was awful, but I had Jack and the kids. She's
alone. What must it have been like to go back to an empty
house after a funeral?"

Glynnis leaned on her elbow. "I doubt she went home
to an empty house. You said she has a circle of friends who
have been helping her. People tend to step up to the plate
at a time like that. It's all the other times—the ordinary
empty days after the funeral flowers have all gone—that
they forget to pay attention."

"That's true." Darcy thought about all the people who
kicked so quickly into "normal" with her, as if the loss re-
solved itself after thirty days like a sprained ankle. There
were people who had asked her constantly about Paul's
condition, who now never even brought up his name in
conversation. *Poof. You die and you're gone. People are always too busy to remember.* Even the articles about those
who'd died on September 11 had stopped showing up in
the papers.

"That's why I think God is asking you to do what He's
asking." Glynnis's voice brought Darcy's thoughts back to
the conversation. "Because *He* pays attention. He knows

what they need, and He knows you know how to give it to them."

"I don't know, Glynnis. I don't think we're any further along in getting The Restoration Project up and running."

"That's not true. You talked again to Meredith at the hospice, didn't you?"

"Yes. She's completely onboard with the idea."

"Well, that's something. And you patched things up with Kate, didn't you?"

"Yeah, that, too. She even came up with the idea for Jack's birthday present."

Glynnis grinned broadly. "I remember. Oh, and I think it's a humdinger."

Humdinger. Who said *humdinger* anymore? For a spry gal, Glynnis's vocabulary would occasionally remind Darcy that the woman was as old—if not older—than most of the grumpy old ladies she knew.

She leaned in toward Glynnis. "It is great, isn't it? You've got to pray hard Friday night, Glynnis. Pray really, really hard, 'cause this has just *got* to work. Everything else won't matter if we can't get Jack to come around."

Glynnis's face registered a look of supreme satisfaction. "Oh, I'm sure it will work. One hundred percent."

Darcy was sure—one hundred percent—she didn't want to ask how Glynnis knew *that*.

Chapter 13

God Is in the Details

October 28 was a mild, clear Sunday evening, perfect for viewing the lights of the city from the corner table where Darcy and Jack sat celebrating. It seemed to Darcy that God had ordered up extra stars for the evening, a private hint of His approval of her birthday plans. She was halfway through the best chicken marsala on the planet, enjoying Jack's face as he savored a steak of monumental proportions. The evening had been perfect. A batting average, she hoped, that would last another two hours or so.

"Is yours as good as mine?" Jack asked, smiling "You've got a smile a mile wide on your face." He eyed her. "Or are you just plotting something?"

Darcy felt that rush of unnamable sizzle, that certain something his eyes could always do to her. Forgotten and familiar. "Both," she replied. She had always loved the way he looked in that tan sweater. His eyes could stop her from across the room when he wore it. Had it been another favorable sign when he chose to wear it? Or luck of the draw?

Jack's smile widened. "Fess up, then. What did you do for my birthday?"

Darcy hid behind her water glass, taking a long drink. "Oh, hon, you told me not to go overboard, so it's not much."

Jack raised an eyebrow. "Your face says otherwise."

"Well, I suppose there's a bit of *otherwise* in there."

"More than a bit."

He was waiting for her to tell. She wouldn't, not yet. She simply rested her chin on her folded hands and stared at him, teasing. It was as if they were in high school, flirting over milkshakes or something. Her heart was doing flip-flops worthy of an eighth grade crush.

"Well?" He toyed with his steak knife.

"Well, what?"

"The suspense is killing me. If you don't wipe that look off your face soon, I'll…"

"You'll what?"

"Actually," he said, "I'm not quite sure what I'll do." He started spinning his wedding ring with his thumb. It was something he did when a situation put him on his toes. He'd done it for a solid week when they were waiting to see if she was pregnant with Mike. It felt splendid to know she'd caught him off guard. Infatuating.

Over Jack's shoulder, Darcy caught the waiter looking at her with questioning eyebrows and a *Now?* expression. He was holding a large tray with one of those domed lids on it. Darcy nodded.

Jack caught her signal and looked over his shoulder just in time to see the waiter bring the tray to the table. The waiter, grinning himself, set the tray down and kept his hand on the dome. He waited for Darcy's signal.

* * *

Jack stared at Darcy, then at the waiter, then back at Darcy again. She was wearing a Cheshire-cat grin, practically squirming in her seat with anticipation. Suddenly, she was twenty again, sitting on his car trunk, holding out the first birthday present she'd ever given him. The woman lived for birthday and Christmas presents. He didn't care much for the presents one way or another, but the way she looked when she gave them—well that was another thing altogether.

"Now," she practically giggled, her chin still perched on her hands.

The waiter, who obviously enjoyed his role in the charade, whipped the lid off in a dramatic arc. There, on the tray, was a large stack of DVDs.

James Bond movies.

"Whoa, Dar. This is amazing." He began flipping through the boxes, calling out the titles as he found them. "This is incredible. There's…there's six movies in here."

"A virtual Bond bonanza," she replied.

How many times had he seen those boxed sets for sale at the video store? How many times had he thought about picking just one or two movies up, trying to calculate if it'd be worth it to own it rather than rent it once a year? How many times had he stopped himself just short of buying one?

How had she known?

She'd known because she was Darcy. And knowing just what to get is what Darcy did best.

"Wow. This definitely counts as *otherwise*." He ran his fingers down the stack of titles. "You didn't have to spend so much—even one would have been great." Jack tried to stop his brain from calculating how much she must have spent, but it ran the numbers without his consent.

"That's the beauty of it—I didn't. Ed Bidwell found them wholesale through a friend of his." Her face told him she'd anticipated his calculations and beat him to the punch. She knew he'd be uncomfortable with the price of the DVDs, so she'd found a way to spend less and still give him what he wanted. Man alive, he loved his wife tonight.

He pulled one of her hands out from underneath that adorable chin, wrapping it in his. She'd kept up polishing her nails since that crazy stint at the spa. She'd kept her hair in that same new style, too. He liked it. He made a mental note to tell her more often.

"These are amazing. *You're* amazing. Thanks. Really."

"You're welcome. My pleasure."

"Oh, count on it," Jack replied, the husky edge of his voice surprising even him. Darcy's mild shock only made it worse. How long had it been since he'd been so eager to get his wife in private like this? This was the stuff of teenage hormones, not the well-seasoned affections of a man with two kids and a minivan.

Who cares? It felt wonderful.

"Let's hurry up and get dessert." He didn't care how it sounded.

"Oh, that's fine, but you're not done yet."

Jack stifled a gulp. "I'm not?"

"Oh, no, that's only half the present."

Darcy felt like a child on Christmas morning as they drove out of the restaurant parking lot. She insisted on driving, which only seemed to make Jack more curious about the second half of his birthday present. Once again, as if God had decided to voice His approval by adding superlative details, the weather was ideal. It was crisp and cool, but not uncomfortable—in fact, it was unseasonably pleasant, and people were out all over the city enjoying the near-perfect evening. That was important, because this time outside—and other people being outside—were crucial elements in Darcy's plan. If God truly was in the details, He was making sure the whole world knew it tonight. Darcy was happy—thrilled even—at the show of divine support.

The part of town she had chosen for the second half of tonight's festivities was a distinct counterpoint to the plush comfort of the restaurant. Out of the corner of her eye, Darcy watched Jack's expression as she turned toward the other side of town. If she had wanted to keep Jack guessing—which had not been her intent but had arisen as a marvelous byproduct—she had him positively stumped. Good. Mr. Sensible Predictability needed a good shake-up in his life, and she had the epitome of all shake-ups in the works.

Please, Lord. Let this work. It's either going to be wonderful or awful. I need it to be wonderful. I need your help.

It had taken her three days to find the right spot. Not a good part of town, but not a dangerous part of town. A place on the edge of uncomfortable. When she pulled into the community center, it was just as she had hoped. Filled, even at this time of night, with several boisterous pickup games of basketball. On several far from perfect courts. Slabs of crumbling asphalt with trash and broken glass piling up along the edges. Most without any nets on the hoops at all, some with the last remains of chain hoops that merely swung and chattered when a ball hit the rim.

A few of the teenagers and adults looked up when the car pulled into the parking lot, but most were too engrossed in their games to care much about a rusting sedan's arrival. Jack's eyes were wide and a bit doubtful as she switched off the ignition. He was trying to

think of a way to ask her what on Earth was going on—
she could see it in the way he squinted up the corner
of one eye. He evidently settled on, "What are you up
to, Dar?"

"You'll see." Darcy took a deep breath and pulled open
the door latch. *Here we go.*

She heard Jack's door open as she came around to the
back of the car. She waited until he was beside her to hit
the trunk release on her key chain. It seemed to take ages
to rise all the way open, and Darcy fought the urge to grab
the lid and push the hydraulic hinges faster. The slow rise
of the trunk lid added a certain drama to the moment.

Darcy waited for Jack to see, feeling as if her lungs had
forgotten how to work.

Jack let out a long, slow whistle—an uncharacteristic
response to be sure—when he did.

It was excruciatingly impossible to judge Jack's response to the sight before him. Darcy sent a silent yelp to
heaven, and let him take it in.

Or, actually, take *them* in. All twelve of them.

A dozen of the absolute best street-play basketballs
money could buy. Nestled like Fabergé eggs in the trunk
of his car.

Get it. Get it. Oh, God, please let him get it.

He looked at her. There was the beginning of something
in his eyes, a spark she hoped to God could be fanned into
just enough flame, a connection just out of reach that she
hoped to snap together.

She took his hand and placed a ball in it. "One's for
you," she said, her voice wavering more than she
would have liked. It felt like her whole world was tee-
tering on a knife edge. "The others are for you to play
hero with."

"Hero?" Darcy could see the thoughts string themselves together in his brain. It was not an instant flame as she had known in the spa, but a slow, grasping revelation. An unsure questioning. A disbelieving curiosity.

Just at that moment, as if God had been listening in the wings, a teenage yell came out over the air. "Man, this ball is the worst. I can't shoot worth—" he added a colorful word here Darcy would have rather avoided, but she wasn't about to second-guess God's stage directions "—with this ball." A chorus of grunted agreements rang out across the court, and one kid even chose to kick the hoop post for emphasis. Its metallic echo pierced the air.

Go with it. Just go with it. Darcy picked up another one of the basketballs and tossed it to Jack, trying to smile. It was hard; she was unbelievably nervous. She had three different speeches rehearsed, but something told her to just hush up and let the moment do its job.

"You're kidding," he said, his tone one of astonishment.

Darcy shook her head.

He paused for what seemed like an eternity. Then, without moving his eyes from her, Jack sent a ball soaring over the chain-link fence behind her. Its crisp bounce made a sweet, clear sound.

"What the…?"

"Hey, where'd that…"

There were a few other choice additions to the clamor of reaction. It wasn't every day brand-new basketballs appeared out of thin air.

It had begun.

But where things went from here would make all the difference.

The group turned, peering in the direction from which the ball came.

"Yo, mister, your ball." One very tall, rather scary-looking teenage boy palmed the ball easily and walked toward Darcy and Jack.

Please, God. Please-please-please…

Jack walked past her up to the waist-high fence. She turned with him, feeling as if she were pulling her feet out of quicksand instead of pivoting on asphalt. The boy—well, you could hardly call him a boy, but he was no man, either—flicked the ball toward Jack with a single, casual move. Jack caught it in the chest.

I swear, I'll do anything, anything you ask just please-please…

Jack shot the ball back toward the group. "Keep it."

Darcy felt as if her entire circulation system had just changed direction.

"You crazy, man?" The group laughed and came a bit closer.

"Could be," Jack replied, looking at Darcy. She thought her stomach would drop out of the soles of her shoes at any second. The whole world spun in the dark of his eyes, as if someone had just turned on a light, or opened the door onto a breathtaking vista.

"Nice ball." The youth turned it in his hands, clearly enjoying the feel of it. Darcy noticed that the ball they had been using—now held by a smaller boy in the back of the group, was near black with dirt and even had what looked like duct tape on it in a few places.

"You bet," Jack replied. Darcy watched something catch fire in his eyes and spread throughout his body, almost visible, until it looked like the man would shoot sparks out of his fingertips. "I got more in here," he added, with the most remarkable look on his face. "Anyone else want one?"

The crowd went wild.

Darcy was near tears by the time all the balls had been passed out, and whoops of joy echoed through the flood-lit basketball courts. Jack himself had been pulled into the first group's game, his hair all ruffled and his sweater sleeves pulled up. It was like Christmas in November. It was amazing.

It was a miracle. Her own, personal, precious miracle. She sat hugging her knees on the trunk of the car, watching her husband turn into a wild-eyed twelve-year-old boy, laughing and carousing with a group of boys who could hardly believe what had just happened to them.

My hero.

Chapter 14

All the Way Home

Mike walked out the door for school at 8:17.

At 8:18, the phone rang.

"SO?" Kate's voice practically exploded through the receiver. Actually, Darcy was a bit surprised Kate wasn't waiting in the driveway when Mike opened the door this morning. She was glad. It had taken a gallon of coffee to get her and Jack going this morning.

"So is Jessica going to sell Girl Scout cookies this year?" Darcy replied, smiling. She knew exactly what Kate was asking, she just felt like kidding around a bit this morning. She felt almost giddy with the afterglow of last night's events.

"So how'd it go with Jack?" Kate yelled into the phone.

"Oh, yeah, that."

"'Oh, yeah, that.' Come on, I've been on edge all morning. Give up the details or I'm going to come over there."

Darcy's response was a sparkling sort of sigh. She couldn't even think of where to begin.

She heard Kate chuckle on the other end of the phone. "That good, huh?"

"Incredible."

"Spill it, girl. Start with dinner and don't leave anything out—well, okay, it sounds like there's a *bit* I probably don't need to hear in detail—but don't leave a speck out of dinner and the basketballs. However you all chose to occupy yourselves after you came home is…well… skippable."

Darcy sat down at the counter and poured herself a fourth cup of coffee. "Kate, it was wonderful. Every last bit of it."

"Jeff Ruby's still a great steak, huh?"

"For sure. Jack was practically glowing over the slab of meat. And the waiter thing, with the DVDs? Went off without a hitch. Everyone in the restaurant stared, and the waiter was great about it. Dramatic presentation and everything."

"Pure Darcy Nightengale. You do this kind of stuff better than anyone I know. So, did he love that you got them at a bargain, too?"

Darcy glanced at the stack of DVDs now proudly displayed on the coffee table. "You know it. I just knew he'd get weird about that—it was the perfect touch to let him know I'd gotten them at a great price. At about two o'clock this morning, he actually calculated that we'd get a full return on our investment over rental fees in under three years."

"You guys were up at 2:00 a.m.?"

"Well…"

Kate interrupted her. "Let's not go into it, shall we? I want to hear about the basketballs. Did it work? Did he get it? You didn't get mugged or anything?"

"It was amazing." Darcy hadn't been able to wipe the smile off her face yet. Even the kids had given her grief about her exhausted state of euphoria. "I thought I'd die just after I opened the trunk. It took forever." Darcy went on to tell the whole tale, from the first hesitant basketball pass to the astonished faces of those boys to the wild games that followed. When Jack had finally held his hands up and pleaded middle age, he was winded, sweaty and downright electrified. He walked back to the car, haloed by the court floodlights, panting and grinning. As if someone had peeled ten years off his soul. He was young and vibrant and athletic and the world was his oyster—the dynamo of a man she'd fallen head over heels for in college. The man glowed from the inside out. Without a word, but just the instinctive sigh of her name, he'd pinned her up against the side of the car and kissed her as if they'd been apart a hundred days.

Once home, they sat up talking for another hour. About what giving those basketballs felt like. What it did to those boys. How that energy that came from doing something so unsuspectedly nice for them was downright addictive, even if it couldn't really be explained.

Her body went into that wonderful meltdown of feeling, just remembering the look in his eyes.

"He *gets* it, Kate. He gets it now. I thanked God a dozen times for you last night—I'd have never thought of something like this. I owe you." She didn't know if it was fatigue or the leftover emotional release of last night, but she found herself choking up on the phone. "I owe you so much."

Kate's own voice faltered. "Yeah, well, I can't let you go around having all the good ideas now, can I?"

"We make a pretty good team, Kate Owens."

"That we do Mrs. Nightengale. Who knows how it will pay off now?"

Darcy narrowed her eyes. "I think we stand a pretty good chance of getting the Restoration Project off the ground now."

"Maybe, but I wasn't thinking of that."

"No?"

"No, I had more immediate gratification in mind for you."

Darcy was puzzled. "Meaning...?"

"Meaning are you forgetting your birthday is a week from Thursday? Think of the payback! I hope he comes to me for advice—I think it's time you got that tiara you've been eyeing. Or maybe a new..."

"Fridge?" Darcy finished for her.

"Not on my watch, girl. Not on my watch!"

Tuesday Morning Prayer in the Henhouse was more like Tuesday Morning Party in the Henhouse. Glynnis was bubbling with excitement. She held Darcy at arm's length. "My, but I'm not sure I even have to ask how it went. The look on your face could light up a room."

"It was wonderful." Darcy felt as if those words had come out of her mouth a hundred times in the last two days.

"Isn't it *wonderful* when God goes the extra mile? I just love it when he exceeds our expectations. Feels like a glimpse of heaven, doesn't it?"

Darcy took her usual chair at the kitchen table. "Well, Jack hasn't actually said yes to the project yet." She was trying hard not to jump to conclusions, not to run off and put everything in the works just because of one wonderful evening. It was pretty hard—her brain seemed to be working overtime ironing out the logistics of The Restoration Project's first wave.

Glynnis looked surprised. "You mean you haven't discussed it yet?"

"Well, sort of. We talked about what it felt like to give those balls away, and why it's worth the—what did Jack call it?—'fiscal irrationality,' but we didn't quite make the jump to going forward with The Project."

Glynnis still looked stumped. "Why ever not?"

Darcy felt like she was turning crimson. "Well, for one thing," she said sheepishly, "he kept kissing me."

Glynnis's eyes took on a sparkle worthy of a woman one-third her years. "Well, there is *that* to consider. A mighty fine reason, if you ask me."

Glynnis sauntered off the stool toward the refrigerator for the requisite iced tea. "You young people think you have the monopoly on romance," she called over her shoulder.

Darcy sucked in her breath. Some thoughts a brain just can't hold without making you wince.

"Ed Bidwell could sweep any woman off her feet. Even now, and even without the fancy car, mind you." Glynnis filled two glasses and returned to the counter.

It was like thinking about Santa putting the moves on Mrs. Claus. Darcy could only roll her eyes, even though she tried to look understanding.

Glynnis could have been insulted, but she merely regarded Darcy with a one-day-you'll-understand kind of look and sighed. "God designed marriage—and the marriage bed, mind you—for the long haul." She spread her hands on the counter and pulled in a long slow breath. "Once you get those kids out from under you,

you'll be amazed at what you can find to do with your free time."

Now Darcy was positive she was turning crimson. The Bidwells were just one surprise after another. Or one shock after another, depending on how you looked at it.

When I grow up, I want to be just like Glynnis Bidwell, Lord.

"You know," she said, rather eager to change the subject, "that wasn't the only reason we didn't get to that discussion. I felt something—a tug, sort of, a hesitation. I wanted to talk to you about it, actually. Every time I tried to steer the conversation around to that, I'd get this weird feeling that I wasn't supposed to ask him about it."

"Really." Glynnis leaned in.

"Yes. It was…well, it was the exact opposite of what I felt up on the church steps. As if that had been a giant green light and this other feeling was a giant red light."

Glynnis pondered the information for a moment. "Well, I gather you're learning to listen better, hon."

"What? To Jack? To my nerves?"

"To God."

"God? Why'd He stop me from talking to Jack about it?"

"Don't you think He can say *stop* if He can say *go*?"

Darcy didn't have an answer to that one.

Glynnis sighed. "Everybody's always looking for an answer to prayer. Trouble is, people often forget *no* is an answer to prayer, too."

Darcy felt her chest tighten. "You mean God is saying *no* to The Restoration Project? He can't do that *now,* can He?"

"God is God. He can pretty much do as He likes." Glynnis reached out and patted Darcy's arm in a motherly gesture. "But no, I'm pretty sure He's already given His stamp of approval to your idea. But maybe He just doesn't want you to push the issue with Jack right now."

"But I need to move forward! So much good has happened—he *gets* it Glynnis, Jack finally gets it—and I know God did that. I'm dying to get started *now*."

"All the more reason for you to sit tight. If God's telling you to sit still, it's because you need to. He's already done heaps for you this week hasn't he?" She waited, staring at Darcy, until Darcy nodded her agreement like a pupil in class. "So you can trust Him, can't you?"

"I supp— Yes." Glynnis had banned the use of *I suppose* two weeks ago.

"Don't you just hate it when God decides it's time to learn patience? I just hate cooling my heels when I'm raring to go on something." She picked up a cookie, pointing it right at Darcy. "But like I said, God has a habit of exceeding my expectations when I do."

"Really." Darcy tried to sound enthusiastic, but wasn't very successful.

"You just watch, Darcy Nightengale. God has whopping big plans for you. You'd better let him get Jack onboard in His own way."

Chapter 15

It's in the Cards

"Jacob the Kindly Lawyer," as Darcy always called him, looked as though he had earned the name. A tall, frog-eyed gentleman in a striped shirt and real bow tie, he was soft-spoken and deliberate in his movements. Jack couldn't think of anyone less like his idea of an attorney than Jacob Foxmore. Still, he looked like a man true to his word. And he had been.

"I don't think I need to tell you this is highly irregular, Jack. There aren't a lot of circumstances where I'd agree to meeting to discuss an inheritance without the beneficiary present." Jacob tapped the thick Paul Hartwell file on its end, lining up the papers inside into precise stacks. "Then again, everything about this particular estate is highly irregular. And, I doubt much as Paul would have minded. But you understand, I hope, why I had to get written permission from Darcy, even if you *are* married to her."

Jack hadn't minded at all, even though Darcy had made a few jokes about "signing enough permission slips for schoolkids" as she wrote out the note. Jack rather admired Jacob's keen attention to detail and protocol.

"And I can understand," Jacob continued, "why she'd want you taking the lead on this. With your background, I'd have probably advised her to do the same thing."

"I appreciate your willingness to speak with me," replied Jack. "I'm just trying to figure out our options here."

Jacob pointed at him with the pencil in his hand. "Good choice of word. You do have options. Paul felt he had no right *requiring* you and Darcy to do anything." The man sharpened his gaze. "But he did make his preferences mighty clear."

Well, Jack expected Jacob to see it that way. "Still," he countered, "I gather there are several ways to do that, and several levels at which to do it." Jack stared back at Jacob to see if he caught the subtext.

He did. "If you're asking me if you have to give all the money away or just some of it, the answer is no. I have no authority to make you do anything here. Darcy's always been a signer on the account, even if she didn't really know it. That's why she could pull from her father's checkbook to go do that beauty thing with her friend. Truth is, there's nothing stopping her from using Paul's money to get her nails done every day for the rest of her life."

"I was wondering about that." It was one of Jack's primary questions: whether or not Darcy had current access to the money, or did she have to go through Jacob. "So if I understand you right, the present setup could still stand. We wouldn't need to move the money into a new account or anything at this point? It's still earning the interest it's earned all along, and we can access it whenever we want?"

"Yes."

For a fleeting moment, the thought struck Jack that he and Darcy could turn around tomorrow and buy a new house cash on the barrel. Never to see a mortgage payment again. That was a rush any CPA would have to be comatose not to appreciate.

"Can we donate it right from where it is? Or do we need to set up some kind of special account?" Jack asked the question half out of honor, the other half out of stopping his spinning capitalistic gears.

"Nope, you could give the whole kaboodle away tomorrow in one check—*if* you wanted to. Of course, if you were asking me, I'd have to say I wouldn't advise it."

"Oh, I quite agree with you there. I think we have a lot of thinking to do before we do anything."

Jacob's face took on a strange expression. "I can't say, Jack, that I wouldn't be slowing down past the boat dealership if I were you. It's a lot of money. You got a lot to think about."

Jack tried not to let his shock show, then realized Jacob was not being judgmental at all. "It's a lot to take in. Your brain wanders a dozen different directions."

"It does at that. Look, I get paid to give advice, so I'm going to give it. Go slow. Do your homework. Look at all your options. And never say never." Jacob steepled his hands.

Had he worked the Bond movie title in there on purpose? It was debatable, as the exact title was *Never Say Never Again,* but the slight twinkle in Jacob's eye made Jack wonder. He made a mental note never to make assumptions about anyone in a bow tie ever again.

Darcy cleaned three closets trying to keep her mind off The Restoration Project the next two days. She boxed up the last of the kids' summer clothes, pulled out and assessed the snow boots and snow pants, and even sent three boxes of hand-me-downs off to the hospital thrift store.

Anything to keep her mind off grilling Jack.

She'd managed—through a supreme effort and no less than six calls to Glynnis—to keep her mouth shut. Her brain, however, had exploded wide-open, and the family computer held a ten-page outline of the Project's pilot testing phase. She'd allowed herself one call to Meredith, asking her to identify five families or individuals who might be good candidates for involvement. It was superfluous, really, because timing was crucial and she still had no idea when The Project would move forward. She'd asked Meredith to humor her, however, desperate to be doing anything while she waited for the Green Light from Heaven that seemed to never come.

"Trust it," Glynnis kept saying. Darcy felt herself chanting it like a mantra whenever her spirit got antsy—which was daily.

Trust it. Trust it.

Trust me. Trust me, God seemed to be asking. It seemed so difficult to do. Darcy found herself moaning to God, pleading with Him to give her enough peace, or to send her more patience. She was itching to act, to move her plan forward. Why wait? What would be gained by not actively pursuing her plan? It would be so much easier if things would just make more sense.

The morning of her birthday, Darcy wasn't sure Jack felt much like celebrating at all. His shoulders were stiff with tension—there must be a big meeting at his office today, and the stress had kept him up much of the night.

She waited all day for him to call and cancel their dinner out.

But he didn't. When he called at 4:00 p.m. to check and make sure the kids were set for the evening, his voice sounded softer. Less stressed. Not excited, more like resigned, but at least not as tense. She couldn't bring herself to ask what had transpired at work.

As she put on the last of her makeup and slid a frozen pizza into the oven for the kids, Darcy found herself almost agitated with uncertainty. She was looking forward to this night, to the time with Jack, but she wasn't at all sure how the evening would go.

Jack chose a lovely little seafood place in trendy Hyde Park. They'd driven by this place a dozen times, wondering to each other if it was any good. It was a Jack kind of place. Small, unpretentious, but with enough flair to make the evening special. He'd done well.

"Wonderful." Darcy let the buttery garlic of her shrimp scampi melt on her tongue. Cholesterol be hanged, tonight was no night for margarine. A woman deserved some crustaceans smothered in real butter on her birthday.

Jack nodded. His swordfish steak was nearly gone already. He was currently digging his way through a baked potato big enough for NFL play. "Ed was right—this place is terrific."

"Ed?"

"I had lunch with Ed Bidwell last week and he mentioned how much he and Glynnis liked this place."

Darcy tried not to let her shock show. Jack? Lunching with Ed Bidwell? That was the last thing she expected. While her relationship with Glynnis had blossomed immediately, Darcy was never quite sure Jack had hit it off with Ed much beyond mutual car affection. Evidently it had. Or was starting to. She opted for a noncommittal response. "Really?"

"He called with tickets to some car show. I told him it would be like taking a diabetic to the candy store. He laughed at that one. Suggested lunch instead."

So Ed had called him. Well, she could have guessed that. It was odd, however, for Jack not to have mentioned it. "How was it?" She tried to sound casual, suddenly finding her Greek salad worthy of intense inspection.

"He's a nice guy. A bit on the odd side, but I think you'd *have* to be to be married to Glynnis."

Darcy smiled. "They do suit each other, don't they?"

"Supremely." Jack got a bit of a faraway look in his eye. "I wish my parents were so happy. Ed and Glynnis are about as far from the grumpy-old-couple mentality as you can get."

"Your parents are together, Jack. They seem happy enough." It felt like a dumb response. As if she'd just negated Jack's very telling remark. But his parents were together. They were *alive,* for heaven's sake, and that counted for a lot in her book. Still, Jack had a point: they were grumpy. Didn't he realize they'd always been grumpy? What, so now a guy can't wish for vibrant parents? Darcy stabbed a cucumber with remorse. When would she learn to hush up, stop analyzing things down to the last micron, and just let Jack talk?

"They're together. But lately, it seems like every conversation with Mom is about something Dad did to tick her off, and every conversation with Dad is about how Mom is nagging him."

"They're in their seventies, Jack. It's what old people do. I suppose we should be happy they can still get around on their own."

"Ed still talks about his wife like she's a pinup girl."

Darcy laughed, thinking of Glynnis's scandalous remarks in the Henhouse. "Tell me about it. Glynnis was giving me *way* too much information about Ed's romantic side the other morning. It's cute, but it's creepy at the same time."

Jack chuckled, and softly sang a verse from the Beatles tune "When I'm Sixty-Four."

Darcy lifted her glass. "Of course I'll still feed you when you're sixty-four. Puree and all."

"And when I'm seventy-four?"

"Definitely."

"Eighty-four?"

"I'll wheel my chair right up beside yours."

"*Ninety-four?*"

"I'll have my nurse pass love notes from my hospital bed to yours." That one made Jack laugh out loud.

"I like them. The Bidwells. They're a bit odd, but I have to like a guy who can set you up with cheap videos and I still can't figure out how he got those basketballs wholesale for you."

"The man knows *everyone*. They're a kooky pair, but it's a nice kind of kooky." Darcy imagined Glynnis would take *kooky* as a compliment.

"He offered to set us up with a financial planner, you know."

Again, Darcy strove to keep her response as neutral as possible. "That sounds like something Ed would do."

"He's offered four times. I'm almost sorry I gave the guy my business card. The man loves to e-mail people."

"Really." So Ed's been e-mailing Jack. Hmm.

"Yeah, and here I can't even get Dad to program his VCR."

Darcy smiled, thinking of the nearly dozen times her mother-in-law had called her asking how to reset the clock on the coffeepot. She'd finally put the instructions in large print on an index card, sneaked it through the laminating machine at Paula's school, and taped it to the wall in their kitchen. She found providing such assistance heartwarming. It was so much different than the large-scale dependence and eventually the dementia she had endured with her father.

When she snapped her thoughts back to the conversation at hand, Darcy noticed Jack was looking at her. Twirling his wedding ring again. She had the distinct impression he was working up the nerve to say something, but honestly couldn't tell if it was good news or bad.

"Speaking of cards, I've got something for you, Dar." He had a sort of smile on his face, but it was an uncertain one. As if he wasn't particularly happy with whatever present was forthcoming. That didn't seem to be a very good sign.

Jack pulled out a box roughly the size of a videocassette. "I bought this two weeks ago, just after my birthday, but I hadn't decided until this afternoon whether or not to give it to you." He pulled his hand through his hair. "*Ugh,* I'm botching this." He took a deep breath, as if to regroup his thoughts. "Um, look…what I'm trying to say is that I thought long and hard about this. And, actually, I talked about it a lot to Ed, and I've come to a…well…oh, why don't you just open it?" He pushed the box across the table to her.

Well now, that was one of the strangest gift presentations Darcy had ever seen. Honest, even to the point of…what was that, reluctance? But heartfelt. She wasn't quite sure what to make of it. Whatever it was, it had been a big deal for Jack, so it must be important.

Lord, she sighed as she pulled the box toward her. *Give me the right reaction.*

Jack put his hand out to still hers as she reached for the bow. "No, wait. I did that all wrong. Let me start over." He kept his hand on hers, his finger making slow circles on the back of her palm. "This…this was hard for me. But I want you to have this. I want to be all jumpy and enthusiastic about this, but I'm not there yet. But I'm trying. I…I just want you to know that."

Darcy did not dare let her heart go where it was racing. She did not want to allow herself to hope. But her heart went there anyway, without permission, full of fragile expectation. Could he?

She pulled on the ribbon and slid her fingers under the tape of the giftwrap. Inside was a beautiful velvet chest— almost like a jewelry box, or a tiny treasure chest, covered in red silk and exotic-looking beadwork. She looked at Jack, and he nodded a silent *Open it.*

The lid tilted upward to reveal two slim silver boxes and a cream-colored envelope.

"Open the one on the right first." Jack's expression was going from contorted to excited. Slowly, but definitely going in that direction.

She picked up the silver case. It was, she realized, a business card case. Stumped, she pressed the small button that popped open the lid.

And lost the ability to breathe.

Inside, on delicate cream-colored cards, was the following inscription.

Darcy Nightengale
President and Founder
The Restoration Project

She ran her hand across the graceful raised lettering and felt life click into place. How much sweeter this moment was for the waiting. How much more Jack's agreement meant because it had not been hunted. It had been given. Freely, with much effort. Out of sheer love. Jack had stepped out of his sensibility—at a time when it must have felt so uncomfortable to do so—because of his love for her and her wish to do this extraordinary thing.

"Oh, Jack."

"Yeah, well, I think you should do this. I think you *need* to do this. I understand it, sort of, but even if I don't, there seems to be a part of you wrapped up in it." He seemed to want to say more, but couldn't quite find the words. "You're not done, yet, though, open the others."

The second silver case made Darcy laugh out loud. Its cards read Kate Owens, Vice President, The Restoration Project.

"Oh, Jack, she'll love this. I love this. Thank you."

The cream-colored envelope held a small note that read in Jack's efficient script:

I ♥ YOU
I.O. TRP $2K

It took her a moment to unscramble the alphabet soup of his wording, but she smiled when she did. It was pure Jack. He'd found a way to offer his approval in a bits-and-pieces approach that his CPA soul could handle. She almost loved him more for his transparent honesty than if he'd told her to give the whole inheritance away. That would have been wrong for him. This meant, to her, that he was taking it very seriously. And that was wonderful.

"Take your two grand and run with it, Dar. Let that pilot project idea of yours fly. Then we'll come back, evaluate and see where we go from there."

She had envisioned the moment when Jack would give his approval. She'd thought of herself jumping with excitement, whooping with victory, even. Instead, what she found was a simple, quiet, almost pure joy. The perfect, silent sound of a plan snapping into place. Of a God engineering all the details to a marvelous outcome. What had Glynnis called it? Exceeding our expectations.

Oh, He'd surely done that.

Way to go, God. Thanks.

She imagined herself high-fiving The Lord Almighty.

Then, better yet, she could picture her father doing the same.

Chapter 16

The Stuff of Legend

Darcy sat in Ernestine's salon, fresh from a trim and touch-up on her hair. She paged through the November edition of *Good Housekeeping*, scanning for Thanksgiving recipes while she waited for Kate to finish her "regularly scheduled maintenance." They'd piled in the car for a celebratory appointment this morning after Darcy had presented Kate with her new business cards. Darcy wasn't sure it was ethical to send up a prayer for openings in a stylist's schedule, but God had evidently granted her some leeway: Ernestine had been booked, but she'd squeezed in "the comfortably drastic girls" as she called them, as a favor.

The magazine's food section served up a stunning-looking turkey with orange-sage dressing. Darcy smiled. To her father, stuffing had always been the whole point of Thanksgiving. He had seven different "secret family recipes." Paul hadn't been an especially good cook—he had kept to the three-ingredient-ground-beef-based basics like most single men—and as Darcy had been in high school when her mother died, he had mostly cooked for one.

On Thanksgiving, however, all bets were off. Paul bought one of those deep-frying contraptions long before cooking turkeys in that fashion became the fad. The man lived to, as he called it, "cook The Bird" every November. But more than that, he lived to concoct the perfect assembly of ingredients to stuff that bird to perfection. Hartwell stuffing was, as Dad liked to put it, "the stuff of legend."

Two years ago, Paul wasn't in perfect health, but he was well enough to make a turkey worthy of his legend. Darcy had offered to help with the side dishes, and they'd had everything at her house—it helped to claim that they couldn't all fit at Paul's small dining table anyhow. Sure, it had been altered a bit, but most of it felt like the traditional Hartwell holiday.

Last year, he'd quietly handed her all seven of his stuffing recipes with a pained look in his eyes.

Jack, God bless him, had gone over to Paul's house, hauled out the deep fryer, pulled the cooking instructions off the Internet (Dad never did keep the manuals to anything), and "cooked The Bird." Dad was bundled up in the mud room on a recliner they'd put there just so he could "supervise."

The realization that this year would be different—that forever would be different—burned in her chest like hot oil.

Thanksgiving without Dad.

Christmas without Dad.

Life without Dad.

Even though she'd gone two weeks without crying, the tears came fast and uninvited. Could she stand the sight of the turkey fryer sending up smoke off the back deck? Would it be a welcome memorial, or a reopened wound?

"Hey, you okay?" Kate's voice came over her shoulder and a hand touched her arm.

"Sort of."

"Not sort of." Kate glanced at the magazine, understanding dawning on her face. "It's going to be different this year. Hard. But you'll make it. You'll make a new kind of Thanksgiving."

Darcy looked up, suddenly feeling like she was five years old. "I don't want a new kind of Thanksgiving." She wanted to stick her trembling lip out and pout.

"I know." Kate pulled a tissue from the box that sat on a table behind her and handed it to Darcy.

Darcy blew her nose. "Can we just cancel the holiday season this year? Go straight to something harmless like President's Day?"

Kate plopped down on the seat beside her. "I'm not so sure Mike and Paula would go for that. Especially since they have the Grand Lady of Great Gift Giving as their mother. Christmas is your prime season, girl."

"Yeah, well everyone may just get department store gift cards this year, I'm warning you." Darcy reached across Kate's lap to snag another tissue.

"Hey," Kate's voice was soft and suddenly serious. "No one would blame you."

There was a stretch of silence. Darcy sighed, feeling the tears subside. "I suppose."

"Just take it slow. Think of Thanksgiving as a warm-up. Do what feels good, and give the rest the boot. Keep the stuff you like and that helps you to remember, and forget anything that feels like it'll hurt too much. Cut yourself some slack."

"You're right."

Kate took a deep breath. "Yeah, well I have just two words for you."

Darcy looked up.

"Extra crispy."

Darcy smiled. "Mmm. I like the sound of that." She folded the magazine back into her purse.

Kate pulled Darcy up out of her chair and hummed "Hail to the Chief" all the way out the door.

An hour later, they were pulling off the exit ramp toward home. "Man," Darcy sighed, "I love this little car. It's such a terrific break from the mom-in-a-minivan existence. I can't remember the last time I was in a car with less than ten cup holders."

"Don took the van to work today. He's stopping at Home Depot on the way home."

Darcy let out a moan of recognition. "What now?"

"New garage shelving."

"Our garage doesn't even *have* shelves, much less new ones."

"Ah, the joys of being married to Mr. Home Improvement." Kate rummaged through the bucket for another drumstick. "You got the sports guy, I got the power tool guy."

Darcy passed her a napkin. "Thanks again for your idea. I'd have never dreamed up the basketballs without you. It was just…wonderful."

"My pleasure."

"Speaking of wonderful, are you free Friday morning? I want to set a meeting with Meredith to pick the test group. I thought I'd invite Doug Whitman, too."

"Whitman? The Pastor Whitman from your dad's church?"

"Yes. I think he can help with the families and he works with Meredith a lot. I haven't told him yet, but I think he'll really buy into the idea."

"O-kay," Kate drew the word out in a skeptical drawl. It didn't take Mike's mathematical mind to see she wasn't keen on the idea.

"Kate, he's an okay guy. And he seems to have a pretty good take on this whole weird setup Dad handed me. I mean, nobody really knew what Dad was doing, what he had in mind, but I think Doug comes close. I trust him."

Kate deposited another drumstick bone in the paper sack. "This is the guy who didn't instantly ask you to fund the new church nursery, right?"

"Yup, that's him."

Kate was thinking, biting her lower lip in that way she did when she was frustrated or uncomfortable. After a moment, she said without taking her eyes off the road, "This isn't gonna get all churchy, is it?"

Well, now, that was the question of the hour. If God was behind this idea…*wait.* Darcy's own internal dialogue made her stop and question herself. She thought God was behind this, didn't she? Really, truly? But was she sure? Could this be just some emotional response to her father's death, his secrets and her desire to make things add up sensibly?

No, there were no doubts. She knew. She knew it down to her toes, even though the knowledge both surprised and scared her. God had exploded into her life, surrounded her, and camped out on the doorstep of her soul until she cracked the door open and finally let Him in.

If faith was supposed to be a comfort, this was the most uncomfortable faith she'd ever known.

But it was also more alive, more captivating and more irresistible than she'd ever imagined. It pulled the rug out from underneath her, but it also sent her soaring.

This God was nothing like she'd remembered. Surely nothing she had expected.

She imagined He rather enjoyed that.

All of which made it rather hard to answer Kate's pointed question. Dear friend and coconspirator that she was, Kate didn't really have an understanding of the spiritual side of what Darcy wanted to do. For goodness sake, *Darcy* didn't even have an understanding of the spiritual side of this crazy endeavor. It hadn't started that way, but God's hand in this was becoming unmistakable. Unignorable.

Would Kate understand?

Was Darcy even ready to try to make her understand?

Darcy settled on the truth. "You know, I'm not really sure."

"Your dad's faith was a big part of his life," came Kate's soft reply. It was an odd, noncommittal response. Not really a response at all, actually. The tiny car grew a bit tense. They had never talked about this kind of thing. It felt like very foreign ground between two friends who shared just about every detail of their lives with each other. Darcy grasped for a comfortable way to broach the subject.

"I'm coming to understand some things. Get a sense of what it is that my dad believed so strongly in. Glynnis has been teaching me a lot." Did Kate tense up at the mention of Glynnis, or did she just imagine that? "Other stuff has just sort of—" she groped for the right verb "—dawned on me on my own." *Eeek, Lord, I'm drowning here. A little help, please?*

"Does it help?" Kate's question was sincere, not judgmental.

And, it was a really good question. Perhaps the most important of all. One, thankfully, with a solid answer. "Yes. It does. A lot."

Kate didn't reply.

Come on, Lord, I can't just leave it like this.

Darcy tried again. "Look, it's true that faith is becoming a bigger part of my life. I'm not one hundred percent used to it yet, but it means a lot to me. And…and I won't deny that it hasn't become wrapped up in this whole project—but I think that's a good thing. I know I'm supposed to be doing this." Darcy looked at Kate. "I know *you're* supposed to be doing this."

Kate got that I'm-not-so-sure-I'm-ready-to-be-dragged-into-this look. Darcy touched her arm. "I'm pretty sure, too, that no one's going to part the Ohio River so we can wander in Kentucky for forty years or anything like that."

Kate laughed. Darcy was glad for it. The tension lifted. "I'm still here," she continued. "We're still us."

"Yeah, only with better hair."

"Well, we've got to practice what we preach, don't we?"

Kate shot her a look. "*Are* we preaching?"

"I have no idea," was Darcy's completely honest answer. "But I imagine we'll find out."

Chapter 17

Anyone Worth Their Salt

"Darcy, I think it's an extraordinary idea. I can't think of a better use for the money." Doug Whitman looked like he really meant it. Underfunded nursery and all.

"Thanks. I appreciate your support."

"I had a feeling there needed to be an unusual, creative end to this. That your dad had more in mind than you whipping a check off to some charity." Whitman's face lit up in a warm, reminiscent smile, as if remembering some great joke Paul Hartwell had told him. "I think this is exactly what he had in mind. He'd be proud, Darcy."

Darcy thought of her father smiling down on the tumble of circumstances that had been her life since September. The image caught in the back of her throat like tears. "Yep," was all she could choke out.

Kate handed Darcy a tissue. Kate was always handing Darcy tissues. It was a good thing in life, Darcy thought, to have someone by your side, ready to hand you tissues.

"We're still not in the clear yet, this is only a test run. Of course, we know the results will be irrefutable evidence for a full-scale project, right?" The four people in the room chimed in their affirmation. Kate smiled. "Just so we're all ready."

Ready? How can someone be ready for something like this? Willing, yes. Able, well, that remained to be seen. Ready? Darcy felt she was both born ready to do this, and that she couldn't be ready for this in a hundred years of preparation.

Meredith produced a sheet of paper, handing copies to each of them. "I've taken the liberty of going ahead with Darcy's request, and identifying five candidates. They are a variety of ages and situations, Darcy, just as you asked. Three of them are from the Center, the other two are members of Doug's church who have ill family members living at home."

"At home?" Kate asked.

"Far more people are dealing with end-of-life care within their own homes than have access to hospice centers like this one. It makes for some unique issues, and in many ways the stress is even greater without a medical staff continually present."

"You're right, Meredith, I hadn't even thought of that," Darcy replied. "I'm sure glad you guys are in on this."

"We've got the salons and spas onboard," added Kate. "Three of them, actually. It was an easy sell—they all think it's a great idea. As a matter of fact, each of them threw in services gratis so that TRP funds will go even farther. Two of them have packages that already include coffee and lunch, so we're good to go."

Darcy ran her eyes down the page. Five lives, five tragedies, spread themselves out before her.

Anne Morton was caring for her father-in-law who was in the middle stages of Alzheimer's. An eighty-seven-year-old man who could carry on a lucid conversation one hour, then be found standing in the garage in his underwear the next. Mr. Morton's other children had sent regular checks, but left the gargantuan tasks of daily care to Anne and her husband.

Jean Tinsdale was caring for a sister, Margaret, in the final stages of breast cancer. A double mastectomy and endless rounds of chemo had failed to keep the beast of a disease at bay. The endema from the operations and treatments had swelled one arm to the point of uselessness. Margaret was running out of options, and running out of time. Now in her late forties, Margaret had never married. Jean was engaged, but the wedding had been postponed twice in the faint hopes of Margaret's recovery.

Darcy knew what it was like to put your life on hold. And on hold again.

Frances Neyburg was watching heart disease take her husband from her one day at a time. He would not live to meet their grandchildren.

Michelle Porter's baby had endured seven surgeries in his first year of life. None had helped. When other mothers were waiting for their babies' first steps, Michelle was steeling herself for her baby's last breaths. Alongside a husband who was not, by any means, coping well with the tragedy.

The last candidate was the most surprising. Noreen McDylan and her husband Ian were a couple in their fifties who had no children of their own, but spent their days caring for a succession of gravely ill foster children. Life had not handed the McDylans this cruel card; they'd taken it for themselves. Darcy couldn't even begin to imagine what kind of person could have the strength to do that.

Meredith must have followed Darcy's eyes, for she caught Darcy's wrist. "I know, can you imagine? The McDylans are angels, pure and simple."

Doug Whitman piped in. "They've been doing this for seven years. I honestly don't know how their hearts can stand the constant loss. You'd think they'd earn admiration—well, this year they've earned a cutback in their support funding, so that now they're just scraping by. Ian's diabetes has been acting up, and they're trying to find enough funds to meet all the medical expenses for both the children and themselves."

Darcy sat there, staring at the profiles, and begged God to make this thing fly.

"To top it all off," Doug continued, his voice sharp with the injustice of it all, "Ian had a nephew who worked in the Pentagon. It took five of us to cover for them so they could both attend the funeral."

"This is really heartbreaking," said Kate, obviously affected. "Talk about trauma. There's a whole year's worth of *E.R.* episodes on this one page." She looked at Meredith with a sort of awe. "How do you handle it? Day after day?"

Meredith shrugged. "Not everyone can."

Kate tapped the page with her hand, "No one gave them a choice, did they?"

Darcy clenched her fists. These people needed to know their toil was noticed. That they were human beings, deserving of rich lives of their own, not just caretaking machines who could give and give and give without cost.

She was about to voice her conviction when her cell phone went off. Her speed dial recognized the number as Paula's school. Darcy snagged it out of her purse and ducked into the hallway to take the call.

Two minutes later she popped her head back into the room, snapping her flip-phone closed in disgust. "Paula just threw up in gym. Excuse me, folks, seems I have a little trauma of my own to take care of."

In a single, swift arc, Meredith popped open the door of the credenza behind her, reached back, and sent an object flying in Darcy's direction. She recognized the industrial gray color and shape immediately, and caught it midair with a chuckle.

Kate looked confused. As Darcy headed out the door, she heard Meredith's amused voice explaining what an emesis basin was, and why anyone worth their salt here at the center could produce one of the "vomit pans" at a moment's notice.

Welcome to my world, ladies and gentlemen, Darcy thought as she left the pair in Meredith's capable hands.

On day three of crackers, ginger ale and ice pops, Paula was just about returning to human state. Mike, however, had let it slip over breakfast that he wasn't feeling so hot. It was 2:00 p.m., which meant that he'd made it through the school day, which was good, because Darcy didn't cherish the idea of stuffing pale little Paula into the van to go fetch Mike from the nurse's office. Darcy calculated Mike would make it until about four o'clock, and then the festivities would begin all over again. Good thing she'd asked Jack to pick up more soda, crackers and half a dozen videos at the store on the way home this evening. At least it was Friday.

Better now than at Thanksgiving, she tried to encourage herself. It wasn't really working. And it didn't really matter that it was Friday, she suddenly remembered, because Jack had to go into work tomorrow. Sometimes it was hard to decide which was worse, the poor souls who got laid off, or the bedraggled souls who had to hold down an oversize workload.

Bedraggled. That was the word for it. She and Jack were both bedraggled.

Darcy kissed Paula's sweaty little forehead. At least Paula had finally fallen asleep, even if it did mean Darcy had lost the circulation in her left arm as Paula slept against it. At last, a respite from another *Arthur* episode. She could practically recite the dialogue, she'd seen it so many in the past three days. And she was getting ready to pledge a second time to her local PBS station just to get those perky pledge drive people off the air faster.

Darcy couldn't get up off the couch—no sense risking that until Paula was more soundly asleep. She couldn't reach the TV remote, not that she wanted it on now anyway. Scanning the room for something within reach to pass the time, her eyes landed on the coffee table drawer. The little side drawer nobody ever opened. She angled her body just so and caught the knob, pulling the drawer open. She couldn't see into the drawer, but her hand found what she knew was in there, her father's letter and his Bible. The other contents from The Box had gone into the fire safe downstairs, but for some strange reason she'd wanted these things up here, close by. Even though she'd not opened the drawer since she put those articles inside nearly three weeks ago. Now, with Paul Hartwell's namesake asleep in her arms, the time seemed right to bring them back out.

It still astounded her how five slips of paper could turn a life inside out. Why keep the lawsuit settlement such a secret? Why go to such extremes? If Paul couldn't give the money away, how could a man of his emotional and spiritual health not handle life enough to make good use of the money? It wasn't as if it were mob hit money or anything—the courts had declared that money justifiably his. Why treat it like such a poison when it had the capacity to do so much good in their lives? The questions buzzed around her brain. She'd never know the answers. Only God knew what had been going on in her father's head.

Darcy fumbled a bit to open the Bible, limited as she was to the use of only one hand. She wandered through whatever pages fell open, wondering if she could interpret it like a family cookbook: you could always tell the favorite recipes by how dirty the pages were and where the book fell naturally open. It didn't seem to work. Some pages held notes and comments from her father, while others looked untouched. She found several more references to forgiving someone named Harry, similar to the one she'd found when she first pulled the Bible from The Box.

Why it hadn't come to her before this, Darcy would never be able to explain. It was so obvious. Harry. Harry Zokowski. The man who had hit her mother.

Forgive Harry. Dad never spoke of Harry Zokowski. He was a faceless, nameless villain to her. She'd always hated him for what he'd done.

As a matter of fact, now that she rolled the name over and over on her tongue, she did remember Dad saying that name. Cursing that name. Long-buried memories of Dad, raging in anger downstairs when he thought she was asleep, swearing vengeance on Harry Zokowski, came floating to the surface of her recollection.

They'd taken him for everything. Without insurance, Harry Zokowski lost his home and savings in the lawsuit.

Yes, she remembered the victory they'd made of it. Harry paid dearly for what he'd done.

Forgive Harry. Had that been Dad's private battle over the years? Why the settlement money seemed so corrupting to him? Darcy was struck by how little she really knew about that dark episode in her father's history.

She'd never know. Even Harry Zokowski was dead now. No family, either. She'd never know the rest of it. The reality stuck its sharp edges into her chest. She was alone. No Dad. No more answers, no more advice. No more Grandpa for Paula and Mike. No more world-class stuffing. So much "no more" everywhere.

Life would be so much nicer if Little Orphan Heiress had a different middle name.

She ceremoniously flipped through the Bible one more time. Her dad—and Glynnis, for that matter—always talked about how the Bible "spoke" to them, how passages would practically jump off the page into their heart for a moment of unquestionably divine intervention. *Come on Lord, show your stuff. Let me see what it is everyone keeps talking about.* Feeling stupid, wondering if the aforementioned was even a legal prayer—wasn't there something about not testing the Lord Your God?—she planted her finger on the next page. Darcy took a deep breath and looked down.

If ye love me, keep my commandments. And I will pray to the Father, and he shall give you another Comforter, that he may abide with you forever. Even the Spirit of truth, whom the world cannot receive, because it seeth him not, neither knoweth him; but ye know him, for he dwelleth with you, and shall be in you.

It was the next verses, however, that made Darcy nearly jump.

I will not leave you orphans: I will come to you. Yet a little while, and the world will see me no more; but ye see me. Because I live, ye shall live also.

Darcy sucked in her breath and looked around, half expecting to see someone playing a practical joke on her. This was far too weird—the hair on the back of her neck was standing on end. How many times could the word *orphan* possibly appear in the Bible? Surely not that many, and surely none in the context of this verse from—she had to look a second time, too stunned to notice the first time—John 14.

Yes, she was orphaned, but she had not been *left* orphaned. Darcy knew, at that moment, that the words were for her. The living nature of the Bible, that missing umph that her father, Glynnis, and others she had heard talk about had finally revealed itself to her. Sure, there were lots of *yes, knoweths* and *dwelleths* in the way, but the message came through loud and clear.

I will not leave you orphaned. I will come to you.

The message was for her. To her, feeding her. Filling a particular hole in her heart that had been aching since September 12. God *had* come to her. She knew it. She'd known it all along, actually, but it was somehow more true now. It was almost something she could feel and taste. It had force and strength. It had life.

She sat there a while, stunned. Suddenly, Darcy realized that the parts of her life collided right here in her lap: Paula breathing softly on her left, Paul's Bible and its living, breathing message on her right. Her past and her future, intersecting over her heart.

Everything was as it was intended to be. Life was taking its intended course. The money could be redeemed. Suddenly, Paul's mysterious why seemed to matter less. What mattered now was what she did with what God had handed her. Because He was beside her.

For a moment, there was no chaos, no fretting over the future, just a still, perfect moment in time. As if God had plunged down out of His heaven, sat down on the couch beside her, and put His arm around her. Truly, it was almost a physical sensation, like a hug around her brain. Around her soul. Darcy smiled at the sappy metaphor, but that's truly how she felt. She wasn't sure she could ever relate to anyone what this moment really felt like. She could sit on this couch, cradling her daughter and these mementos of her father, for hours.

The sound of the school bus rolling by the kitchen windows brought her out of her reverie. She counted down, like a rocket launch, the ninety seconds before Mike burst through the door.

He threw his backpack down on the kitchen floor, sat on the steps, and leaned against the wall.

"Mom, I don't feel so hot…."

Chapter 18

Fluffheads under Fire

By Wednesday of the next week, round two of the stomach virus had finally ended. Darcy sighed happily at the prospect of a child-free morning, spent—how else?—with Kate.

"Glad to have Mike back in school today?" said Kate, sipping the last of her tea as Darcy finished loading the dishwasher.

"Yep. Finally. I really wanted to send him yesterday and make our meeting, but his fever had only just gone down. I'm probably pushing it today, but he's got to get his work to catch up over the holiday." Darcy loaded the cups from both bathrooms into the top rack—everything that could even *think* of hosting a germ was going to get a good washing today. Sheets and towels were already in the washer on Scalding.

"So that leaves you, what, twenty-four hours to get ready for Thanksgiving?" The two of them were braving the warehouse shopping club to stock up at the last minute. Costco the day before Thanksgiving was no place to venture alone.

"Twenty-three if you count the time I'll spend chatting with you."

"With my luck the store will be out of sweet potatoes by this afternoon. And mini-marshmallows will be out on the black market."

Darcy clicked the dishwasher door shut and pushed the button marked Sanitiz-R Rinse. She pretended she didn't hear the strange clanking noise as the machine kicked on. She reached for a stack of recipe cards, and fanned them in front of Kate. "Pick a card, any card."

"Huh?"

"No, really. Just pick one."

Kate plucked a card from the middle. "Why?"

Darcy flipped the card over. "That settles it. We're making Dad's corn sausage stuffing this year. I had all seven of these recipes to choose from. That is, of course, providing I can actually get my hands on the ingredients." Darcy snagged her shopping list off the fridge and proceeded to add the necessary items.

"Corn bread? On the Wednesday before Thanksgiving? You're brave."

"I know." She grabbed her purse off the counter and drained the last of her tea. "But we make a good team and it's only 9:00 a.m. You can tell me how the meeting with Meredith and Doug went yesterday as we drive."

"Oh, yeah, that. Well, it didn't go so well. Come on, I'll tell you in the car."

Meredith and Doug had each informed their respective Restoration Project candidates. The group was getting back together to go over initial reactions, identify logistical challenges such as getting baby-sitters, and match women with salons. It was going to be a great meeting—a first chance to watch The Restoration Project's real implementation. Darcy was frustrated to miss it.

"What do you mean, 'It didn't go so well'? Why didn't you call me last night?" Darcy unlocked the car.

"I didn't see the point. I knew I was going to see you today."

"Well, come on, what happened?"

Kate pulled her car door shut and snapped her seat belt into place. "Actually, I may be overstating things a bit. Most of it went well. Really well. Four of the five women were really excited. A little wary—you know, I think they suspect they're walking into an episode of some reality makeover TV show or something—but mostly excited. Glad, I suppose, that someone notices what they're going through. It's going to mean so much to them, Dar. Such a boost."

Darcy revved the car into gear. "Good. That's good."

Kate's entire body language shifted. "That young mom, though, Michelle Porter? She…well, she didn't take it so well."

"What do you mean by 'so well'?"

"She was angry. 'Bitter,' Doug called it. I think even he was taken aback by her letter."

Darcy looked at Kate. "Her letter? She wrote a letter?"

"A scathing one. She's…um…not very happy to be chosen. She thinks…" Darcy could see that Kate was trying to smooth over whatever that letter had said.

"Just tell me." Darcy could feel her already too short temper shrinking. She didn't care for the way letters had so much power in her life these days.

"Look, you shouldn't let this get to you. Doug said we

shouldn't take her lashing personally. She's mad at the world for what's happened to her son."

"You're stalling, Madam Vice President. And why don't I have a copy of this letter?"

Kate slumped down in her seat. "Okay, okay. I *do* have a copy for you. But I agree with Doug, I don't think we should be discouraged by this."

"Kate, either show me the letter or tell me what it said. *Now.*"

Kate sighed. "She said we were wasting money on stupid things when it could be better spent on research. 'A good haircut can hardly bring my son his life back' was one of the better lines. 'Vain misguided fluffheads' was my personal favorite."

Darcy felt like someone had just punched her in the stomach. Twice.

"Look, Dar, she doesn't get it. She's up to her earlobes in grief and anger and she can't see the value of anything right now. Meredith said it was bound to happen now and then. People respond to grief in so many different ways."

Darcy cut a corner closely, her grip viselike on the steering wheel. Of all the nerve…

Kate continued. "It's the *other* women you should be paying attention to, the ones who are so grateful and amazed and surprised. We're giving them something they don't even understand they need yet. This is good, Dar, really good. Amazing things are going to come from this. You should see the looks on Doug's and Meredith's faces— they're as excited as we were in the beginning."

"You mean *before* someone lambasted us as vain fluffheads?"

"See? That's why I didn't call you last night. I knew you'd get like this."

"You'd think—" Darcy's cell phone ring cut her off. She pulled it out of her purse and flipped it open.

"Hon?" Jack's voice was thin and strained. *Oh, Lord, what now?*

"Jack? You sound awful." Darcy panicked—had he been laid off? Were they cruel enough to do something like that the day before Thanksgiving?

"I'm on my way home. I feel awful."

"Oh, no…" Darcy wanted to scream, but kept her voice sympathetic. How did she not see this coming? Oh, that's right, she was an optimist.…

"Oh, yes." He coughed horribly. "I'm getting out of here before I get sick again."

"Come home, Jack." Sick *again?*

"See you soon."

Darcy pulled off the road and laid her head on the steering wheel. "Kiss my corn bread goodbye."

"What?" Kate sounded panicked.

Darcy tried to laugh, she really did. "Jack."

"I *know* Jack. Jack what?"

"Jack's sick. He just threw up at work. He's on his way home now." With an enormous sigh, Darcy edged the car into a three-point turn to head back. With any luck, she'd make it home just before Jack.

"You're going home?" Kate wailed. "Jack's a big boy, you know. He can find a bathroom all on his own. We can still get you the basics in half an hour. Plus extra Pepto-Bismol."

"No way," Darcy countered. "Jack's an even bigger baby than Paula when he's sick. I thought he looked, well, not himself this morning, but I just assumed it was stress."

Kate groaned. "Turkey Day's going to be a real turkey for you this year, huh?"

"I could just cry."

"Don't cry. Send Paula and Mike over to our house for dinner—what's the difference between twelve people and fourteen? I'll send home a plate of fixings for you. Jack can eat chicken noodle soup and saltines—that is, if he can keep anything down."

Darcy simply nodded, wanting to sob.

"Do we need to stop for supplies on the way?" Kate was trying to be helpful.

"No, we're all stocked up. We've got enough ginger ale, saltines and chicken soup to feed half the city."

"This rots, Dar. It just rots."

The two of them yelled "Rots!" at the top of their voices the whole drive home. Kate would just have to go into the Costco battle alone. The Nightengales were under attack.

Right beside the "vain fluffheads."

Happy holidays, all right. The Stuff of Legend.

Saturday morning, Darcy Nightengale filled her travel mug with tea and organized her sale circulars. Jack's stomach had calmed, the kids were happily installed in front of Saturday morning television and Mom was going shopping.

Power shopping.

Thanksgiving had been a complete washout, saved only by the fact that her family now possessed no less than twelve hours' worth of James Bond movies. It didn't have quite the same romance as Jack's birthday, but she made herself an enormous bowl of popcorn and worked her way through four movies.

In between responding to calls for care from Jack, that is.

Suffice it to say the Pause button on the DVD remote got a supreme workout.

Today's workout, however, would be all about the mall. It was going to take an all-out war to make this holiday season a decent one, and this heiress was up to the challenge. Darcy had spent a whole day nursing the wounds of Michelle Porter's letter, and it only added to the undercurrent of pain that lingered over the prospect of a Christmas without her father.

The solution, as Darcy saw it, was to have the absolute best Christmas. A really meaningful holiday season. She'd been up half the night, combing the ads, scanning the magazines. She had meals, baking, cards, presents and even new Advent traditions planned out to the tiniest detail. She had a decorating theme for each room. This would be the year she finally made those hand-cut gift cards she'd admired from a television show. She'd downloaded four different churches' Christmas Eve schedules off the Internet—including, of course, Ohio Valley where Doug was pastor. If the Nightengale household had budded back to life this fall, it was going to blossom into full bloom this Christmas.

Four stores, then lunch, three more stores, then tea with Kate, then two final stores with a swing by the China Pavilion for takeout to bring home. Darcy stacked her flyers, her list and her timetable on the passenger seat beside her.

The Beach Boys were belting "Merry Christmas, Baby" through the car stereo as Darcy zipped out of the driveway. Today, she would get to show her family just how much attention she had for *them* now. It was a new beginning. The birth of new traditions, a time to find new ways to pamper her family and make them her priority.

Stand back, world, Darcy Nightengale is ready to have a full-blown Christmas!

Darcy checked items off her list with an efficiency that would have made even Santa jealous. She'd not only scored the planned items on her agenda, but halfway through the second store she'd found two gifts that were even better than the ones she had planned. She'd stood there, in the back corner aisle of Dillard's housewares department, and debated if it made more sense to return the previous items now, or wait until later. She'd opted, in a rush of clarity, to do none of the above.

She would return neither.

Kate and Glynnis would get both gifts—the good ones, and the better ones as well.

Yes, folks, this year, everybody was going to get everything. She added two more pairs of mittens to the care package she was sending to a local homeless shelter. And the stock of food she'd send to the food pantry? Well you can bet it would include honest-to-goodness Oreos. If there was ever a year for the queen of presents to claim her throne, this was it.

Darcy stared down at her collection of bags. Suddenly the pressure of plastic handles wasn't cutting off her circulation; she was simply feeling the weight of her generosity. The lines weren't annoyingly long; they were simply time to chat with strangers. The holiday season sucked her up in its marvelous momentum, and she reveled in the joyful bustle.

It hurt more to be still. To ponder and remember all those tiny Yuletide details that would never be here again. The fifth stocking unhung. Movement was the antidote to that undercurrent of pain. This was her weapon—the giving, the adorning, the crafting, the rejoicing—her shield against those things which she could not change.

By three-thirty, she was brimming with a deliciously useful exhaustion as she plopped down opposite Kate in the window table at J.L.'s. "Behold," she said stretching her arms out and rolling her aching shoulders, "I came, I saw, I holidayed."

"Had a good day, did you? Nice to get out and play with all the grown-up, unsick people?"

Darcy rested her chin in one hand. "I never did that to my mother. I was never that sick, and I never made my brother or sister sick only seconds after I recovered. Never. Not once."

"You're an only child. There was no one to infect. That's hardly an accomplishment."

"You can't hold my sibling deprivation against me. And I surely never infected the wage-earning parent the day before Thanksgiving. I was a model child."

Kate peered over her shoulder out the storefront windows into Darcy's van. "I'd say you were the model consumer today. That's quite a haul you've got there."

Darcy grinned. "I'm making up for lost time."

"Looks like you're making up for the national trade deficit in there." Kate sipped her tea. "I've got to hand it to you, though, all your shopping done in one day—and on the Saturday after Thanksgiving no less. That's the mark of a true professional."

"Well, now, I'm not exactly sure I'm done yet. There are two more stores to hit yet today, and then I'm not sure where I'll take it from there. I found some decorating ideas I may want to try. And we haven't even gotten to the food yet."

"O-kay," Kate drew the word out again, the way she did when she got all weird. "I suppose you're entitled to a little retail therapy."

"What's that supposed to mean?"

"Nothing. It's perfectly fine to blow off steam with a credit card. Sort of."

"I was Christmas shopping. A perfectly respectable holiday pastime. Normal behavior. Seasonally appropriate."

"Yeah," Kate replied skeptically.

"Okay, I guess I went a little overboard. But you know what? It felt so good—so just plain marvelous—to have fun again. To act happy. I don't think there's anything wrong with that."

"There's not. I'm just saying you might want to make sure you don't…overdo it." Kate laughed a bit too forcibly. "Well, overdo it more than usual. On the Darcy scale of things. Which is kind of over-the-top to begin with, so…"

"I'm *fine*, Kate. Enthusiastic, granted, but fine." Darcy eyed Kate. "Besides, trust me, you don't want me returning the fabulous gifts I bought you."

"Well, since you put it that way…"

Chapter 19

Hens with Antlers?!?

"No, really, Glynnis, I'm fine. I mean, I have moments—times when I remember some Christmas or some present, or when I look at the fireplace mantel and it just looks wrong with four stockings on it—but I'm okay for the most part."

Glynnis just nodded in response.

"And why does everyone keep *asking* me that? I swear, if I hear that overemphasized 'How *are* you?' one more time…"

Glynnis took a bite of cookie. "Because it's hard to *lose* a loved one around the holidays. They're just concerned about you, that's all."

Darcy snatched a cookie of her own off the plate. "If they were so concerned about me, why didn't they show it before? When things were really messy and ugly and hard? Why now in the nice clean aftermath?"

Glynnis looked at her. "I think you just answered your own question, hon. Death is a messy business. People don't like to get too close to it. Makes 'em realize they'll have to muck around in that mess, too, someday. Not exactly a cozy thought."

"Still, I'm sick of people looking at me as if I've sprouted antlers or something."

Glynnis chuckled. "In a way, you have."

Glynnis was always coming up with the strangest metaphors. Darcy couldn't always keep up. "Because..." she cued, half dreading the explanation.

"Antlers are a sign of maturity. The passage from—what are they called, fawns? I don't know, whatever Bambi was—to adult deer. You've made it through a rite of passage of sorts. Become the senior generation—the survivor, if you will. Everybody dreads it, wonders if they'll make it through it. You have. Or, are still making it through it." She shifted in her seat. "In our generation, it's losing your spouse. All of us well-seasoned human beings dread how we'll cope when our husbands or wives die. Some of us handle that fear well, others don't. I have friends who absolutely dread it. Ask any widow you know, and she'll name a handful of friends who simply stopped talking to her once her husband died. They run in fear."

"There's a real friend for you," Darcy replied.

"You end up either forgiving them for their human frailties or just counting them as lost." Glynnis's eyes brightened, and Darcy knew another metaphor had just popped up in her brain. It was funny how you could actually see this woman get an idea. It was that plain on her face. "They are lost, in lots of ways, 'cuz faith is what enables the good friends to stick it out with you. I can't imagine how I'd handle it without my faith. I'll be mighty lonely if the Lord calls Bid home first. But I know I'll see him again, and I know God will stand by me until I do."

"Yeah, I've thought about that." Darcy stirred her tea, seeing not the brew but an image in her mind. "Seeing Dad, I mean. I found a picture of him and me from a couple of years ago—before he got sick—and I thought that's what he'll look like." Darcy felt a lump rise in her throat. "Not all thin and pale, but stocky and tanned and running." The tears welled up in her eyes. "Full of life, not fighting for it. I think of him…in heaven…that way." She was crying now, ambushed by the sudden force of emotion. "I want to see him like that again. I know I will."

Tears brimmed out of Glynnis's own eyes. "It'll be even better than that, hon. Better than we can even imagine. You hang on to that thought. That's how you can hold those antlers high."

Antlers, chickens, who knew what images Glynnis would conjure up next? Darcy realized it was one of the reasons she loved the woman.

And she did. She had come to love Glynnis as a mentor, and, well…as a mother. Could you adopt a mother like you adopted a child? Darcy had a friend who adopted a little girl from China, and she called her the "child of my heart."

That's what Glynnis was. The mom of her heart. There weren't enough Christmas presents in the whole wide world to repay her for that.

"Thanks, Glynnis," she heard herself say, "I love you."

With that Glynnis's eyes overflowed. "Oh, hon," she said in a thick voice as she pulled Darcy into a gigantic hug. "That's the whole point. The whole blessed point of it all."

Two weeks later, Darcy sat in the kitchen updating a new 2002 calendar with school break and early-dismissal days.

Jack's voice bellowed from somewhere upstairs. "Dar!"

Darcy turned her head in the general direction of the stairway. "What?" Such calls were usually preceded by "Mom!" and were almost always the precursor for questions like "Where's my jeans with the flowers on them?" or "I can't find my baseball cleats!" You'd think such helplessness would be confined to children, but Jack would occasionally—and most especially in times of stress—fall into the same pattern. *Mom, find my everything* mutated all too easily into *Hon, find my everything!*

Dar had a friend who was always saying it takes both eyes and estrogen to find most household items. She wasn't that far off. Darcy would frequently find Paula, Mike or even Jack howling to help them find an object when they were standing right in front of that very thing.

"Dar!" came Jack's voice again, more sharply now. "Come up here!"

She tried to stem her anger as she started up the stairs. Jack's work had been miserable. Rebounding from missing five days down with the stomach virus, he had been a ball of tension. Even though it was Sunday afternoon, and Dar had made not one, but *two* of his favorite meals, he still hadn't loosened up.

Darcy turned into their bedroom only to find it empty. There were sounds—the rustling of plastic and paper bags—coming from the guest room. She looked down the hall and saw the guest room door open. What on earth could Jack be looking for in there?

Stepping into the room, she found Jack surrounded by shopping bags. Her Christmas shopping. She'd been picking up things for the past few weeks, tucking them inside the guest room closet where she always stashed her

Christmas shopping. Jack had evidently pulled it out of the closet.

And the pile was enormous.

Surely she'd not bought that much, had she?

"What is all this?" Jack's face broadcast that he already knew the answer.

"Christmas presents. Decorations for the house."

"How many presents are in here?" Jack's voice was tight and precise. The tone he took when he was threatened or angry.

"I don't *count* them, Jack." How dare you get on me for this, after all we've been through, she thought as she bit back her growing anger. She couldn't believe his attitude.

He pulled four more bags out of the closet, practically sending them airborne as he did. "Okay, then, do you have even the *vaguest* notion of how much you've spent so far?" He was patronizing. That really made her mad—she hated when he did that, explaining things as if she had Paula's ability to grasp economics instead of a grown woman's. As if she were irresponsible or something.

"No," she countered, getting defensive. "I don't. I've spent a lifetime bargain hunting, making Christmas as cheap as possible. Making do, buying knockoffs. I'm tired of it, Jack. We've been through enough already this year. I just wanted—*once*—" she almost spit the word out, she said it so harshly "—*once*—to go all out for the holidays. We need it."

"Need? Need? There's not a thing in this room we *need*, Darcy." He snatched a bag from the Lazarus department store and held it up in front of her. "Can you even tell me what's in here? There must be fifty gifts in this room. More maybe."

"So I bought a lot of gifts. I like to buy gifts. You know that. Now you want to tell me I can't?"

"This is not a lot of gifts." Jack stabbed his hand around the room, pointing at pile after pile. "This is way too many gifts. This is over the top, even for you, Dar. It's too much."

"Why can't you just let me enjoy this holiday?"

"That's not what I said."

"That's exactly what you're saying!"

"All right, you want to know exactly what I want to say? What I think? I think this isn't about Christmas at all. You're—what do they call it?—you're overcompensating."

She crossed her arms and glared at him, furious. Since when did he pull pop psychology into an argument? Had he been watching too many talk shows while he was home sick?

Jack blew a breath out in exasperation. "I'm trying to see it your way, Dar, I really am." He waded through the bags, pacing the room. "But you do something like this and I don't get it. You want to give your dad's money away like water, and you want to spend ours like we've got millions." His eyes narrowed at her. "Which do you want? You can't have it both ways."

Oh, that really sent her over the edge. She wasn't going to let him play Scrooge. Not this year. "We have more than enough. We can afford *one* really nice Christmas. I won't do what Dad did. I won't sit on my money like some miserable old miser. We're alive and healthy and our kids are here *and it's Christmas*."

"Wise up, Darcy, we're alive and our kids need to go to college and the economy's in the toilet and we're about to go to war and…and—" he turned to look at her, his eyes intense and almost painful "—and all this isn't going to make your dad come back."

His accusation hung in the air, knocking the breath out of her.

"You can't see it, can you? Look around this room. Can't you see what you're doing here?" He softened his voice. "This is way too much. Wake up, Dar, and see what's going on here."

"It's not too much." She knew it was, though, the moment the words left her mouth.

She recoiled when Jack tried to pull her into the room. He pulled her in anyway. There were packages everywhere. There were even still more in the closet he hadn't even gotten to. Piles upon piles of it. He was right—there were things she couldn't even remember buying. "Stand here. Stand here and look at this, honey, and tell me it's not too much."

Darcy couldn't answer.

Jack turned her toward him, tucking her head onto his shoulder. "We can't do this. Somewhere down inside I think you know that. I know you love to give gifts, but this is…this is about something else." He pulled her away to look into her eyes. "We can't do this, Dar. Not with things the way they are."

"Jack…"

"He's gone. He's gone and he won't be here for Christmas." Darcy started to cry, the sharp truth of it twisting inside her. "Your dad is gone and all this isn't going to change that."

"It's not…"

"It is. It is."

"I…" She couldn't even begin to actually say it. To speak it would bring it all back up to wash over her and drag her under again and it was Christmas.

Christmas.

The pain would not stay down. It swirled up around her until she felt flooded by it. She clung to Jack as if he were a lifeboat in a hurricane. "I—I m-miss him so much. So much." Darcy melted into sobs on Jack's shoulder.

He just held her.

"I miss both of them." She continued, unable to stop it now even if she wanted to. "I want my parents back. I don't…I don't want to be *alone*." The last word came out as more of a wail than a word. "I can't do Christmas without Dad. I can't."

"I know. I know." Jack stroked her hair, speaking softly, the way he did the night Paul died and she just didn't have any more words or sobs. "We all miss him. There were times I could barely stand the guy but I miss him, too. And that's just how it's going to have to be this Christmas." He pulled his arms around her more tightly, as if sensing her need to feel his strength. "Our Christmas has a hole in it. But this isn't going to fill that. It'll just make things worse."

Darcy sniffed and looked up at him. The anger was gone out of his eyes, replaced by a tender sadness. "I don't know," she offered, loving him so very much at that moment, wanting to give him the whole world and everything he ever wanted. "Some of this stuff is pretty neat."

He laughed. She could feel it ripple through his chest. "Oh, I'm sure it is."

They stood quietly for a moment.

"I think," said Jack in his I-will-save-the-day voice, "that we need to find the middle ground between *celebratory* and *fiscally reckless*, wouldn't you say?"

"That's somewhere between here and the Returns counter, isn't it?" Darcy sighed.

"I'm afraid so."

Darcy looked down at the nearest bag, poked it with her toe and sighed. It was a fabulous sweater just the color of his eyes. With a pang she remembered that he already *had* a fabulous sweater just the color of his eyes. She winced.

"Let's not do this now." Jack let his hand slide down her arm until it wrapped around her hand. "Go downstairs, make a pot of tea and we'll sit down and figure out a number between *celebratory* and *fiscally irresponsible,* okay? I'll use my manly skills to see if I can get all this back *into* the closet."

Darcy eyed him, pasting a look of mock indignation on her face. "You're going to put me on a holiday budget this year, aren't you, you cruel man?"

Jack laughed again, his arms now full of bags. "That'd be a bit of a reach. I'm a realistic kind of guy. I was thinking more in terms of an *x* number of gifts per person equation."

"Holiday algebra?"

"Think of it as more of a game plan."

Darcy groaned. "Oh, it's so much more *appealing* that way." She turned to go downstairs, then stopped and poked her head back into the guest room door. "What'd you come in here for in the first place, anyway?"

"My dark-blue socks."

Sure Jack, I always put your socks in the guest room. It's a game I play. It's so much more interesting than just putting them in your sock drawer. Did everyone in this house think the laundry magically floated back upstairs into drawers once it was clean? "Downstairs, blue laundry basket, left-hand side. Five pairs at least." She pronounced herself the noblest of all women for not adding *like always.*

Chapter 20

Pithy But Engaging Holiday Greetings

Darcy loved the city done up for Christmas. Churches glowed like those ceramic village buildings they had in gift stores. Over on Fountain Square, even the fountain—the symbolic city centerpiece—glittered in a coating of tiny white lights next to a magnificent tree. Crowds still streamed out of the Tower Place Mall. It was just the perfect kind of cold—seasonal but not brutal. It was the Friday before Christmas, and downtown Cincinnati looked like it belonged inside a snow globe.

"It's a perfect night." Jack had kept his promise. Once she'd done all the returning, whittling the Nightengale family Christmas down to four perfect presents per person—she'd haggled Jack up from three—they went out for a night on the town together. Nothing fancy, mostly just a time to step away from the holiday bustle and enjoy the season as a couple. After sitting through no less than five holiday choir programs, orchestra concerts and dance recitals, Jack and Darcy were ready for a little adult conversation.

Darcy stopped in front of a gift store window. "These are all right, but their window display last year was much better."

Jack gawked at her. "You remember their window displays from last year?"

"Sure. They had a north woods kind of theme, with ironware mugs and stuffed bears and such. Elves just don't cut it. They should leave the elves to the toy store."

Jack touched the holly pin on her coat lapel. "Sometimes I forget just what a holiday nut you are."

"I admit, I enjoy the season." She tucked her arm into Jack's as they walked farther down the block.

"You obsess the season. You *are* the season."

"Not really."

Jack hip-checked her as they turned the corner. "How many other women do you know who have a different Christmas pin for every day in December?"

"Some of those were gifts. You know how people get—they see you with two or three of something and then everyone assumes you have a collection and suddenly you get them all the time as gifts." Darcy thought of Glynnis's chickens. She remembered that Glynnis was praying for her and Jack tonight and the plan the two of them were hatching. For the important step they were taking. "Oh, Jack, look."

In one store window was a stunning white porcelain crèche. The figurines had a remarkable grace and beauty, lifelike and yet unearthly all at the same time. The artist had somehow given special touches to each figure. The three wise men were off to the far right, making their way down a green velvet mountainside. They had robes that swished and flowed in some imagined wind, and you could just picture them out on the desert landscape, walking, seeking. A trio of shepherds, awestruck and humbled, knelt near the manger. One's head was turned back toward a companion, as if they were still asking each other questions, still struggling with the wonders they had seen that night. The angels billowed like clouds, their bodies caught in motion, their hands spread in joy. She thought, as her glance returned to them, that they had moved since the last time she'd looked at them.

Darcy caught herself with her nose pressed up against the window like a child. She'd read the Christmas story from Luke's gospel five or six times in the past weeks. It echoed deep in her heart now in a way it hadn't before. Jack wrapped his arm around her shoulders and pulled her close. The two of them stood and admired the display.

Joseph stood under a balsa wood barn silhouette amid tiny wisps of straw. He leaned over his new family with a protective stance. You could not tell if his eyes were on Mary or Jesus, but his expression was one of wonder and love. His hand held tight to a staff, as if saying to the world that this child was under his protection and would come to no harm if he could help it.

In the center, reclined, cradling her child in the smitten love of a new mother, was Mary. Proud, fragile, willowy in stature, Darcy's mind recalled the verse "Mary kept all these things, and pondered them in her heart." Darcy's own heart was full to bursting with pondered things as well. With a surprising peace, and a growing seedling of faith. She stared again at the figure of Mary. She was beautiful, young and innocent, but with a face that looked comfortingly familiar. As if she knew her.

And the child—he was the best of all. This Jesus was not a peaceful, iconic child, but a child of life. A chubby, joyful baby. She could almost see him wiggle. Tiny fingers reached out for his mother's cheek, his eyes were wide and his mouth open in such as way as she could just imagine his exuberant squeal. This was a Christ Child glad to be in the world, eager to "Let Earth receive her King."

"I don't think this was here last year," said Jack from beside her.

"No," Darcy whispered. "This is new."

It was *all* new this year. Or so it seemed. Sure, there were gaping "holes" as Jack put it; bittersweet memories and missing pieces. Yet, there were new things, fresh things, parts of the holiday that had powerful meanings that had never been there before. Darcy couldn't help thinking that last year she might have passed this crèche by without a second thought. This year, it captured her imagination and warmed her spirit. Her faith was no mere mustard seed anymore. No, it was growing. Spreading, taking root, taking hold.

Jack kissed her forehead, and the world seemed an absolutely perfect place.

There!

She and Jack heard it at the exact same time. The rhythmic ping of the Salvation Army bell. There must be a kettle just around the corner, in front of the bank building.

They caught each other's eyes, sparks flying between them. The moment had come.

It had been Jack's idea, initially, thrown out more as a joke than anything else. But the minute he suggested it, something clicked between them and they knew it was the perfect solution. The key to "between celebratory and fis-cally reckless." And it was; knowing it was in the works enabled Darcy to return all the extra gifts without a moment's remorse.

Darcy watched Jack's hands slip to his coat pocket. "Got 'em?" she whispered, her face close to his.

Jack patted his pocket. "Got 'em." He leaned his fore-head in to touch hers. "Ready?"

"Yep. You ready?" Darcy could hardly believe Jack agreed to the scheme, much less be the one who pro-posed it. She kept waiting for him to call it off, to come to his Jack the Numbers Guy senses, but he seemed to get as much of a thrill out of it as she did. That was the beauty of it, though; Jack had come up with a sensible half and a celebratory half—something for each of them. In the perfect symmetry of it, it had become something for *both* of them.

And that was nothing short of amazing. Miraculous, actually.

Jack held out his hand. "Let's do it." They started up the block together, Darcy fighting the urge to run or even skip like a preschooler.

They turned the corner, and the ringer came into view. An older gentleman, wearing a red-and-green-striped stocking cap with a matching scarf. He bounced up and down on the balls of his feet as he swung a rather large gold bell—either enjoying himself immensely, or perhaps just trying to keep the bottom of his feet warm and off the pavement. There were three or four people around him, looking at the window display the bank had put up. It was the ideal scenario.

Darcy heard Jack exhale. They both made a pitiful at-tempt to look casual and natural. To Darcy it felt like walking down the church aisle to get married—trying to look calm, peaceful, and joyous, even though it felt like a gallon of goldfish were doing somersaults in her stomach. They strolled by, Jack pointing out this and that—rather stiffly, like a bad actor—in the window display. Darcy held her breath as she watched his hand slip casually into his coat pocket, palm a coin, and wish the ringer a Merry Christmas as he slipped the coin in the kettle.

The coin.

The solid-gold Krugerrand from her father's bank box.

The one worth serious money. One of two they would "casually" slip into Salvation Army buckets tonight, just like the ones they had read about in the newspaper. The other two of her father's coins had been sold late this afternoon, their proceeds deposited into college funds for each of the children. Two coins sensible, two coins celebratory. Perfection.

She and Jack kept their steps deliberately slow and natural as they walked on down the block, pretending to examine the other window displays. They made it all the way to the end of the block, where Jack broke into a run and pulled Darcy around the corner. They laughed like kids who just made a prank phone call. Jack's eyes were wide, his smile brilliant in the shadows.

"Do you think he saw?" His tone of voice could have been Mike's, it was so excited.

"No, no, you were perfect. You couldn't even see the coin. You were great. Just great."

Jack pushed her up against the building. He kissed her. Hard and long. With the same fervor as he had in the basketball courts. "I can't believe I just did that," he said breathlessly when he finally pulled back for air.

"What, kissed me on a street corner?"

"No, no, *that*." Jack cocked his head back in the direction of the Salvation Army kettle. He caught her expression, and added, "Yeah, well this, too, but mostly that."

"You're good at this." Darcy was enjoying his excitement. Jack wasn't exactly the kind of guy who "twinkled," but his expression came mighty close.

"What, kissing you on the street corner?"

Now it was Darcy's turn. "No, no, *that*. Yeah, well this too, but mostly that."

Jack laughed and nuzzled her in a way that she felt down to her toes. "You do the next one," he said into her neck, this voice deep and tingling against her skin.

"Me? No way. I'm not sneaky enough to pull this off."

It was Jack's turn to act insulted. "Should I take offense at that? Are you saying I'm sneakier than you are?" He was trying to sound agitated, but the smile on his face just wouldn't go away.

"No, no." She was laughing now, pushing him off her so she could get a clear thought. "It's just that I could never look normal doing that. I'd fumble it or talk too much or drop it on the ground or something."

"Come on. You hid a dozen basketballs from me for hours on end. You can do this." He brushed an errant strand of hair off her cheek. "We each do one. Come on, do the other one."

Who could say no to those eyes? "Okay." The two of them set off around the corner, looking for another kettle. Four blocks over, they paused as they heard the familiar bell chimes. They ducked into an alcove half a block away, and Darcy practiced hiding the coin in her mitten until she felt she could place it in the red kettle without being seen. Jack promised to say something pithy and engaging to the bell ringer, distracting him or her while

Darcy sneaked the coin into the kettle. When they had their plan, they set off down the block.

The gallon of goldfish returned to Darcy's stomach, until they came within a few feet of the woman.

Surely God had a great sense of humor, for manning this kettle was an older woman and her dog.

Her *seeing eye dog*.

It was all Darcy could do to keep from laughing out loud as Jack employed his pithy but engaging holiday greeting and Darcy slid the coin into the slot. She could have easily dropped the Hope Diamond in there for all the stealth it required—no one else was around at just that moment. Once again, Darcy felt as if God had arranged the universe to meet her individual needs.

A blind bell ringer. On just this corner on just this night. God had sent his stamp of approval on Christmas philanthropy, Jack and Darcy style.

The next night, as the evening news reported the mysterious appearance of two gold coins in Cincinnati's Salvation Army kettles, Jack kissed Darcy up against the steadily clunking refrigerator.

"Ewww," pronounced Paula, unwrapping a package of Ho Hos.

"Ewww yourself," said Jack, and kissed his wife again.

Chapter 21

*'Twas the Night Before Christmas,
and Down in the Kitchen...*

"God Rest Ye Merry Gentlemen" was playing over the stereo at J.L.'s. Larry and Joyce, who owned the place, had a thing for jazz. They had a stack of jazz recordings two feet high and it was always playing in the background. It lent a hip-sophisticated air to the place, and was part of why Darcy and Kate loved it so. At Christmas, with J.L.'s decked out to its Christmas extreme thanks to Joyce's touch, it was extra wonderful.

"It *was* you!" Kate exclaimed as quietly as her shock would allow. "I *knew* it was you. The minute I saw it on the news I practically jumped off the sofa." She sat up straight, rocking her head as she teasingly sang, "I know the coin droppers, I know the coin droppers."

"Shhh!" countered Darcy. "I knew I shouldn't have told you. Except that I was sure you'd hound me mercilessly once it made the news. You can't tell anyone, understand? I'll make you link pinkies if I have to...."

"Okay, okay." Kate held up her hands. "And 'link

pinkies'? You've been spending too much time with Paula, girl."

Darcy pulled a pair of wrapped boxes out of the shopping bag at her feet. "Yeah, well wrap your grown-up pinkies around these, partner. Merry Christmas."

"Whoa, these are huge!" Kate's eyes widened. "Looks like the Grand Lady of Presents is hitting her stride this year."

"Open them first, then gush. Smaller one first."

Kate tore the wrapping off as fast as any six-year-old would. Darcy watched her reaction as she opened the gift certificate from a local portrait studio. Kate had been griping for years about not having a decent family portrait, and Darcy had decided the best way to show off Kate's spiffy new look was to capture it forever.

"Wow! I mean, really wow! This is over-the-top, even for you, Dar." She looked up at Darcy, the corners of her eyes crinkled up with a wide smile. "You know how much I've been wanting one of these. Don's been dragging his feet on spending the money—he claims a snapshot captures all we need—and now he has no excuse. Thanks."

"Don't thank me yet, you've another box to go there."

"Ooo, you bet!" Kate tore the second set of wrapping to uncover a lime-colored mohair sweater. It was one Kate had admired in a store window, but wouldn't go look at because she claimed she had no business buying anything that needed dry cleaning. "The green sweater! You got me the green sweater! You are so amazing. You never miss a trick."

"Well, what's the good of having your picture taken if you don't have something really wonderful to wear?"

Kate reached across the table to hug her. "You're the best friend ever. This is really nice. Thanks."

"You're welcome. Really. I had fun getting them."

"I'll bet you did." Kate bent over to reach into her own enormous purse. Actually, Kate's purse was more of a back-pack—the woman carried tons of stuff with her everywhere. If you needed a Band-Aid or gum or even a screwdriver, chances are Kate had it in her bag. It was like having Mary Poppins and her magical carpet bag as your best friend. "Now," said Kate, her head dipping as she groped around in the capacious handbag, "I've long given up trying to match your gift-giving abilities, but I did rather well this year, if I do say so myself." She produced a small, oblong package and pushed it across the table toward Darcy.

She undid the bow—a real cloth bow tied in a fancy knot. Evidently Kate had gone upscale this year. The velvet box opened to reveal a gorgeous fountain pen. Engraved with Darcy's name on the side. It was a deep green with gold flecks, trimmed in gold. Darcy picked it up; it felt heavy and important in her hands.

"For signing Restoration Project checks," Kate offered. "And greeting cards, and even permission slips. Consider it a presidential pen."

Kate was right: she had done well. It was just perfect, and Darcy told her so.

"I'm glad you like it. It suits you. You look good holding it." She held up her teacup. "Merry Christmas, Dar."

Darcy clinked her cup gently against Kate's. "God bless us, every one."

"You know, I think He has." Darcy was sure that was the first time she'd ever heard Kate even allude to God. She felt her smile broaden, if that was humanly possible—for she felt as if she was already grinning ear to ear. After a sheepish grin, Kate added, "Hey, Larry, can we get some more hot water here? And what do you have that's chocolate and gooey?"

* * *

Jack rolled over to have his hand fall on an unoccupied pillow. The sensation woke him up. Darcy wasn't in bed. Squinting his eyes, he rolled over to look around. She wasn't in the chair by the window. He cast his eyes out the bedroom door and down the hall, but he could see the wedge of night-light glow coming from out of the bathroom door—she wasn't in the bathroom, either. Slowly, rubbing his eyes, he pulled himself upright. Where was she?

A small sound from downstairs gave him his answer. What was Dar doing in the kitchen at—he glanced at the clock—2:00 a.m. on Christmas Eve? Well, actually, it was Christmas morning, wasn't it? Even if it was, 2:00 a.m. was early to be up and placing out presents—even for Darcy. He reached down to the floor next to the bed and picked up his T-shirt.

Tugging it on and yawning, he padded down the hallway. Sure enough, he could see the kitchen light on downstairs. He peered into the room as he came down the last of the stairs.

She was there, at the kitchen counter, eating cereal. Next to her were a box of tissues, and her father's Christmas stocking. Six or seven tissues were out and crumpled on the counter beside her. She had been crying. Still was, by the sound of it.

"Hon?"

She startled a bit at his voice. Her eyes and nose were red when she turned to look at him. "Um, hi."

"Honey, what's wrong? It's two in the morning."

"Actually, it's 2:17." She gave a huge, shuddering sigh. She must have had one good cry down here—he was surprised he hadn't heard her before this.

"Okay, it's 2:17 a.m., and you're crying. Want to talk about it?" He pulled up a stool.

Tears brimmed anew in Darcy's eyes. "We didn't go to church. It was Christmas Eve and we didn't go to church."

"We haven't gone to Christmas Eve service in years, since your dad got sick. We've always spent—" and as the words left his mouth, he put the pieces together "—the night with your dad."

Darcy nodded, the tears running down her already wet cheeks. Jack cursed himself for not seeing this coming. He'd tried to think of all the places that would be painful for Darcy this week, tried to see the rough spots coming— but he'd missed this one. And it was a big one, too. *Nice going, guy.*

"I'm sorry this Christmas is so hard for you." He didn't really know what else to say. There was no way to fix this. The only way to get through it was to simply get through it.

"It rots," she replied.

Jack wasn't quite sure what to do with her remark. He was pretty sure Christmas didn't actually "rot," just felt rotten at the moment. He just needed to let her get it out—ideally now rather than in front of the kids. He'd expected scenes like this to come about now anyway. "It doesn't *all* rot, does it? I thought you loved Kate's gift. I don't even have a pen that nice, and I sign most of the checks in this house." He touched her cheek.

"Well, no, it doesn't *all* rot. Just big, huge parts of it. I wanted to go to church tonight. I thought about going to church, even planned it out, but then somehow I couldn't get myself to make it happen." She started to cry again. "Then it felt like if I didn't think about it, then it wouldn't happen, then I wouldn't have to *not* go to see Dad and I could pretend things *weren't* different and…" She looked up at him. "I'm not making any sense, am I?" she whimpered.

He pulled her to him. They both yawned.

"Then come back to bed, hon."

Chapter 22

Just the Tiniest Bit Willing

Glynnis wrapped her in a big hug. "I've missed you. How does it feel to have made it through the holidays?"

"Some good, some bad." Darcy added sugar to her ice tea. "I lost it a few times, but I sort of expected that to happen."

Glynnis sighed. "The first holidays—all of them, for the first year—are hard. But then you make new memories, find new ways to do the things you can't do anymore and it gets better." She lifted her ice tea glass in a toast. "You make new friends, who give you splendid new gifts, so you can do your favorite things in new ways."

Darcy laughed. "Oh, so you like the sun tea jar, huh? I wasn't sure you'd give up your kettle so easily. I actually found a chicken teakettle, Glynnis, and came—" she put her fingers up together "—*this* close to getting it for you, but the salesman said it made the most awful noise."

Glynnis burst out laughing as she stood up and went to a corner cabinet. She opened the door with a "Ta da!"

and exposed the exact kettle Darcy had been discussing. Someone had beat her to the punch.

"Oh, he's right," Glynnis chuckled. "It does. Ed thought I was *butchering* chickens in here the first time it went off, not making tea. I like your gift much better. Wherever did you find one with hens on it?"

Darcy smiled. This gift had been one of her better inspirations. She was glad Glynnis was enjoying it so much. "Actually, I had it made. The woman at the pottery shop told me she had a special technique for painting on glass. So I bought the jar and had her paint the chickens on it. She liked how it came out so much that she decided to stock the jars for other customers. And thank you for the hankies, by the way, I love carrying them. It's so much more elegant to weep into a hankie than to sniffle into Kleenex."

" 'Weeping may endure for a night, but joy cometh in the morning.' Psalm 30. Your joy is coming, Darcy dear, I think even you can see that."

"There are days where it feels like it's been years that Dad has been gone. Then there are times when it feels like it happened yesterday. I don't remember it that way with my mother."

Glynnis selected a particularly well-frosted Christmas cookie. "It's more complicated when you're an adult. You've got different people pulling on you for different things, you understand things in a different way. You can see, I think, farther down the timeline in both directions— past and future—and get a glimpse of how someone's death defines part of your life."

Darcy grunted. "I don't feel like I can see toward the future at all. I have no idea where things are going."

"Nonsense," Glynnis countered, swallowing the last of her cookie. "You can see very clearly. You just want to see farther than you ought to right now. Like I said, sweetie, they call it—"

"Faith, not agreement," Darcy finished for her. The woman had a way of drumming theology into you with sugarcoated accuracy. "I understand that, but if I can't see, how can I plan? How do I know the things I'm doing are what God has in mind?"

"Well, now," replied Glynnis. "That's the harder part."

Darcy choked on her bite of cookie. "It gets *harder?*"

Glynnis didn't seem to think that question required an answer. Her eyes were two whopping pools of *course it does, hon* as she said, "When you start stepping out in faith—like you're doing—you've got to be careful to watch who's doing the planning."

"Well, that's exactly what I mean. How am I supposed to know if I'm just making my own plans or if I'm looking to see what it is God is asking me to do? I mean, this whole thing has sort of felt like one long argument with God. Weird stuff plopping down in front of my face that I'm suddenly supposed to deal with. I don't exactly have a clear set of road maps here, Glynnis. I'm pretty much making this up as I go along."

"That's good, that's good!" For a scary second Darcy thought she was going to clap hands or give her a gold star. "Uncomfortable, yes," she added, seeing Darcy's look, "but good. Let me see if I can explain it better." She sat for a moment, drumming her fingers against one another, her lips pursed. "Okay now, just give me a minute." More silence, then a slight nod. "Ah, I know where to start." She shifted in her seat to face Darcy more directly. It was then, for some reason, that Darcy noticed Glynnis was wearing a pin.

The Standard Issue Grandma Gaudy Rhinestone Bee Pin.

It seemed as if every old lady on the planet owned a gaudy rhinestone bee pin. The one where the outstretched wings were gilt silver, the bee's body made up of black enamel stripes and rhinestones set in gold, its shiny little legs spread across the wearer's chest, lapel, whatever. Entirely too big—beyond bumblebee life-size. Every older woman somehow had one. As if it came free with the purchase of every *Old Lady Handbook*.

Why would Glynnis own one? Then again, why *shouldn't* Glynnis own one? The woman was such a contradiction. A fabulously vibrant person, elegant, fashionable, but with the oddest touches of "standard old lady" peeking out here and there. Darcy found herself wondering if her own mother would have come to own one had she lived. Would Darcy herself wake up one morning to discover she, too, had become one of the bee-pin-wearing old ladies? Was the butterfly pin she bought last spring just a warm-up? The gateway drug of elder-jewelry?

"...so you have to keep asking yourself if...Darcy? Darcy? Where did you go, hon? You were miles away."

Darcy shook herself back to the conversation at hand. "Ugh. I'm sorry, Glynnis, my brain just seems to take off in its own directions these days. It's terrible, I'm sorry."

Glynnis actually looked pleased. "No, no, as a matter of fact that's exactly what I'm talking about—in a way."

"I'm not following you, Glynnis."

Glynnis scrunched up her forehead in thought. "Let me see. Let's see. Oh, I've got it. Do you ever feel like a particular thought is chasing you? When it feels more as if the thought found you than you having the thought? More as if you've been given the thought rather than having made it up on your own?"

Darcy had to think about it, but yes, she had. "Yes. You know, I have. The whole Restoration Project idea. It just sort of *came* to me. Details and all. Like someone opened up the top of my head and poured it in, completely formulated and everything. And yes, it *did* feel like the thought found me. I never thought about it in that way before, but that's *exactly* how it felt."

"And how did it feel, to have that thought find you?"

"Well, before we got into the messy business of actually making it happen—which was scary—it felt wonderful. Like…um…how I'd imagine love at first sight feels. All warm and energized. Like I couldn't wait to get started. Like I'd just plugged into something really, really important."

Glynnis was smiling. "It's a real kicker, isn't it?"

That woman had the funniest expressions. "Yep, Glynnis, a real kicker."

"The easy ones—the pretty ones—are always a kick. It's the hard ones—the tough ones—that feel more like a kick in the pants. Those are how you really know."

Darcy shot Glynnis a look. "You know I'm not following you. You're going to have to offer more of an explanation than that."

Glynnis took off her glasses and pinched the bridge of her nose. "Okay, Lord," she said as if He'd just walked in off the back deck or something, "I'm gonna need a little help with the words. This isn't exactly a clear-cut concept." She squinted her eyes, thinking hard. Darcy found herself wondering if she was supposed to say Amen or some such thing.

"Near as I can figure, God tries to be as clear as He can with us. Trouble is, we're not exactly the world's greatest listeners. We spend lots of our time telling God what we want, and not too much time hushing up so He can tell us what He wants from us." She opened her eyes. "With me so far, hon?"

"Uh-huh. I get that part."

"Where the real work of heaven happens, though, most times isn't in the stuff we want. Lots of times it's in the stuff we'd rather *not* do. The messes we'd rather not touch, the people we'd rather leave alone, the folks and ideas that rub us the wrong way."

Glynnis looked at her, checking for understanding, but Darcy didn't really have a response to that. She purely motioned for Glynnis to go on.

"It's easy to jump on the bus when it's going your way. It's when you feel the bus turning down a street you hadn't planned that you need to make sure you stay on."

"You lost me on that one."

Glynnis squinted her eyes tight again, searching for words. "You love this project, right? It makes your heart beat faster, you couldn't walk away from it if you tried. Feels as if it lives right in here, doesn't it?" She tapped her heart, just under the bee.

"Yes."

"That's good. And I've no doubt—not one at all—that this is what God had in mind for you. What I want you to be on the lookout for, though, is the part of it that isn't so attractive. The one thing that's really gotten under your skin."

Darcy knew the answer even before Glynnis finished her explanation. It was the thought that had been hounding her for days, despite every attempt to shake it off. Michelle Porter. The angry young mother who refused The Restoration Project.

Glynnis eyed her. "You already know what it is, don't you. Look at your hand. It's just about choking that napkin."

"It's Michelle Porter. The mom whose baby is dying. I can't get her out of my head. I can't just brush off that nasty letter she wrote rejecting The Restoration Project."

"Really got under your skin, didn't she?"

"She was really vindictive about declining, that's for sure."

"Lashing out?"

"Big time. That was one bitter woman. Angry. She actually called me a misguided fluffhead or something."

Glynnis was still eyeing her. "And you know nothing about lashing out in grief, about being angry with people whose lives look like they have all the corners neatly sewn up when yours is coming apart at the seams?"

"I never acted like that. Glynnis, she was downright mean."

"I know. People can get vicious when they're really hurting, can't they?"

"She doesn't want to have anything to do with this whole thing. She's made that pretty clear, if you ask me."

Glynnis sat back and folded her arms. "And you think she's just a miscalculation, an error in judgment? That God steered her into the path of this project just so she could get run over?"

"Let me get this straight. You're telling me that I need to listen, because God may be telling me to get cozy with a woman who wants to bite my head off?"

Glynnis clapped her hands together. "Yes-siree. And you might not see a speck of satisfaction from the whole deal. But sometimes, that's where we really put the feet on our faith. Like Jesus said, it's a piece of cake to love the people who love you back. It's the folks who tick you off that are the hard ones to love."

Darcy shot her a look. "I'm pretty sure 'piece of cake' did not enter Jesus' vocabulary."

"Yes, well, I do like to paraphrase."

Darcy rested her chin in her hand. "Glynnis, I'm *done* growing for now. I ache from all the growing I've done. From all the stretching and mucking and grieving and learning."

"Good."

"No, not good."

"Yes, good. That's just the kind of place where God does His best work. This week, try spending time just *listening* to the Lord. Letting Him know you're trying to listen, that you're available, and even just the tiniest bit willing."

"But Glynnis, this is the week—"

"So God doesn't know what's on your schedule? You can't even *begin* to know what the Lord Almighty has planned for those women and their lives. How about you just hush up and let the Lord have the floor? You might be amazed at what you see."

Chapter 23

Every Woman Should Own One

January 9, 2002. A nice day for fresh starts. Of course she hadn't actually chosen the day—Jean Tinsdale, The Restoration Project's very first recipient, had. Still, Darcy felt a proprietary sort of approval.

Nice day or not, Darcy was extremely nervous. They'd had no less than six recommendations for this particular salon, but Darcy couldn't help thinking that only Ernestine could pull off something like this. Visions kept invading her brain of a fragile woman, bawling her eyes out in front of a salon mirror, wearing the most atrocious haircut imaginable.

"But dah-ling, it is time for something with drama! Time to be bold!" her imaginary stylist would be saying, waving his scissors like a rapier. "Wait till you see what we do with you in makeup! No one will recognize you."

And the imaginary recipient would cry harder. In her brain, Darcy would hear slews of curses sent up to heaven on her behalf. Distraught, overdyed women calling all of

heaven down on Darcy Nightengale's misguided med-
dling head.

Why had she ever thought staying anonymous would
be a good idea? It meant she had to stay out of sight, out
of the picture when the women received "their days."
They'd come to call them that—simply "their days." Spas
always had elegant little names for these kinds of packages, these full-day full-tilt indulgences. But they never
fit the quiet, important purpose they had for The
Restoration Project. They became, simply, "their days."

By "her days," though, it was simply a Thursday, and
school had started back up that week. Darcy discovered
she was all but useless—forgetting to pack Paula's lunch,
unable to find Mike's field trip permission slip—locked in
a fog of preoccupation. It was all she could do to keep
Mike from missing his bus, but finally at 8:16, quiet de-
scended upon the house for sixty full seconds before the
phone rang.

"Happy Inauguration Day, Madam President," came
Kate's voice over the other end of the phone. She hummed
a few bars of Hail to the Chief, now a habit of hers. "I think
I'm going to go out of my mind today."

Darcy poured herself a third cup of tea. "Me, too. I'm
brain dead. Nervous. It's like having to watch the birth of
your baby from behind a secret window. I've wiped the
same counter down at least ten times."

"I can't stand not being there. You know, we could just
happen to book ourselves a couple of manicures there. No
one would know—they've never been told who funds
the project. We could even wear hats and sunglasses or
something."

Darcy was just about to put the milk away in the
freezer before she caught herself at the last minute.

"Tempting, but too risky. If we did it once, we'd convince ourselves we could do it every time, and someday someone would put the pieces together. No Kate, we've got to stay clear of this. Maybe it will get easier as time goes by."

Kate snorted into the phone, then yelled as Darcy heard a glass shatter on the other end. "Not a chance, Dar. Great, now I'm down to three water glasses. We'll be drinking out of paper cups if I keep this up."

"A tea date isn't gonna cut it today. We need to do something more drastic. Something more engrossing."

"We could try doing our taxes?"

"Very funny."

"Drive to Kentucky and play the ponies?"

"It's *January,* Kate. And since when do either of us bet?"

"I don't. But I was thinking it had to be something really drastic."

"Let's stick with *comfortably drastic*—it's practically our theme song." Darcy realized she'd left the sink tap running for the last ten minutes and sighed as she turned it off.

"Tiny tattoos with our company logo?"

That made Darcy laugh so hard she spit tea out over the counter. "What kind of brew are you drinking this morning? It sounds like you've been hitting something harder than the Tetley's tiny tea leaves. And we don't even *have* a company logo."

"We should."

"Sure, fine, but not today."

"If we don't do something big today, Dar, I'm gonna crawl out of my skin. I haven't been this nervous since my wedding day."

Darcy found that hard to believe, but then again maybe not. She was hard-pressed herself to think of a day when her stomach had been in this many knots. What to do? What to do? Why hadn't they seen this coming and planned something?

It popped into her head, an unwelcome idea she'd have dismissed in a nanosecond before her earlier talk with Glynnis. *No,* she countered, *that'd surely be a bad idea.*

The thought persisted. Darcy resisted. She wasn't ready for this. There wasn't even a solid reason, just a knee-jerk of reluctance, a purely emotional response. Unbidden, Glynnis's words came back to her. No, this isn't what she would have planned to do today. Somebody Else, however, seemed to want it on the agenda.

"Kate," Darcy began, squinting her eyes shut, "how would you like to meet Glynnis today?" She didn't even expound upon it with "I think you two would like each other," or "I've been meaning to get the two of you together." She just let the question hang nervously in the air.

"You know," Kate said, after what seemed like a disastrously long pause, "I've kinda been wanting to meet her. Why not today?" Darcy could tell by the slight edge to Kate's tone of voice that she had been rather aware of the fact that Darcy had not yet introduced them. That it might have even become a sticking point had she let it go on longer.

Touché God. Lord Almighty 1, Darcy Nightengale 0. Game, set, lunch.

"It's settled, then. Rockwood Pottery, eleven-thirty."

"I'll call Glynnis. Whether or not she can meet us, I'll meet you there at eleven-thirty. We can stay and shop until it's time for the kids to come home." Darcy put the last of the breakfast dishes into the dishwasher.

"Only one problem now, Dar."

"What?"

"How am I supposed to kill the three hours until then?"

Darcy chuckled. "We could do something radical like clean our houses?" She punched the buttons to turn the dishwasher on to soak and scour. The waffles hadn't exactly been cooperative. Or maybe the chef hadn't exactly been on the ball this morning....

"What? High-level presidential types like us? No way, I'm going for Chips Ahoy! and an episode of *Oprah*. Maybe even Judge What's-Her-Face."

"You do know how to kill an hour well, Mrs. Owens."

"Don probably wishes I knew how to kill a germ better."

"I'll make you a deal—one clean bathroom, one episode of *Oprah*, then lunch. Best of both worlds." Darcy opened the dishwasher again—she'd forgotten to put the soap in.

"Can I drag the television into the bathroom?"

"How you clean your bathroom is your own business. Eleven-thirty, then?"

"Got it."

"Okay."

"Dar?"

"Yep?"

"We're doing something wonderful today. You know that, don't you? It's amazing."

"It is, isn't it?"

"Yep. See ya, girl."

Darcy hung up the phone and sighed, thinking that maybe the two parts of her world were going to collide, not combine. Still, she somehow knew that this was the right path, even if it was wildly uncomfortable. She looked up at the sky as she punched in Glynnis's number. *Okay, Lord, your serve. Am I allowed to point out that I'm not really thrilled about this?*

Darcy wasn't the least bit surprised that Glynnis was free. Now even more nervous, Darcy decided to skip *Oprah* in favor of cleaning two bathrooms. She was sure today's episode would be something like "Women Whose Friends Can't Stand Each Other."

Darcy was halfway through spraying the bathtub with Scrubbing Bubbles when the phone rang. She pulled off her rubber gloves and snatched the cordless phone up from the bathroom floor. "Hello?"

Jack's voice responded, humming "Hail to the Chief."

"Oh, great, now you're picking up Kate's habits. Very funny."

"Just wanted to say hi on your big day."

Darcy hunched the phone up on one shoulder and pulled her glove back on. One of these days she was going to get one of those headset phones before her shoulder became permanently cocked under one ear. "I wish. It's not really *my* day at all. I don't get to do anything but just sit here and be insanely nervous. What if she hates her hair? What if she has some kind of allergic reaction to the skin care products and we end up putting her in the hospital?"

"You're being ridiculous, Dar. None of that's going to happen." She heard Jack's other line start to ring.

"Do you need to get that?"

"No, I'll let it go into voice mail. So I forgot to ask you, what are you going to do today? Want to have lunch?"

Darcy winced and bit her lip. She should have thought of that first. "Oh, no, I just made plans. Kate's as nuts as I am, so we're meeting for lunch. I'm going to introduce her to Glynnis. It's a rather terrifying prospect."

"They haven't met yet? Really?"

Darcy blasted the toilet bowl with white foam. "Yes, really. They're a bit different from each other, don't you think? I'm not at all sure this is going to work."

"I think they're a lot alike, Dar. They'll probably love each other, and you'll call me at 2:00 p.m. saying 'What was I worried for?' and telling me how you could barely get a word in edgewise."

"Are you sure you don't want to join us for lunch? We promise not to discuss hair color." It was a poor joke, and she wasn't surprised when Jack didn't laugh. He didn't sound like he was in much of a joking mood.

"No, thanks, it's probably better that I stay here anyway." His phone rang again. "The phones are going nuts and people keep running into each other's offices with the latest rumor. Best I stay close."

"Okay." She didn't envy Jack one bit. He sounded tense. She was sure Canterbury Manufacturing Industries was not a nice place to be these days.

The morning dragged by. Darcy's mind skittered a thousand different directions, pondering Jack's work, what Glynnis would think of Kate, what Kate would think of Glynnis, what was happening to Jean and her friend at the salon. Were they going through the same experience, the same coming back to life that she had felt with Kate? What if it was awkward and forced? What if the massage felt invasive or the person doing her facial made some disparaging remark? Doug and Meredith had gone over with the salon staff—twice, in fact—how fragile these women were, how neglected the nurture and social sides of their lives had become. For some of them it may have been their first "nonnecessity" outing in months. The first time they'd done something—anything—for themselves.

They have their best friends by their sides, she re-minded herself. That can make anything better. This par-ticular woman, as a matter of fact, had asked a dear friend to come visit for the occasion. They'd been close years back, still talked by phone, but visited each other far too infrequently. Darcy liked that her idea had rekindled a friendship as well as a spirit. She was glad Jean was the first recipient, and that it had already seemed to spur changes in her life like calling this friend. She was lucky, though; the friend had the time and resources to hop on a plane and come. Not every woman would have that op-portunity. Would The Restoration Project one day be large enough to fly in friends? Restore relationships that miles had broken?

Darcy stopped what she was doing and laughed at her-self. She'd wiped the same faucet four times now, was dreaming up expansion plans for The Restoration Project, and they hadn't even made it through their pilot run. Whoa, girl. Life is complicated enough as it is.

By the time she pulled the back door shut and drove to lunch at the Rockwood Pottery Restaurant, no disaster had come calling. No salon called to report the cata-strophic results of any treatment, no assistant principal called with yet another "issue" regarding Mike's behavior, and no one within one hundred yards had thrown up or contracted any virus. Darcy considered that the day might just prove itself successful, and tried to calm her stomach for lunch.

She got there fifteen minutes early, determined not to let Kate and Glynnis meet each other without due super-vision. When she thought about it, Jack was right—Glyn-nis *was* kind of like Kate. Slightly unconventional, fun loving, direct. But Kate was Major Babe to Glynnis's Mrs.

Claus—Kate was smart and sassy to Glynnis's warm and gooey. Then again, Glynnis had her smart and sassy side. Kate, however, didn't seem to have a warm and gooey side. You could imagine, if you really let your mind go, that Glynnis may have been a bit like Kate when she was younger. Maybe they would get along.

Stop kidding yourself, Dar, you know the real reason you think they'll clash. Lunch with Glynnis is like tuning into the all-God-all-the-time channel. Sure, she wasn't pushy about it, but God was such a pervasive part of Glynnis's life, such a constant in her everyday existence, that two minutes didn't go by before spirituality came up in the conversation.

She didn't think Kate was ready for that. Darcy had barely brushed up against the topic in conversations with her, and it was always uncomfortable when she did. Darcy thought to call Glynnis back several times this morning to ask her to go easy on Kate. She realized, though, that Glynnis knew an awful lot about Kate and their relationship from Tuesday Morning Prayers in the Henhouse. And, when it came right down to it, asking Glynnis to go easy on the God stuff was rather like asking her not to breathe.

She checked her watch—11:20. She'd done worlds of worrying in the space of five minutes. Then she heard Kate's infectious laugh coming through the doorway and turned just in time to see her arrive.

With Glynnis.

Arm in arm.

Laughing like they'd known each other for decades.

"Oh, there she is!" Glynnis cried with embarrassing glee. "Quick, Kate, get it out!"

Kate produced a bright-red shopping bag, thrusting it toward Darcy.

"How did you two…?"

"Oh, we'll tell you in a minute, just *open* it!"

With no small amount of trepidation, Darcy slipped her hand in through the tissues to produce a twinkling, princess-worthy tiara.

A tiara.

"Isn't it just grand?" Glynnis cooed. "I decided to come a little early and do a little shopping, and was in the store when I saw a woman asking about this." She elbowed Kate with a clear air of conspiracy.

"*Oprah* wasn't very interesting, so I cut out early and went shopping. I found this in a store and was explaining about it to the clerk, seeing if I could get him to come down on the price—you know these antiques stores have a huge margin and they expect you to try and—oh, well, anyway, I'm telling a bit of the story and *she* comes up behind me saying, 'Oh, my, you've just *got* to be Kate Owens.'"

Darcy tried not to feel trumped. She tried to remember that although she'd spent no less than seventeen minutes crafting the proper introduction, it was far better that they'd introduced themselves and struck up such an instantaneous friendship. Really, it was better that way. Really. She held up the sparkly crown. "Well, um, it's lovely. Remind me to watch what kind of jokes I make around you, Kate. Why didn't you call me to come out early with you?"

"What? And admit that I skipped out on cleaning my bathroom? Not on your life. Well, you are going to put it on, aren't you?"

"Umm…"

"No," said Kate, grinning, "you *have* to."

Darcy shot the pair of them a look. "Won't it be kind of embarrassing, doing lunch with Cinderella? The Miss America pageant is in May, ladies, and it's January."

"Oh, no," giggled Glynnis, with that look Darcy had come to recognize could only mean trouble. "You'll fit right in."

With that Kate produced a second bag, from which emerged two other tiaras. Kate and Glynnis quickly helped each other don their crowns and then stood, hands on respective hips, waiting.

It was hopeless.

Sighing, then finally laughing, Darcy inclined her head toward Kate's outstretched bobby pins. She tried not to turn a dozen colors when the hostess, not to mention half the waitstaff, applauded.

Lord, I told you I wanted a distraction, but…

In her head, as the waitstaff led this little spangled trio to their corner table, she heard Glynnis's motto, "Don't you just *love* it when God exceeds your expectations?"

Chapter 24

The Oreos of Life

"Oh, you're kidding." Jack stared at the tiara in disbelief.

"No, really. They both had one, too."

Jack finished the last of his soda and tossed the can into the recycling bin. He loved sitting in the kitchen at this time of night. Darcy—with a little "help" from Paula—had put away all the dinner things, the kids were in bed and she just had a few lights on here and there. It was cozy and quiet.

Well, except for the fridge. That thing had a month to live, maybe two. And now, Darcy told him the dishwasher was making odd noises. He stared at the stove, daring it to join in the conspiracy. It was January already, and Mike's final orthodontist bill—the big one—would be coming due next month. They'd feel the pinch, all right, if all of that kicked in within weeks of each other.

Still, lean as the checkbook seemed, Jack couldn't help but snicker at his wife twirling around the kitchen in jeans, a cardigan sweater and a tiara that looked like something from one of Paula's Barbie dolls. Of course, once she laid eyes on the thing, Paula'd wanted her own "princess crown." Evidently there'd be no worries about coming up with a theme for Paula's February birthday party now, would there? Which also meant party purchases and a birthday present. It was going to be a tight month, all right.

All the better to talk to her now.

"Aren't you glad you didn't come to lunch with us now? Can you just see yourself in the restaurant, surrounded by royalty?"

"Yes, I must admit, eating with a pack of nervous accountants is looking mighty good by comparison." He caught Darcy's arm, pulling her to him as she twirled past him with a roll of paper towels. She looked up at him, smirking. She'd spent the whole day in that silly crown. She might have groaned publicly about hating it, but she was like a queen traipsing around the house all evening. Mike was completely mortified, naturally, and that was particularly entertaining. "You're having a lot of fun with this."

"It's silly."

He leaned back against the counter, settling her in front of him with his arms around her waist. "If I want to have a serious conversation, do I need to remove it?"

Her smile faded. "No, you don't. What's going on? How bad was it at work?"

"Things are tense, but that's not really it."

Jack took a deep breath, making his case as clearly as he could. "I checked in on my retirement program this afternoon, and my 401-K has taken a nosedive of monumental proportions. Everybody's has. I've been reading some of those investing magazines. You know, just to bone up on this kind of stuff. From what I've read, the economy isn't going to turn around anytime soon. There's talk of war, tourism failing, all kinds of stuff. Three of our major customers have cut their orders down to the bare minimum, and I've got another two hanging on by their fingernails."

Darcy looked at him, a bit panicked. "Your job?"

"Is still on solid footing, but who knows? We have an appropriate—well, according to the finance guides, we're on the lean side of appropriate—amount of money set aside, but those funds have taken a beating as well. Between Mike's braces, Paula's birthday and Christmas, and you not working anymore and—" he cocked his head toward the fridge "—our near-death appliances, we're in for a lot of expenses soon."

Darcy stilled against him. "I need to go back to work, don't I?"

"Well, we need to look at the whole picture here. I think we need to explore all our options."

"Meaning…"

"Meaning that I think we shouldn't rule out accessing some of your dad's money if it means this family will have better options." The moment he said it, he felt her spine stiffen under his hands.

"You want me to ignore Dad's request?" She pulled out of his arms.

He knew she'd jump to this conclusion. "No, that's not what I'm saying, Dar. I think what you're doing is important. Today was a big day, and I don't want to make all that go away, but why do we have to think in absolutes?"

She turned to face him, leaning against the other counter, arms folded in defiance.

"Don't you think there might be enough money in that pot to do more than just fund The Restoration Project?" he continued. "Do you really think, if your Dad were here now, facing what we're facing, that he'd insist we give it all away? If it meant Mike couldn't go to a good college or you had to go back to work full-time?"

"Dad's seen us have tight times before. He never offered the money *then*." Her voice had a sharp edge to it. The pain of that secret was still fresh, to be sure.

"Nothing like this. Dar, he never could have expected 9/11. *No one* expected what's happening now."

She didn't answer.

"Will you hear me out?"

She stood still for a moment, and he thought about crossing the room to her, but opted to stay where he was. Eventually, she hoisted herself up to sit on the counter, and nodded.

Jack smoothed his hands over his jeans. "I want us to talk to a financial guy. That guy that Ed Bidwell told me about. Let him explain to us what the long-term and short-term options for that kind of money are, and evaluate how the funds are currently invested." She unfolded her arms. "Jacob did a commendable job, but there are people who specialize in this sort of thing. Would you agree that we need to pull in some people who can tell us what we're really dealing with?"

"Maybe."

Maybe was good. It wasn't great, but he'd take it.

He'd never told her about his final conversation with Paul. About how Paul told him there was so much in his life he regretted not sorting out. About his own promise—his sincere, heartfelt promise—that he would always take care of Paul's little girl. "She's all I have," the frail old man had said, tears filling his eyes. It made Jack's heart twist in two. "You need to be all for her now. Thank you for lending me your wife so she could be my daughter so much."

That had been his goodbye from Paul. An agreement between them. The next day Paul's lucidity began to waver and he could only recognize Darcy. After that, Jack's main job was to keep life at bay so Darcy could go about the business of death.

Now, he would keep chaos at bay so that they could get about the business of life.

He took her hand. "Just think about it. We don't have to decide anything right now. Promise me you'll mull it over, okay?"

"Fair enough."

Suddenly, Jack remembered the little gift he'd bought on Tuesday, tucked away in the top cabinet especially for today. "Oh, and by the way, Your Royal Heiressness, I completely forgot about my little memento of the day. Sir Jack's attempt to keep up with the ultimate gift lady. Close your eyes." She resisted, and he pulled her off the counter, waltzing her around the room a bit. The mood definitely needed lightening, and he knew just the way to do it. "No, really, you're going to have to close your eyes. You know I don't gift wrap."

Reluctantly, a smile just catching on the corners of her mouth, she stood in the center of the kitchen. That ridiculous tiara sat a bit off-kilter on her head. She made a show of shutting her eyes.

Jack turned around to the cabinets above the refrigerator—the ones too tall for Darcy to reach or see into without his help—and produced a bag of Oreos. Not store-brand "chocolate sandwich cookies," but Oreos.

Gift-wrapped at just his speed: one adhesive bow stuck on one corner. He rattled the cellophane wrapping, watching the sound intrigue her.

"Put out your hands, my lady."

She did, her head cocked at an *oh, puh-lease* angle.

"Open 'em."

It was a slow smile that spread across her face. He had a million things to say, a dozen speeches about how *he* wanted to give her the Oreos of life, that he didn't want her to have a life of making do and knockoffs, but in the end he opted just to open up the package in her hands and feed her an Oreo. Somehow, watching the look on her face as she ate it, Jack guessed he would never be able to look at those cookies in quite the same way again.

That was the great miracle of Darcy—she changed everything she touched.

Pastor Doug and Meredith were already at the table in Meredith's office when Kate and Darcy came into the room. It had seemed like an eternity over the weekend, waiting to hear how the first recipient's "day" had gone. They'd decided, beforehand, that Meredith would get a report from the spa and Doug would meet with the recipients, so that frank and honest appraisals could be gained. Also, their help was necessary if Kate and Darcy were to keep their identities out of the picture. They'd go through all five recipients in this manner, using each experience to further tweak the program for the next person.

"Sorry for the sweatshirt, folks," Darcy offered, pointing to her bright-yellow Churchill Cheetah's sweatshirt. "It's spirit day at Paula's school and I have to go straight there."

"And you wonder why I never volunteer to be room mother?" Kate quipped. "Can you imagine what *that* would look like on me with my red hair?"

Meredith and Doug still said nothing, just sat at the table with odd looks on their faces.

"Well?"

Meredith fairly beamed. "I think we can declare recipient number one a complete success."

"Details, we need details," Kate cued, her smile as wide as Meredith's. "Who, what, when, where, how short, what color?"

"We didn't exactly take 'before' and 'after' photos, Kate."

Kate glanced around the room. "Why not? That's a pretty good idea."

Darcy spoke softly. "Because this is more about what's happening on the inside, than what's happening on the outside."

"Granted, but it's the outside seeping in that makes the difference."

"Still," countered Meredith, "I agree photos are not a good idea. This is a respite, not a makeover."

"Okay, you have a point there. Let me rephrase the issue. Does she like the way she looks?"

"According to the spa," Meredith reported, "she was immensely pleased. Her friend went for a really drastic change, which made the day extra fun, but Jean mostly just took care of things that were long neglected."

Doug flipped through a notepad in front of him. "She used a particularly striking image, let me see…oh, here it is—'I feel softer around the edges. Not so brittle anymore.'"

Darcy could only nod. She knew what that was like. Her fervent wish had been granted; this woman had the same experience, the same reawakening she had known. It felt wonderful—*deep down* wonderful—to know she'd found a way to share that.

"Actually, we've uncovered a surprise benefit, ladies. The salon people got as much out of it as the recipients. They were choking up just talking to me. They took their job very seriously. When you think about it, these are people who have always known the value of pampering. Now they get to apply their craft in a way that makes a huge difference. All six of the people who worked with Jean and her friend just about begged me to do it again. And you can imagine how they reacted when they heard Jean was engaged. Two of them offered to come primp her for her wedding for free."

"Wow." Darcy just couldn't find the words for what she was feeling. As though she'd found her perfect spot, her unique place in the world. She'd always thought she had that as wife and mother, but this went so much further. "Wow."

"Any glitches?"

"Well," began Meredith, "if you can call it a glitch, we needed to reiterate several times that all the tips and such had been already taken care of. Jean and her friend kept trying to tip the salon workers, even though we'd told them several times that all costs had been covered. We worked it out, finally. It just became one big hugfest at the end of the day. Fun to watch, actually."

Suddenly noticing the peachy-rose color of Meredith's fingernails, Darcy teased, "Got in on the fun, did you Meredith?"

Darcy had never actually seen Meredith blush before. It was rather satisfying. "Who could resist?" she said sheepishly.

"They look great," admired Kate. "Your hands work hard. Why shouldn't they get a little pampering now and then?"

"Well, don't count me in on that little trend," offered Doug. "I'm sticking with my good old barbershop on Sycamore. I'm strictly here in a professional capacity."

"Reverend Whitman," Kate countered, "real men get manicures."

He eyed her skeptically. "Not in Ohio."

"Give us time," Kate replied. "We're just warming up here."

Doug rolled his eyes, and everyone laughed. They spent the next half hour going over details, passing along reports, discussing if the plan had met its expectations. By all accounts, The Restoration Project had exceeded expectations. Darcy smiled—Glynnis would eat this up when she told her tomorrow.

The next hurdle was arranging for all the child care needed to cover Mrs. McDylan's day. It took quite a bit of scheduling, but thanks to Doug's church Ladies Guild, they had a trio of ladies who agreed to cover the day, including an extra day to spend with the McDylans just going over all the tasks—those kids needed unbelievable amounts of care. Darcy found herself wondering why Mrs. McDylan hadn't keeled over in exhaustion long before this.

Over the next two weeks, the other recipients would have their "days." She, Kate, Doug and Meredith scheduled in two more evaluation meetings for the individual recipients. They couldn't schedule a final evaluation, because the fifth recipient had declined, and hadn't been replaced.

Ah, yes, the troublesome issue of Michelle Porter. If The Restoration Project was an idea that found Darcy, Michelle's reaction was an idea that *pursued* her. Darcy's heart pounded when the subject of the fifth recipient came to the table.

"I've got a few ideas for a fifth recipient," Meredith began, passing out sheets of profiles as she had done at the first meeting.

"Wait." The word seemed to jump out of Darcy's mouth of its own accord.

Everyone around the table stared at her.

"I…um…I'm just not ready to give up on Michelle yet."

Kate did a double-take. "You? You were maddest of all. That letter didn't exactly leave a lot of room for renegotiations."

"I know, and I'm not even sure why, but I just know I'm not ready to write her off." The tone of that woman's letter echoed in her heart. There was something there. Something that had grabbed at her and refused to let go.

Meredith looked at her. "Are you sure that's wise?"

Darcy had to be honest. "No, not at all. But I just want a little time to mull this one over." Which was, of course, a lie. Darcy knew exactly what it was that she needed to do, and it wasn't wise at all. As a matter of fact, it was downright terrifying. Unavoidable, unignorable and wildly uncomfortable.

That's what you get, Darcy chided herself, for hushing up and letting God do the talking.

Which is why, after saying goodbye to Kate and Pastor Doug in the parking lot, Darcy walked right back into the Center, and right back into Meredith's office.

"Meredith, I think I need to visit Michelle."

Chapter 25

Advanced Discipline for Rambunctious Upstarts

Glynnis was delighted to hear all the good news of TRP's first successful pilot recipient. You'd think it was her own project, the way she cheered and smiled at Darcy's report. She listened just as carefully when Darcy shared how she was planning to meet with Michelle Porter. Glynnis seemed so confident that Darcy was doing the right thing—Darcy wished some of that confidence would rub off on her.

"But Glynnis, there doesn't seem to be any good reason for me to see Michelle Porter. I don't know what to say to her. Why on earth would God plant such an idea in my head without any hint as to what I'm supposed to do when I get there?"

"Because sometimes, honey, all you need to do is show up. He'll take care of the rest."

"How am I supposed to call up a woman I don't know, who's in the midst of a heartbreaking crisis, who wrote me a nasty letter and ask to come by and chat? Who'd say yes to such a dumb request?"

Glynnis scooted the plate of cookies closer and selected one. "Her response is God's problem. Your job is just to do the asking." She considered the cookie. "What's your favorite cookie, Darcy?"

Darcy didn't see how this was relevant. "I don't know, it'd be a toss up between Oreos and Mint Milanos, I suppose."

"Why don't you take Michelle a package of each when you go?"

"Cookies? Store-bought cookies? Shouldn't I come bearing a bundt cake or something?"

Glynnis laughed. "Bundt cakes. I didn't think people your age even knew what a bundt cake was anymore. Do they even sell the pans still?"

Darcy cocked an eyebrow. "Do I look like the kind of person who would know? You're talking to the queen of slice-and-bake here." She straightened in her chair. "I do, however, make a mean quiche."

Now it was Glynnis's turn to raise an eyebrow. "Would you have been as happy if Kate picked you up in that little red car of hers after the funeral with a *quiche*?"

"You've got a point there." Darcy reached for another cookie herself. "If God has been so blunt about asking me to go, I figure I can trust Him to be just as clear about what to do when I get there. And you're right—if He wants me there, He'll get me in the door. Right now I suppose I just need to trust and pick up the phone, huh?"

"Bingo." Glynnis smiled. "Now that we have that settled, Ed tells me you and Jack are going to see one of our financial advisors, Craig Palmer."

"Yeah." Darcy didn't bother to hide her lack of enthusiasm.

Glynnis shot her a look over the top of her glasses. "I'm glad you agreed to see him, Darcy. I do think it's a smart move. God tells us to be 'wise as serpents,' too. If nothing else, you owe it to Jack. His sense of security is important to who he is. You should respect that. God'll respect it, too. Craig is a fine man. A good Christian, and a smart advisor. Ed wouldn't have recommended him if he didn't think so highly of him."

"I don't like it. I told him so."

"Then he'll appreciate your going all the more."

Darcy changed the subject. "Hey, the next recipient gets her 'day' next week. It's Anne Morton, the woman whose father-in-law has Alzheimer's."

"Ugh." Glynnis recoiled. "Nasty disease. I don't think I ever want to be found somewhere confused and in my bathrobe. I love my little gray brain cells, and I don't want them going anywhere anytime soon."

Darcy couldn't think of too many people sharper than Glynnis Bidwell. "Relax, I think yours are all in fine working order. But it's sad, isn't it? Meredith said it's like taking care of a ghost in the body of somebody you once knew." She ran her finger around the top of her glass. "Dad's dementia was bad near the end. It was frustrating. His eyes would get this incredibly vacant look, and it was like he wasn't even there. I had so much to say to him, and he wasn't even there to hear it."

Glynnis shook her head. "That woman needs a break, sure as anything." She smiled, a warm, enormous smile that seemed to fill the whole room. "And you're going to be the one to give it to her. Doesn't that feel *scrumptious?*"

"Yes." Darcy laughed, once again baffled by Glynnis's choice of words, "that's exactly the word I'd choose."

"Is not." Glynnis poked her gently. "If you've got that school meeting at eleven-thirty, we'd better get to praying or we'll run out of time." She pushed the cookie plate out of the way and took Darcy's hands in hers. "Where do you want to start?"

"With Mrs. Anderson. That school meeting is with Mike's algebra teacher. It can't be good."

"I know we probably made you anxious by calling you in here this morning, Mrs. Nightengale, but I think you'll actually find this a good meeting." Evidently Darcy's surprise—or perhaps concern was a better way to put it—was clear on her face when she walked in to find Mr. Tortman alongside Mrs. Anderson. *Ms.* Anderson, actually. Her first impression of the woman, from when they were introduced at parents' night in October, still held: she looked about nineteen years old. How young *were* college graduates these days? She was young and hip and frighteningly perky. Darcy thought she looked more like a flight attendant than an algebra teacher. Oh, now there's thinking that will really help the situation, she silently scolded herself. Come on, Dar, stop judging and see what these people have to say.

"Good morning, Mrs. Nightengale," said Mr. Tortman formally. Don't call him Torture Man, don't call him Torture Man, Darcy pleaded with herself. For a man who commanded such fear among eighth-grade boys, he looked rather harmless. He didn't look like the kind of guy who could torture anyone—not even his own conscience. A small, lean man with unfashionable glasses and thinning hair. The stereotypical Vice Principal.

"Good morning, Mr. Tortman, it's nice to meet you face-to-face." *You said Tortman, good.* "And nice to see you again, Ms. Anderson."

"Thanks for coming in. Can I say first, Mrs. Nightengale, that I'm sorry for the loss of your father. Mike tells me it was a long illness." Ms. Anderson had warm, caring eyes. Framed in a lot of mascara and eye shadow, to be sure, but warm and caring nonetheless. She imagined lots of mascara and eye shadow probably looked pretty cool to the majority of eighth-grade boys.

"Yes, it was, thank you for your concern. We're all handling it as best we can."

"As you can imagine," Mr. Tortman began, "we're here to talk about Mike."

"I gathered that." Darcy folded her hands in her lap, trying to look like a committed, involved parent. Appearing cooperative and duly concerned. Which she was, of course, but wanted to make sure it showed. She leaned in a little, to show interest. She hated these kinds of meetings: they always made her so nervous.

"Mike has exceptional skills in mathematics. He's been chewing through the high school math books we gave him last month. And Mr. Davis tells me he's showing the same promise in science. You should be very pleased."

"We are. We're delighted that he has such a fine mind." Fine mind? What kind of thing is that to say?

"His behavior, however, has been a bit more—shall we say—difficult. I think it's safe to say we all agree that Mike needs more challenge than he's getting. Better channels for his talents and energy." Mr. Tortman was making sure he got all the educational buzzwords in, that was for sure.

"I thought things were getting better in that department." Darcy pushed her hair behind her ears, trying to hide her anxiety.

"Actually," offered Ms. Anderson, looking at Mr. Tortman, "they are. But I think we're going to see cycles of this.

He'll be good for a couple of weeks, then he'll get tired of things and the behavior starts up again." She directed her gaze to Darcy again. "It's a rather natural pattern for boys of his age and abilities." Somehow Darcy was sure she was going to cite some textbook called *Questionable Algebraic Behavior for Gifted Young Men*.

Mr. Tortman didn't look like he much agreed. He looked like the textbooks on his shelf read more to the tune of *Advanced Discipline for Rambunctious Upstarts*.

"In any case, Mrs. Nightengale, I called you in because I'd like to make a few suggestions to help Mike along in his studies. I don't know what the family resources are, but I think you may want to consider…"

And thus it began. A list of private tutoring programs, three computer software programs, four community college courses and one very ritzy summer math camp. *Congratulations on your boy's fine young mind, but it sure is gonna cost you.*

Oh, Jack was going to have a field day with this.

Chapter 26

Little Boy Blue

No one was allowed to throw up today.

No one was allowed to break, sprain or deeply cut anything, no cars or refrigerators were permitted to malfunction, even hair was warned to behave.

Darcy needed every ounce of energy and brainpower she had to meet the tasks at hand. There were only three tasks, but they were whoppers. This morning, she was going to visit Michelle Porter. Sure enough, the woman had said yes. Darcy could not remember a single snippet of the conversation because she had been so incredibly nervous and unsure of herself when she made the call. She'd rehearsed three different versions of the call, none of which actually took place. Darcy was thankful she'd written down the address and directions to Michelle's house, because she could remember nothing else from the exchange. Nothing except the general impression that the woman had been baffled, reluctant, but agreeable in the end.

Darcy thought back to the days when Mike was a baby. He'd been a good baby. Agreeable, a cooperative nurser, able to sleep anywhere, anytime. Except, of course, at night. Jack often referred to Mike as "the nocturnal animal" because of his exasperating habit of waking up happy and playful at 3:30 a.m. On the dot. Almost every night.

Darcy smiled. Where was that internal alarm now? Getting him out of bed took superhuman effort these days. Get him to *go* to bed took negotiating skills worthy of the United Nations. Back then, it had seemed both so much harder and so much simpler.

The desperation of too little sleep came back to her, as if her body instantly remembered what it was like to walk the upstairs hallway with a squirming nocturnal beast chewing on her shoulders. The swaying, the wet sleeves, the sounds. Yes, when Mike was a baby, and she was a new mother, she remembered saying yes to *anyone* who came calling. Adult conversation was priceless, even someone to hold the baby so she could actually go to the bathroom by herself. Maybe it wasn't so strange that Michelle had said yes after all—especially with such a challenging baby as hers.

Such a visit was enough to fill anyone's day, but Darcy had to ferry Mike to the orthodontist for a lunchtime appointment, then meet Jack at the finance guy's office. Jack was so eager to set this up that he actually arranged to take the afternoon off. "That way," he had said, "we can go grab a cup of something and talk it over." Jack was pulling out all the stops on this one.

The day's final task was to remain focused on the first two, knowing that Mrs. McDylan had her "day" today. Recipient number two. The one who would prove recipient number one hadn't been a fluke. Jean had been close to her demographically, but Noreen McDylan was a much different woman. Plus, there were all the child-care logistics to deal with, all the people who were involved in covering that end of things. So many places for children to get sick, people to be late or no-shows, things to go wrong. Just looking at the plan for the day had driven up Darcy's blood pressure.

When Jack mentioned he'd scheduled the financial appointment for today, she'd wanted to wave a white flag. Then Darcy decided to surrender to the odd symmetry of it. If you're going to freak out, she told herself, you might as well confine it all to one day.

Still, it could all come crashing down in one "Mrs. Nightengale? This is the school nurse calling…" phone call.

"And that's the way it is with motherhood," Darcy lectured a squirrel standing in the driveway. "One wrong phone call and you're sunk. At any time, any day, they can just pull the rug right out from under you." She pointed at him with her cell phone, just for emphasis.

And she was sure it was a him. You could tell by the unsympathetic way he simply turned and ran away. A momma squirrel, Darcy reasoned, would have eyed her in universal maternal sympathy.

Darcy pulled the car door shut and looked skeptically in the rearview mirror. "Big day, and I'm talking to squirrels. Not good." She roared the engine to life, warning it not to show one shred of disobedience today. "Might as well get on with it."

Michelle Porter's home was small and unassuming—the classic New-Family-Just-Starting-Out model. The Christmas decorations were still up in the yard, and the newspaper hadn't been brought in from the front steps when Darcy went to ring the doorbell at ten-thirty. She remembered those baby days, when the mail sometimes wouldn't make it inside until dinner, and the newspapers might pile up for days on end. Actually, she didn't ring the doorbell, but just knocked softly, as there was a Shhh—Baby Sleeping sign posted in the door window.

Michelle had put on a clean shirt and pulled her hair back in a tortoiseshell barrette for the occasion. Darcy recognized the this-is-about-the-best-I-can-do uniform— she'd donned it herself dozens of times. The house was on the edge of neat, with baby toys and laundry baskets stacked in corners. The kitchen counter held a plastic box containing at least two dozen prescription bottles. A daily regimen was taped to the fridge. She recognized all the caretaking details from Dad's early days at home.

"Robby's asleep," Michelle offered. "This is a good time." She moved a laundry basket from off the sofa and motioned for her to sit down. Michelle looked wary and very tired.

Come on, God, I'm going to need a bit of help here….

You're a mom. Be a mom. Was the cryptic response that came to her.

"There's never really a good time with a baby, though, is there?" Darcy commiserated. "Here, I brought you *my* version of the Mommy Survival Kit." She passed over the gift bag she'd recycled from the now famous tiara.

Michelle let out a surprised little laugh when she opened the gift, drawing out the several bags of cookies. "Oh, this is great. These are really great. I swear, I was thinking we were going to drown in booties and casseroles." Her expression was one of sincere thanks. "Why does everyone think people need macaroni in a crisis?"

"Everyone's got to eat, I suppose," Darcy offered.

"Well, I'd much rather eat *these* any day." She picked up one of the bags. "Shall we?"

"Twist my arm," replied Darcy. "But you don't have to share. You could hide them and eat the whole lot in the bathtub later if you wanted to."

"A bath? What's that? Ever since Robby started crawling I haven't had a bath. Ever since Robby started *breathing* I haven't had a bath."

"Keeps you running, hmm?"

"Between the standard baby stuff and all Robby's medical business, this is a full-time job." She handed the bag to Darcy after taking two cookies for herself. "There's no breaks." She saw the woman's defenses raise ever so slightly. "And I wouldn't want one. I need every moment I can get with Robby. Every scrap of time." You could see emotion well up inside her. "I need to be here. There can't be any breaks. Not with…" Michelle broke off, not wanting to finish the sentence. If you could draw a definitive picture of someone who *needed* a break, Darcy felt like she was sitting in front of it. This woman was worn raw, and bone tired.

Darcy took a deep breath. "That's sort of why I'm here, Michelle. I know you don't like the idea of The Restoration Project, but I wanted you to see that the Project isn't the idea of a bunch of big-haired beauty queens who think a good makeover can change your life. I'm a mom, just like you. Only instead of watching my son die, I watched my father."

"It's not the same," Michelle said sharply.

No, it wasn't. The pain of losing a loved one was bad, but to compound it with the injustice, the sheer unnatural act of burying one's child, well Darcy couldn't begin to know how it would feel. "I won't pretend that it is." She answered after a pause. "I can't imagine what it's like. I don't know what I'd do in your shoes. But I think I have an idea of how tired you are. How much it hurts. How people don't have a clue—even though they think they do. How this kind of thing eats away at your family before you even realize it."

Michelle grew tense. "I don't know why I let you come here."

I do, thought Darcy, determined to get her thoughts out before the door of communication with this woman slammed shut. "I felt like I was dying right alongside my dad. And you know what? I thought that was the right thing to do. I poured everything I had into taking care of him, tried never to miss a minute, put him before everything else. I didn't want to regret a single missed chance. I wanted to do the right thing."

Michelle's glare wavered. She shifted focus to the cookie in her hand.

"And what I regret most, now that it's done and Dad is—" Darcy was surprised at how much she choked on the word "—gone, is just how *much* I poured into it. Because I discovered, Michelle, that if you pour everything into it, there's nothing left over."

That wasn't the comment Michelle was expecting. Darcy knew it, because it wasn't the outcome she had expected from the hospice, either. Darcy took a deep breath. "Robby's going to die, isn't he?" she asked very quietly.

Michelle nodded, sniffling.

"No one ever dares to ask that, do they? Nobody ever wants to talk about it. It's too scary, too messy. But you and I—we know it. We live with it, every day. So we try to be noble and selfless and muster up hope, and all the time we're dying inside, too. And everyone's so focused on Robby. And they should be. He needs it. But what about you?"

"I get to live." Michelle whimpered after a long silence. "And that's not fair."

"It rots, doesn't it?"

"Yeah, it does."

"I can't make that part better. There isn't any 'better' to be had in all this. But The Project is a way that I can help people get one day where it *is* about them. Where you can remember that you still have friends and your body will feel normal again one day and you are stronger than it feels right now. This isn't about hair color or any of that spa stuff. None of that is what really matters. I'd pay for twelve gallons of ice cream delivered straight to your door if I thought *that* would make a difference. It's mostly about giving care to what's been neglected. Giving you a day—just *one* day—away from all this, with someone you probably haven't had lunch with in months, is a start, a foothold toward having something left over. And I know it is because I've been where you are. And 'nothing left over' is an awful, awful place to grieve. I just wanted you to know that. You can still say no, but I just wanted the chance to tell you myself."

There was an awkward stretch of silence. Darcy reached down slowly for her purse. Perhaps she was wrong in coming here. Michelle was entitled to her bitterness; life had handed her a raw deal. The acme of all raw deals. Who was Darcy to think she had any answers to coping?

"Tony won't choose a color," Michelle said quietly.

Darcy froze, her hand still reaching toward the floor. "What?"

"We can get Robby a custom casket, painted with sailboats and whales—he loves boats, Robby does." Michelle still stared down at her cookie. "There is a woman who'll paint a special casket just for him, and I want him to have it, but Tony won't let us choose a color."

Darcy couldn't find words. She didn't think the whole English language had the words for this. All she could do was just put her hand on Michelle's arm.

"Tony says I'm wrong to give up on Robby. But I'm not giving up on him, I…just want him to have a pretty casket." She started to cry, and Darcy could feel the tears running down her own cheeks. "He's not going to get a pretty life, so I want…I want him to have a pretty death. Is that so hideous? Why does everyone think it's so awful that I want that?" Her voice took on the bitter edge Darcy heard in the letter. "Why can't I want that? He's my son, why can't I want to give that to him? Why?" Michelle tossed the half-eaten cookie down on the coffee table and swore. "It's bad enough that I have to be picking out caskets at all! Why can't I have the one I want?"

"I think boats sounds nice," Darcy offered, trying not to sob. "I think I'd want them, too."

"Why can't we have blue boats?" The question trailed off into a sob, and Darcy simply pulled the woman onto her shoulder, letting her cry.

"Blue boats sounds nice." She repeated, stroking Michelle's shaking shoulders. "I think blue boats would look beautiful."

Even after she returned Mike to school, Darcy had yet to remove the lump from her throat. The mournful wail of Michelle Porter's questions seemed to hang inside her chest, aching there, keeping Darcy on the verge of crying for hours after she left that home. Death was such a lousy business. She wondered about the people who said they envied her chance to say goodbye to her dad. Did they know the cost of that good long goodbye? The toll it took? The wide swath of pain it left?

With a sigh, Darcy thought that she might be safer with someone throwing up today. The tasks at hand were proving just too huge. She fished in her purse for the address of the financial planner, and took the car out of Park. *Stay close, Lord, I'm going to need you.*

Craig Palmer's office looked surprisingly like the orthodontist office she'd just left. A small, one-story, redbrick structure with plate glass front windows. Palmer and Associates was painted on one window in trustworthy white lettering.

The finance magnate inside, whom Darcy was certain would be wearing a sharp dark suit and a trust-me expression, ended up being an ordinary guy in a broadcloth shirt and a pair of Dockers. A round-faced, balding man about ten years older than Jack, with bright blue eyes and wire-rimmed glasses. Friendly. Decidedly nonpredatory. Definitely an Ed Bidwell kind of guy, Darcy thought, remembering from whom the recommendation had come.

"Jack's filled me in on the basics," he said as he brought in three cups of coffee and a little china box filled with sugar packets and those tiny creamer tubs. "Jack also told me you drink tea, and I thought we had some, but evidently we're out. I hope coffee's okay until I stock up again."

After today's events, a stronger brew seemed like a good idea. "Coffee's fine, thanks." Darcy chose the chocolate-flavored creamer, though, and used two of them.

"You know," Palmer remarked, stirring his own coffee, "that's some unusual set of circumstances you've got there. I don't mean to sound forward, but guys like us dream of things like this. The possibilities. The options. The challenges. It's enough to make any number cruncher's heart beat faster." The guy was genuinely excited. Not a greedy kind of excited, but an unassuming, this-is-gonna-be-fun kind of excited.

Funny, Darcy thought, *fun's* not the word I'd use for it.

"It goes without saying, though, Mrs. Nightengale," he continued, his tone of voice changing completely, "that I'd much rather you had found this on the street. I'm sorry for your loss. The intricacies of estate management are difficult enough. I can't imagine having it made that much more difficult by all you've gone through. Please, don't ever let my enthusiasm let you think any differently." He really meant it. You could see it in his eyes. Maybe this wouldn't be so bad after all.

"Thank you," Darcy replied. "Please, call me Darcy."

"I'd like that," he said, his smile warm. "Welcome to my office, Darcy. I hope we'll be able to give you some really valuable help here. Coffee okay?"

Darcy took another sip. She liked people who went through the trouble of using real creamer. Especially flavored creamer. "Fine, thanks."

"I've heard the basic facts from Jack on the phone, Darcy. Why don't we start with your story? Tell me how all this happened, and what your thoughts are on where to go from here."

Craig Palmer listened attentively, his mechanical pencil busy jotting notes and figures as Darcy told the story as best she knew it, from beginning to end. He seemed impressed by her idea of The Restoration Project. He asked sensitive but important questions about the source of the funds in the first place, and double-checked his notes of portfolio balances and current holdings. He complimented Jacob the Kindly Lawyer on his job of managing the funds with only an attorney's grasp of financial planning. Most revealingly, though, he told Darcy that her father must have been a unique and extraordinary man to have left such a challenging bequest.

"I'd like to meet with you again in about two weeks—if you're so inclined," Craig concluded, pushing a pair of small bound booklets for each of them across the desk. "In there you'll find a set of references, and some questions that will be crucial to our planning process. It's not a test—" he laughed, evidently catching Darcy's concerned expression "—they're mostly questions to help you think through your goals and needs."

"That makes sense," said Jack.

"There's another major topic I want to put on the table here. Darcy, I know you left your part-time job to take care of your dad. That's had its toll on your family finances. I can only begin to imagine the mental war going on in your heads with the needs, resources and demands you're facing. These are dry times, and you've just been handed gallons of water."

Darcy's heart nearly stopped. Hadn't she used that very image the first time The Restoration Project exploded into her life? There was no way Craig's choice of wording had been chance. She fought the urge to shake her head in disbelief, dragging her attention back to what Craig was continuing to say.

"…You've got kids heading into college and I'd be willing to bet your 401-K looks as sick as mine. Nobody knows what's going to happen in the next few months. Still, you've got to contend with Paul's wishes and the emotional side of things." Craig came around to sit on the front corner of his desk. He tapped the booklet Jack was holding.

"What I want you to see is that I believe there's room for it all in there. I especially want you to consider setting up a formal foundation. It sounds complicated, but with the right guidance it can have lots of benefits. Sure, you could just write checks off the accounts like you've done with your—what'd Jack call it? The pilot test group?—but you'll need the structure of a formal charitable foundation in the long run. A foundation that will need someone to run it."

Craig looked straight at Darcy, and there was something in his eyes that made her stomach do flips. A connection, an understanding, a something. "What I'm saying, Darcy, is that I don't think you should have to choose between your dad and your family. Your new job can be as head of The Restoration Project on a part-time, salaried basis. That means you'll not only have the time that will need to be devoted to get this project off and running well, but also that you will have complete control over your schedule and workload. The project gets the attention it needs, and you can meet the needs of your family." Craig smiled a huge, warm grin. "Everybody wins."

Craig Palmer had seen her needs, her family's needs and her dad's vision, and pulled all three together in a spectacular solution.

And Jack had been wise enough to call him.

In her mind's eye Darcy saw God, standing in Glynnis's hen-coated kitchen, leaning against the counter with his arms folded. *Do you see now, child? Would you give me just a little credit for knowing how to do things? Could we have a little conversation about your trust issues?*

The image struck her as irreverent at first, but Darcy decided it was intimate and loving instead. She had no doubt God hung out in The Henhouse. She was coming to see He hung out just about everywhere she went. In that instant, Darcy realized her earlier prayer had been answered. Hadn't she just asked God to stay close?

What a relief to know He had no plans to leave in the first place.

Craig extended a hand. "It's a lot to take in. Look over the booklets, talk it over, see what your gut tells you. I think there's a happy ending for a lot of people wrapped up in this. I'd like to be the guy who makes it happen."

Darcy clutched her booklet and shook Craig Palmer's hand firmly. "Thank you, Craig," she said.

And she meant it.

27

The Evil of Unemployed Elves

While she was volunteering in the school library the following Monday, Darcy's cell phone went off. It was Kate, begging for a tea date as fast as possible, and not taking no for an answer. She wouldn't say why, only that it was a pleasant surprise.

By the time Darcy entered J.L.'s, Kate had already secured the table and a pair of steaming mugs. "I want to know what you did," she burst out.

"Did what to what?"

"It's to *whom,* not what. Your answering machine has two messages on it. One's from Meredith, and the other's from me. I decided, however, that I'd much rather tell you in person."

Darcy dunked her tea bag, surrendering to the force of nature that was Kate Owens. "Okay, so what did I do to *whom?*"

"Michelle Porter."

Oh. Darcy should have guessed. Given the way that

visit had gone, communication from Michelle could have meant a dozen things. If the woman had chosen to contact someone else, Darcy could only guess her visit had done more harm than good. Still, she couldn't get that conversation, those tears, the image of a little hand-painted casket, out of her mind all weekend. Darcy had sent up a hundred tiny sighs of prayers, her heart aching for the young woman handed such a cruel indoctrination into motherhood. Most of those prayers didn't even have words, just moans of "Oh, Lord…" for who could *know* what her needs were? Who could survive such a situation? It was the best example of *God only knows*…ever conceived.

"Oh, Kate," Darcy moaned, "it's heartbreaking. And I made it worse, didn't I? I knew I made a mistake going there, letting her know who I was…I thought I could help her. I thought I knew something of—"

"Dar." Kate's hand clamped down on Darcy's. "Dar, she said yes. You convinced her. You." Kate's broad, warm smile spilled out over the room. "You done good, girl."

"She said yes?"

"Well, I admit that according to Meredith she's still mighty nervous and not at all sure, but she's willing to try, and that's a big step." Kate took a big sip of tea. "What did you say to her?"

"I don't even remember. It was so awful. So much unfair pain. She looked like she was hanging on by her fingernails." Darcy looked at Kate. "Do you remember those newborn days? How you thought you'd never make it through the day, how you'd never sleep again? Now imagine all the medical stuff and grief and strain piled on top of it. It hurt just to look at her, Kate. Her eyes were this horrible, empty, hopeless place. I was on the verge of tears for hours after I left her house."

"But you must have gotten through to her somehow."

"I guess so. I don't know how. I just told her how much it hurt, I suppose, to see the empty aftermath when Dad died. How I needed a life to go back to, and woke up one morning to discover I didn't have one. At least, I think I said that. Kate, I don't remember anything except wanting to cry."

"I think," said Kate, staring into her tea, "that it's just the fact that you've been there. That you know something of what it's like. The rest of us, we can only guess, but you've been there." Kate looked up. "Does she have any friends? You know, someone she'll take with her?"

Darcy was struck, suddenly, by the tone of Kate's voice. A thin wisp of "second fiddle," a sense of not being the major player in this project. Nothing could be further from the truth. There would be no Restoration Project without Kate, exactly because Kate was the force of nature she was. It was Kate who pulled her from the wreckage when Dad died, just as much as Jack had—maybe even more so. Kate had been the lifeline, the glimpse of hope, the person to walk her back from the edges.

"I hope she has a Kate," Darcy said, her voice catching. "Everybody needs a Kate. You can't do this without a Kate."

Kate didn't respond.

"Don't you see? *You've* been there, too. You're the only one who knows what it's like to *watch* someone go through this. To see the—" she stumbled for the right word "—the disintegration happen and not be able to stop it. To lose your friend to a crisis. You know when to step in and shake them up, and when to let them wail."

Kate blinked wet lashes and pointed a cookie at Darcy. "Don't you make me cry."

"I can't help it." Darcy grabbed Kate's hand and squeezed it.

They were silent for a moment, catching each other's wet glances. Then Kate took a deep breath. "Do you think The Restoration Project should put out its own brand of waterproof mascara?"

They laughed. Kate could always make her laugh. And oh, how many times they had laughed with wet lashes in the past months. She was a lifeline.

"Yep. Right behind our own brand of chocolate-covered graham crackers."

"What? And put the Keebler elves out of work? That'd be heartless."

Later that night, Darcy found Jack in the dining room, Craig Palmer's brown booklet spread open before him. Jack had his laptop open to his left, a stack of scratch paper to his right and a pile of Monopoly money spread out in front of him. Darcy leaned against the doorway, the school sweatshirt she had picked up off the steps still in her hands, and took in the amusing picture. Jack was being Jack. Running numbers. She was always amazed at how fast he could work a numeric keypad—it was like typing for him, instantaneous and as quick as his thoughts. Over the years, she had come to love the *tic-tic* of Jack's hands over a calculator—or lately a keyboard— as he worked through his numbers. Jack. Solving. Finding order. Analyzing. Securing.

The Monopoly money, though, was a new twist. She walked into the room and picked up a pink five-dollar bill. "Visual aids?"

Jack didn't even look up. He gave a grunt of sorts, that universal male signal for "I know you're in the room," but it was clear he hadn't heard a word.

"Do not pass Go, do not collect one million dollars?"

Grunt. *Tic-tic-tic.*

"Jack?" Pause. "*Jack!*"

"Hmm?" Jack blinked and looked up, pushing his glasses back up from where they'd slid down his nose.

Darcy folded the sweatshirt over one of the tall backs of the dining room chairs. She leaned over the chair, gesturing toward the sloppy piles of play money. "What's with the Monopoly money?"

Jack blinked again, as if he hadn't quite understood the question. Then, as if he had just come back from Imaginary Number Land, he suddenly became aware of his surroundings. "Oh, that."

"What's up?"

"The kids were playing in here earlier. I just pushed it aside so I could work."

Darcy laughed. It was just like her to create connections, draw relationships when none were really there. To assume a simple mess was a premeditated strategy. But it *was* funny to see Jack crunching numbers surrounded by imaginary millions.

And millions that were all too real.

She pulled out the chair and sat down, collecting beige one-hundred-dollar bills into a pile. "So what do you think?"

Jack took off his glasses. "Palmer's good. He's on top of things. There's a lot of intricacies to this, and he seems to know his way around them. Plus, anyone who handles Ed's portfolio has to be top-notch, I'd imagine."

"He looks like he'd be Ed Bidwell's finance guy."

Jack grinned. "One of four. Can you imagine? Having a finance *staff*? No wonder the guy drives the car he does."

Darcy tapped the pile of bills into a neat stack. "Jack, you're drooling."

"Am not." He put his glasses back on, then shot her a playful look. "But the thought has occurred to me. Who knew I married into money?"

"Little Orphan Heiress is not amused. In fact, she's considering beaning you with her tiara at this very moment."

"Hey, watch out. My finance guys can beat up your finance guys."

"Your finance guys *are* my finance guys. And they're not even our guys yet, Jack."

Jack's face took on a serious look. "They should be."

Darcy folded her arms. She was coming to the very same conclusion. She liked Craig. Craig's solution sounded just too good to be true. Were they taking Dad's last request and twisting it to their own liking? Or was it just that Craig could see more clearly, unencumbered by all the emotional baggage of grief? She'd pored over the brown booklet herself the past few days, and it seemed to make such sense. Trouble was, she didn't trust her concept of sensible when it came to the subject. "I do like him," she offered, "and he seems to make sense. But doesn't it feel just a little too good to be true? Too easy."

"Well, I don't think I'd call it easy," Jack replied. "This is some complicated management. He can see more possibilities because of his skills. And he of all people knows the work involved in managing—and in giving away—that kind of money. You and your dad, you both have all kinds of emotional issues tied up in this money. Craig's objective. He can see things differently."

Darcy ran her hands through her hair and blew out a breath. "I suppose. I don't know why I'm hesitating."

Jack closed down the spreadsheet program and shut off his laptop. "Your being on staff for The Project means that not only will you be seeing to the needs of this family, but you'll be taking the time and energy to make sure your dad's wishes come true. So much good can come out of something so regrettable. I think that's exactly how Paul would have wanted it. I mean, really, if your dad was in the office with Craig and you and me, what do you think he'd say?"

"Don't you see, that's just it? I thought I knew him. I thought I knew everything about him. Now I discover these big huge things that he kept from me. I don't know how to answer that question anymore."

"You know, it would be ideal if we could find out why your dad did this. Why he didn't feel he could touch that money." Jack pulled his papers into a neat stack. "We're all just guessing at why he didn't touch it and didn't tell you. And I don't think his letter clears it up much, either. If you knew that, it might tell you what he'd do now in your shoes." He held the papers still for a moment and looked at her, his face intent and serious. "But…"

"But what?"

"You may never get to know, Dar. I mean, really, there's no one to ask. Pastor Doug doesn't seem to know, most of your dad's friends didn't know, your mom's gone, Aunt Jenny's downright dangerous. There's no one left to ask. Face it, Dar, there may be no way to find that out. Ever. We need to think this through with what we've got here and now, because I think we may never know the why of it."

Jack was absolutely right. And that was an awful thought. "I hate that I don't know. I hate that he kept this from me. I—I'm trying really hard to let it go, but I can't forgive him for that yet." The emotion welled up in Darcy, grabbing at her throat with greedy fingers. "I don't know what it's going to take to let it go."

Jack stood up and came behind her, wrapping his arms around her shoulders. He kissed the top of her head before he let his chin rest there. "Time, I suppose."

"Why, Jack? What would possess him to do something so strange?" She let the tears come, unable to stem the pain that seemed to come up from out of nowhere. "Why would he think of that money as so evil it couldn't be touched? Who would argue with him deserving it? He lost his wife. I lost my mother. That driver lost control of his car and he hit Mom. It's not our fault that he wasn't insured. That money was rightfully Dad's. There's so much he could have done, travel, comforts, things he deserved. Why? I want to know *why?*" Darcy buried her face in Jack's arms, gripping them as they held her. Try as he might, even sensible Jack would never be able to make sense of this. It would never make sense. Ever.

"I don't know," he said softly, his cheek against her hair. "I don't think we'll ever know." After a while, he added, "So we've got to go on without knowing. You and I. We've got to work through this together. We don't know what Paul would do. So we've got to decide what Jack and Darcy will do." He came around on one knee in front of her, stroking her hair. "You could twist yourself inside out, Dar, trying to figure out your dad's motivations. But if you ask me, it'll just make you crazy. It'd be better for everyone if you and I just try to decide where to take it from here."

It sounded right to Darcy. Jack's voice had the solid ring of truth. It was a scary thought to think it was all up to her, but it was the truth. Jack was right; she could make herself nuts trying to figure out her dad's strange relationship to that money. She might never know the whole story. And she could either choose to let that eat her alive, or choose to move past it.

"Look at it this way, Dar. Would Paul have ever come up with The Restoration Project?"

"Dad?" Darcy sniffled. "Never."

"And look what that idea has done so far. You told me yourself the women in the trial run have been really helped by it. That was *you,* Dar. *Your* ideas, *your* way of doing what your dad asked." He stroked her hair. "Trust yourself to know what to do. Trust yourself to take it from here." He looked at her as if she could run the world. For the first time, she realized how much The Restoration Project had amazed him. You could see it now, in his eyes, that he believed in it. That he believed in her.

"I trust *you,*" she offered, sliding her hand over his.

"I think we can trust Craig, too. Your Dad loved your creativity, how you connected people together to make something happen. How you made sure the kids always had what they needed. I think he'd give his blessing, if he could."

"Maybe he has." Darcy thought about the Bidwells and Kate and Michelle and Meredith, and each person who had come into her life over the past year. What an astounding, amazing adventure it all had become. What a blessing each person was. "Maybe he has."

Jack pulled her up off the chair and wrapped her in his arms. She felt his sure strength seeping into her, melting away the shivers of uncertainty. She pressed her cheek against his chest, listening to his breath, taking in his heartbeat. She closed her eyes and breathed, pulling in the solid air around him. Around them.

"Jack?" she said quietly.

"Hmm?" he answered, his chest humming against her cheek.

"I think Craig's our guy."

"Me too, hon. Me, too."

Chapter 28

The Virtues of Kooky But Amazing

Glynnis clasped her hands together in utter joy when Darcy told her about Michelle. "I knew it, I just knew it. Darcy honey, I'm not surprised at all. When did you hear?"

"Yesterday. We met at the center to go over the final recipients. Norene McDylan's kids were just fine and her husband even got in a round of golf during the day. Norene said he hadn't played for two years. I wouldn't be surprised if we come up with some sort of Restoration Project Men's Auxiliary someday."

"Oh, don't let Ed hear you say that! That sounds like just the sort of thing he'd get all excited about. Me, I'm so excited about Michelle Porter that I can hardly stand it." She poked Darcy in the arm. "See? See what God can do when you're willing to go into the scary places?"

"Yeah, yeah, exceeding my expectations, I get it, Glynnis. It's just that I'm knee-deep in scary places. I keep trying to tell God I've developed all the character I can stand at one time."

Glynnis laughed. "Oh, I've tried that one, too. God doesn't seem to pay much attention to that one."

"No kidding."

Glynnis added more cookies to the plate. "A little bird told me Jack was very impressed with our man Craig. I've always liked that boy."

Darcy had to laugh. Craig Palmer must have been in his late fifties to say the least. Boy was hardly the term that came to mind. "He had lots of ideas."

Glynnis must have caught the hesitation in her voice, for she arched an eyebrow up over her glasses at Darcy. "A bit too many ideas perhaps? What'd he say?"

Darcy took a long sip of iced tea, fighting the sudden secrecy that sprung up. Money was private. But then again, no, her openness about money is what made Glynnis so wonderful. It didn't seem to have that power over her that it did over so many people. Money never seemed to complicate Glynnis's life—even the gobs and gobs of it Darcy suspected she and Ed had. No, Glynnis was just the person to confide in over money.

"Craig thinks Dad's estate can be invested to give more return. Enough to create a charitable foundation and do lots of projects, not just The Restoration Project. And it could provide a salary for me as a staff person as well. 'Everybody wins,' as he put it."

Glynnis stared at her. "I'm waiting for the downside, honey. I'm not hearing one."

"Don't you see?" replied Darcy, trying to keep the exasperation out of her voice. How could Glynnis see everything so simply? "That's going beyond Dad's request. He asked us to give it away. Now Craig is suggesting that I take a salary from the money to help give it away. It's not the same thing."

"I agree. I think it's better."

Why did Darcy just know Glynnis would see this without conflict?

"But it's not what Dad asked."

Glynnis jumped on that, pointing her finger at Darcy. "Ah, right there's an important point. He didn't demand you do this, did he? He *asked.* I remember thinking the wording you told me sounded mighty deliberate. If Paul had wanted to make sure you did things in some exact way, he could have put it in his will, couldn't he?"

For some reason, that simple fact had never occurred to Darcy. Her dad *could* have made it a requirement of the estate. But he didn't. She'd never thought of that before.

"Would you characterize—" her Southern accent pulled the word out into long, rich vowels "—your daddy as a rigid man?"

Darcy laughed. Paul Hartwell could change his mind in a heartbeat. Her impulsive nature didn't materialize out of thin air—no, it was in her very DNA to pounce on a new idea.

Pounce on a new idea.

He would. Dad loved new ideas, new ways of doing things.

Which is why he left it up to her.

"No," Darcy replied, her voice hushed with the clarity of this new realization. "Not at all."

Glynnis seemed to be right there beside her thoughts. "And was Paul the kind of man who went where God led him? Even if it was, shall we say, unusual?"

"Yes. Always."

"Well, honey, what makes you think he wouldn't want the same for you? He's handed you a grand adventure, Darcy girl, why are you so afraid to go on it?"

You know, there just wasn't a good answer for that question. Darcy opened her mouth, then shut it again, unable to refute the simple truth in what Glynnis said. The woman simply smiled—her sunshine, butterscotch, come-on-over-here-and-hug-me smile—and squeezed Darcy's hand. God must delight in her, Darcy thought; His joy is just oozing out of every one of Glynnis's pores.

"You're amazing, Glynnis. How many other women have you helped like this? How many Henhouse alumni are there?"

Glynnis's smile widened. "Eleven."

"I think I'd like to meet some of them."

"You can meet all of them. We have lunch the third Wednesday of every month. I've been praying for weeks now for God to show me the right time to invite you."

Darcy grinned. "Sounds like now's the time. And I've been thinking about church, too. I think we'd like to start coming to Ohio Valley."

Glynnis fairly sparkled, putting her hands on her chubby little hips. "No time like the present. Come Sunday! And bring that feisty redheaded friend of yours with you."

"Kate?" Darcy sputtered.

"Yes, Kate. Quite a looker, that Kate. I wouldn't want her sitting beside me at the hotel pool—these old girls might hardly measure up." The woman shifted her bosom and winked at Darcy, who practically choked on her cookie. "'Course, like Ed always says, 'It ain't what you got, it's how you use it.'" She elbowed Darcy, who willed her mouth shut from its current fishlike position. Only Glynnis Bidwell could invite you to church and flaunt her abundant figure in the same paragraph. Why on earth had she ever thought Glynnis and Kate wouldn't get along? They were both bold-hearted women who liked stirring up a bit of trouble.

I need to get me some normal friends, Darcy thought to herself.

"I've thought about coming to Ohio Valley for weeks," Darcy admitted, and it was the truth. "I'm just not sure Jack is ready."

"Have you asked him?" Glynnis said, as though this were a simple question.

"It's a bit more complicated than that," Darcy started.

"No, it's not. Don't go making it all complicated. Just tell Jack the reasons you'd like to go, and ask him what he thinks. Honestly, you young people talk about sex quicker than you talk about God."

"Glynnis!"

"Darcy Nightengale, Ed and I want to take Jack and you to brunch after service on Sunday. The kids can come, too. Service starts at nine-thirty. You coming or not?"

"I guess we're a-comin, ma'am," Darcy conceded. "Unless Jack has objections."

"Oh, I doubt Jack will have objections."

Now Darcy's hands went to her hips. "And why is that?"

"'Cause Ed asked Jack earlier this morning over the phone at work and Jack already said yes."

If Darcy had a white flag, she'd have waved it.

"Don't you just think God's over there in the corner, smiling and saying 'How do you like them apples, Darcy Nightengale?'"

"Yeah," said Darcy slowly, "sure…just like that."

Craig Palmer's office wall was covered in charts. Pie graphs. Bar graphs. Income projection thingies. Annual yield thingies. Adjusted gross income tables. It was a forest of numbers and formulas, and Darcy was struggling to take it all in. Craig and Jack had been bantering back and forth in energetic accountantese for the last fifteen minutes, their mutual excitement reaching almost amusing levels.

"Darcy," said Craig, taking in what must have been the baffled expression on her face. "I'd bet you'd like this in English."

"I don't know," retorted Darcy, "you guys look like you're having way too much fun. I hate to break the mood." It *was* fun to watch Jack light up like a Christmas tree at all these charts and figures. This was Jack's world, Jack's native tongue.

"No, really. Let's break it down into four areas." Craig picked up the first pie graph. "This is how your father's estate is currently set up. If we keep it this way, we can expect it to produce this—" he referred to another line graph next to it "—kind of income over the next twenty years. That is, as much as we can guess. No one here has a crystal ball, or we'd be out sailing our yachts instead of here crunching numbers for you. Do you follow so far?"

Darcy nodded. This part, she could understand.

"But your philanthropic goals, not to mention the current world situation, presents us with some unique opportunities. Stocks are incredibly low. We can buy assets that we know will return to their former value, but buy them at an incredible bargain because of the current market. Plus, we can shift assets around to new kinds of financial products, tweak formulas, stuff like that, to get an even greater yield. If we think creatively, we can increase that original income to—" Craig held up a new chart with the

same sort of pride a new father would hold up baby pic-
tures "—this. Or, if things really go our way—" he produced a third chart, looking as though he fully expected
a drum roll "—this."

Jack had the look on his face he usually reserved for
sports cars or two-inch steaks.

"Now," continued Craig, who was actually rubbing his
hands together, "watch what those kinds of assets can
do." A new chart appeared. "Even assuming a fair to mid-
dling market with a very slow comeback, these assets can
fund thirty-six Restoration Project recipients per year on
an ongoing basis."

Darcy smiled. That was three women a month. Forever.
Boy, if that wasn't enough to make your head spin.

"Plus," continued Craig, "a nice part-time salary for its
current and permanent president."

Darcy sucked in her breath. Just as a preparation for
today, she and Jack had gone over the family budget, identifying how much new income they'd need to get back
onto what Jack felt was solid footing.

The salary in Craig's chart was almost twice that.

Exceeding my expectations again, Lord?

Craig wasn't done yet. "If you can divert half of this salary to education, Darcy, it means Mike can attend Simmons Math Academy beginning next year. And, assuming
he garners a couple of math scholarships—which, I understand is a pretty safe bet—he can attend any number
of colleges without you refinancing your home or selling
the dog."

"We don't have a dog," Jack said, laughing.

"Sorry." Craig smirked. "It's just an expression we use.
Bad financial humor, I suppose."

Financial humor, mused Darcy. There's two words I don't put together often.

"This section over here shows how we'd save for Paula's education, which is slightly easier because we've got more of a head start. This is all doable, Jack and Darcy. You've got a solid future ahead of you." The guy was beaming. "But I've got another little surprise for you."

Darcy could hardly imagine anything more surprising.

Craig pulled another chart from a folder on his desk. "This section," he said with a mile-wide smile, "outlines a small pool of funds I want you to consider." Craig looked straight at Jack. "With the proper management, a subset of Paul's money can provide sixteen dozen professional-grade basketballs annually to the community centers of your choice."

Jack looked as if he stopped breathing. Darcy felt as if her heart was going to explode right there on the spot.

"Ed Bidwell made a few calls after he told me the extraordinary story of your most recent birthday party, Jack. Seems you have a few people ready to give you top-notch balls at a huge discount—that is, of course, if you'd like to make this more than a one-shot deal."

Darcy looked at Jack. His mouth was hanging open. His eyes were huge. He looked, quite truthfully, just like she felt. Stunned. Astounded. Thrilled.

Of course. Who said this had to be all about *her* giving? Hadn't she already seen—in the basketballs and even in the gold coins—how much they could do *together*? How each of them fit into the puzzle that made this crazy scheme possible? Suddenly the Jack Gives Away Basketballs Project seemed like the most natural, wonderful idea on earth. That glow—the same warm glow that filled her with the first thought of The Restoration Project—now filled the room.

Craig Palmer was, without a shadow of a doubt, their guy. And God, well, it was becoming obvious that He was too.

Sunday's visit to Ohio Valley Community Church was delightful. At least for Darcy. She kept waiting for an assessment from Jack, who said nothing telling during the visit or the car ride home. "Well," he said finally as he pulled the kitchen door shut behind him, "that wasn't half bad." The kids had already plunged past him, in a hurry to get upstairs and out of church clothes. "Your Pastor Doug seems like a normal guy."

Darcy set her purse down on the kitchen counter. "Could this have something to do with the fact that he likes basketball? Or that the Men's Ministries has a pickup league?"

Jack pulled a Coke from the fridge. "Well, that's part of the 'normal' part. I always think of pastors as playing golf or fly-fishing or something. A pastor with a mean jump shot, well, that I can handle."

"Who told you Doug has a mean jump shot?"

"Ed. Hey, you should have seen Doug's eyes light up when Ed told him about my birthday. I think The Restoration Project's gonna lose a committee member once we get my basketball thing up and running. He looked more excited than Craig did when he suggested it."

Darcy laughed. Evidently the tour Ed gave the guys had different stops than the tour Glynnis gave the women. She was glad. She couldn't explain it, but the church seemed different than the one her dad had taken them to so often. Today, it didn't even really feel like the same building her father's funeral had been in. She loved her father, loved his faith even when it frustrated her, but could never get to a place of comfort inside Ohio Valley Community Church. Now, suddenly, it felt like the church had been waiting for her to come back. "It feels so different," she said half to herself.

"I know. I can't figure it out—Paul took us there a dozen times, but it never felt as easy as it did today." He took a long swallow of soda and leaned up against the fridge. "Why do you suppose that is?"

"Beats me. The church is the same, so the only thing I can figure is that we've changed. You know, our viewpoint and all."

Jack's hand found hers and pulled her toward him. "I know I sure like the new and improved Darcy." His voice grew soft as he stared at her. "I like what's happened to you. On the outside for sure, but on the inside, too. You're different than…than you were. I don't know that I can really explain it. It's just…there."

Darcy sighed. "We're coming up for air, aren't we?"

"Hmm?"

"When Dad was really sick, on some of those long nights when it felt like he'd go at any moment, I used to wonder what it would be like when life went back to normal. 'Coming up for air,' Meredith called it. Surfacing after all the crisis stuff. Coming up on the other side of all of it. I used to wonder what that would feel like."

"Is it what you expected?"

"Sort of. Parts are completely different from how I thought they'd be. Other parts are—"

"Quit it Paula! Get out of my room and stay out! Daaad, make her stay out of my room!" Mike boomed from above them. A door slammed.

"Well, fine, Mr. Smarty-Pants, see if I care!" Paula returned fire, her own door slamming.

"—are pretty much the same as always." Darcy laughed. Jack hugged her to him.

"I think we're gonna come out of this okay, Dar."

She nestled her head under his chin. The warm afternoon sunshine poured on them from the kitchen window. Even the sound of Mike's high-volume stereo couldn't put a damper on the moment. "Me, too."

Jack blew out a breath. "Life is still far from perfect."

"I'm okay with it."

"What do you mean by that?"

"Well, I think we can ride out whatever comes. I mean, look at all that's happened. We were able to handle the awful parts, and so many good things ended up coming out of it. I'm beginning to understand, I think, how it was that Dad's faith enabled him to take so much in stride." Darcy waited. Normally, a remark like that would have brought a snide remark from Jack about Paul's "never-ending God stuff."

Today, Jack ran his hand across Darcy's shoulder. "Your dad was an amazing man." Darcy looked up at him, grateful for the words. "Kooky," Jack added, poking Darcy's nose the same way he always teased Paula, "but amazing. Kind of like this wife of mine."

Darcy put on her best Zsa Zsa Gabor voice. "When you're wealthy, dah-lings, it's not kooky, it's eccentric."

"Nope," retorted Jack shaking his head. "I stand on kooky."

"I'm insulted."

"I staked my 'kooky' and I'm not backing down."

"Traitor!"

"Tyrant!"

"You…ugh!" Darcy yelped and picked up her foot as cold water seeped into her sock. She caught Jack's eye. On cue, the fridge let out a death rattle and a very final-sounding thud. In perfect unison, they looked down together to see a large puddle of rusty water expanding out over the floor. No doubt about it this time, the refrigerator was a goner.

"Handle anything that comes our way, huh?" Jack called over his shoulder as he spun several feet of paper toweling out of the holder.

"Well…"

"You better watch what you say next, Little Orphan Heiress." Jack lay the towels down on the floor and pulled open the fridge door. He began handing food and containers to Darcy.

"Why do you say that?" Darcy was accepting items with one hand, while the other hand was already picking up the phone to call the Owens to borrow all their picnic coolers.

"Because evidently, hon," said Jack's voice from inside the dearly departed fridge, "God is listening."

Chapter 29

The Snazziest New Customer

Darcy leaned back in the pedicure chair, letting out a long sigh as she did. "What color did you pick?"

Kate handed her a bottle of the reddest red Darcy could imagine. "It's called Vivacious—I like the color, but it's the name that sold me. Pass the cookies, Madam President."

"Ooo," called Glynnis, reaching over Darcy's lap to the bottle Kate held out, "let me see that one." She held the polish bottle up, examining the shade. "Nope, too daring for me."

"What do you mean?" Darcy laughed. Darcy "You can't get much brighter than the pink you chose."

"That's different," Kate and Glynnis replied at the same time. It made all three women laugh.

"Well, this is quite a party!" Ernestine stood looking at the trio, her hands on her hips. "If you bring anyone else in here to hold court, I'm going to need to buy another pedicure chair. You ladies do know you're going to have to take off those tiaras if we're going to do your hair?"

"It's regrettable," said Kate in her best royalty voice, "but we understand. Cookie?"

Ernestine accepted a cookie from Glynnis's outstretched hand. "Thank you. Now you all have ten minutes to get this silliness out of your systems before I start on Lady Kate. Then Darcy, and then finally our newest customer, Glynnis." Ernestine let out a rich, deep chuckle and shook her braids. "It is going to look like a beauty pageant by the time I get through with each of you." She snatched another cookie out of the bag and headed off into the other room.

"This is such heaven," sighed Kate, pulling one foot from the bubbles to examine its newly exfoliated beauty. "No wonder Frances Neyburg won't stop talking to Meredith about getting her first pedicure at fifty-eight. I'm hooked, that's for sure."

"Did I tell you, Glynnis," started Darcy, "that Anne Morton had glowing reviews for her day? And you'll especially like this—the woman doing her hair color has a father in about the same stage of Alzheimer's as Anne's father-in-law. They became friends instantly. They're having lunch next week, Anne told Doug."

Glynnis adjusted her crown. "Don't you just love it when—"

"God exceeds your expectations," chimed Kate and Darcy in perfect unison, which only brought forth more giggles.

The trio was celebrating Darcy's announcement that The Restoration Project was up and running full-blown. Somehow, there didn't seem to be any other way to celebrate than booking a day of cookies, tiaras and the works at Ernestine's. It hadn't taken much convincing to get Glynnis to come along.

Glynnis reached out and squeezed Darcy's hand. "I think your dad would be so very pleased at what you've done. You could light a whole room from the glow in your eyes."

"What I can hardly believe," Kate added, her eyes wide, "is that what's been set aside will fund thirty-six recipients a year forever. Three lives a month! It's astounding. When I think of all that's going to come from this—" Kate fell back in her chair "—I feel like Queen of the World."

"Me, too," said Darcy.

"There was no stopping this idea from the start," Glynnis confirmed.

Suddenly Darcy shot upright in her chair. "Oh! Glynnis—I completely forgot to tell you!"

"Tell me what, hon?"

"Michelle Porter has scheduled her day. And it was at her husband's insistence. Could you imagine? Meredith called me last night to let me know."

Glynnis smiled as if she knew it all along. "I'm so glad you didn't give up on Michelle, Darcy."

"Me, too. I think this is going to be such an important step for her. Meredith's been trying to hook her up with this support group run out of the hospital—one for parents of terminally ill children. Meredith said she thinks Michelle may finally join."

"That's fantastic news," said Kate, passing the cookies around again.

"It is, isn't it?" said Glynnis. "It's all wonderful news today."

"It's a good day to be an heiress, don't you think, Madam President?"

"I guess so," said Darcy, hoisting a cookie in a chocolate-mint toast. "I'm starting to think there aren't really any bad heiress days."

With that, Darcy's cell phone rang, and the number of Mike's middle school came up on the screen.

Darcy winced. Just goes to show how wrong a girl can be....

* * * * *

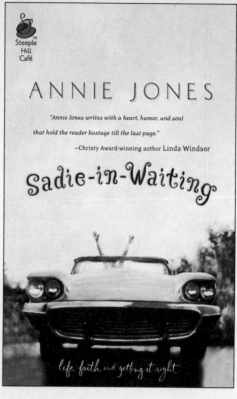

"I'm going to have a baby. Me. Ann. My dad is not gonna understand."

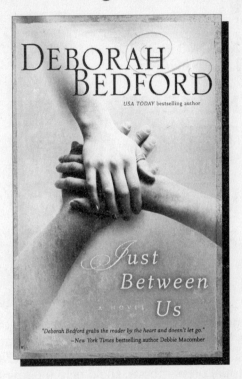

Fourteen-year-old Ann was right. Richard Small didn't understand. Nor did he know how he and his daughter could have grown so far apart. Missing his late wife more than ever, he arranged for a Big Sister to offer Ann the support he felt incapable of giving himself.

What he didn't count on was falling in love with the wonderful woman he brought into Ann's life or that the very person who brought them together could ultimately keep them apart....

Visit your local bookseller.

Steeple Hill®

Love Inspired

PAY ANOTHER VISIT TO
THE FLANAGANS...

UNLIKELY
HERO

BY

MARTA
PERRY

Planning her best friend's wedding was one thing;
working with teens was another. But since that was the onl
way Pastor Brendan Flanagan would assist Claire Delany i
the nuptial preparations, she'd help the rowdy kids find
jobs…and try not lose her heart to the opinionated—
and handsome—pastor in the process!

THE FLANAGANS:
This fire-fighting family must learn to stop fighting love.

Don't miss UNLIKELY HERO
On sale February 2005

Available at your favorite retail outlet.

Love Inspired®

FIRST MATES

BY

CECELIA DOWDY

Cruising the Caribbean was just what Rainy Jackson needed to get over her faithless ex-fiancé…and meeting handsome fellow passenger Winston Michaels didn't hurt, either! As a new Christian, Winston was looking to reflect on his own losses. Yet as the two spent some time together both on the ship and back home in Miami, he soon realized he wanted Rainy along to share his life voyage.

Don't miss FIRST MATES
On sale February 2005

Available at your favorite retail outlet.

Love Inspired™ ®

MAN OF HER DREAMS

BY

PATT MARR

Was her childhood crush really the Mr. Right she'd been praying for? That's what Meg Maguire wondered when Ry Brennan sauntered back into her life. Their relationship soon blossomed, until Meg learned Ry planned to become a doctor—she'd always dreamed of a husband who would always be around, unlike her own physician father. Could Ry convince Meg that, despite long hours of residency, their love could flourish?

Don't miss MAN OF HER DREAMS
On sale February 2005

Available at your favorite retail outlet.

AGAINST THE MAJESTIC BEAUTY
OF THE ROCKY MOUNTAINS
DURING THE 1860s LAND RUSH
COMES AN UPLIFTING ROMANCE
ABOUT THE POWER OF FORGIVENESS....

On sale January 2005.
Visit your local bookseller.